D0046480

# PERFECT FOOLS

# PERFECT FOOLS

## EDITH PIÑERO GREEN

Gre
223

E. P. Dutton | New York

Published in the United States by
E. P. Dutton, Inc., 2 Park Avenue,
New York, N. Y. 10016

Library of Congress Cataloging in Publication Data

Green, Edith Pinero.
Perfect fools.

I. Title.
PS3557.R367P4     1982     813'.54     82-1387
AACR2

ISBN: 0-525-24122-1

Published simultaneously in Canada by
Clarke, Irwin & Company
Limited, Toronto and Vancouver

Designed by Nicola Mazzella

10 9 8 7 6 5 4 3 2 1

First Edition

*To the Piñeros:*
*Manny*

*Jean*

*Danny*

*Linda*

# PERFECT FOOLS

# 1

Dearborn was humming as the taxi wended its way through Central Park. The past ten days had been a delight. No Benjamin. No Otto. Both his son and his lawyer were away. No one checking on him. No accusations or recriminations. He let his mind wander back over the previous eighteen hours with Kittie Addlebogen.

"Fetching, Kittie," he had said.

"But so expensive!"

He had sat on the gray banquette in Bergdorf Goodman's fur salon with his hands and chin resting on the knob of his walking stick while Kittie stared at the silver fox the salesman held up.

"I can't let you buy it for me, Dearie. I don't know why I let you talk me into it."

"Nonsense. After all, a lady turns forty only once or twice in a lifetime."

Kittie had giggled and slipped her arms into the sleeves. "No, no, a thousand times, no."

"Now, now, you shouldn't worry about how I spend my money." He had gotten to his feet and circled her, stimulated by her scent, which was a combination of Lily-of-the-Valley cologne and Spring Mist hair spray. Agreeable little creature, so unassuming, so simple. He had addressed himself to the salesman with authority and just a touch of condescension. "Miss Addlebogen will take the fox."

Ah, yes. Kittie Addlebogen. So pink, so plump, so exceedingly grateful. It had been quite a night.

"Grosvenor House," the taxi driver announced.

Dearborn paid him, got out of the cab, and nodded to the doorman. "Morning, Jaime. How's tricks?"

"Yes sir. Very fine."

"Things going well, are they?"

"Like always."

"What are you doing on duty, Jaime? I thought you were off Saturdays."

"I am fillin' in for George. You know, to make a few bucks."

"Need money, do you?"

Jaime shrugged.

"Mrs. Huysman still paying you to walk that revolting Pekinese of hers, is she?"

"Five dollar a week. That ain't gonna make me rich."

As Dearborn spoke he rummaged through his pockets, slapping himself here and there. "Damn. I've misplaced my keys. Oh no, here they are. Tell me, Jaime, have you seen anything of Mrs. Woolley this morning?"

"She just went out to do the shoppin'."

"When she comes back, mum's the word on when I arrived home."

"You can be sure."

"Even if she asks you point-blank."

"I won't say nothin'."

"Good man, Jaime."

Dearborn started into the lobby but paused when Jaime called after him, "There was somebody lookin' for you this mornin', Mr. Pinch."

"Really? When was this?"

"Just after Mrs. Woolley went out, about half an hour ago."

"Did he leave his name or say what he wanted?"

"He say his name's Tribble."

"Tribble? Did he leave his card?"

"No, but he say he was comin' back."

"Today?"

"Yes sir. I told him I don't know when you was comin' home but he say he was comin' back."

2

"Tribble," Dearborn repeated. "I wonder what that's all about."


Mrs. Woolley returned at noon to serve Dearborn an uninspired lunch of cold cuts, salad, and chocolate pudding. He was stabbing his spoon into the pudding bowl when the doorbell rang. Mrs. Woolley, hennaed curls bouncing, passed through the dining room on her way to the door.

"Rubber!" Dearborn complained as she flew by. "B. F. Goodrich might be interested in talking to you about this concoction, Mrs. Woolley!"

"Not now, Mr. Pinch. I have to go to the door."

Dearborn twisted around to catch a glimpse of her substantial derriere. Too bad she was such a stick-in-the-mud. It wasn't only the pudding that could use a little less starch.

The dining room was a long way from the front door. Dearborn couldn't make out the conversation beyond the initial greeting, but he could tell from the deep voice that the visitor was a man. He wasn't surprised when Mrs. Woolley trotted back to report that a Mr. Tribble was at the door. "He's from the State Department. He says it's important. He says he has to see you about your son."

"What about my son? Benjamin has been gallivanting around Cuba in his gym shorts for the past ten days."

"It wasn't my job to give him the third degree," Mrs. Woolley snapped back.

"No doubt Benjamin has committed some horrendous diplomatic faux pas and you may be sure it involves a woman. That son of mine can't walk from here to Madison Avenue without falling in love. Imagine him loose among those hot-blooded Latin ladies for ten days."

"Don't tell *me* about it. Are you going to see the man or not?"

"Yes, I shall see him."

Dearborn sauntered into the library. His first impression of Tribble was that in black chesterfield, black fedora, and black gloves, he looked more like an undertaker than a government employee.

3

"Mr. Pinch," the man announced, "my name is Tribble. I'm with the State Department."

"So my housekeeper told me. What can I do for you?"

"I've come in regard to your son, Benjamin."

"What about him?"

"May I sit down?"

Dearborn wasn't eager to encourage this man or to prolong the interview but he nodded curtly toward the couch and lowered himself into the armchair opposite. "Benjamin, I assume, has gotten himself into some kind of difficulty?"

Tribble nodded, and Dearborn went on peevishly. "Who is she? Castro's mistress? Somebody's sister? Some high official's daughter?"

Tribble reached into his coat pocket and extracted a folded wad of yellow paper. Smoothed out it proved to be a strip of perforated teletype. "The actual complaint from the Cuban government came through official channels, 'Eyes Only,' but we received this from the Interests Section attached to the Swiss Embassy in Havana. We don't have an embassy of our own down there, you know."

"Give it here."

"It won't mean anything to you." Tribble handed the strip to Dearborn who stared at it uncomprehendingly, then got up, fetched his reading glasses from the desk, and looked at it again. "What is this gibberish? Fampridpustgaltobay?"

"Code."

"I can see it's code. I'm not a half-wit, Tribble. What does it say?"

"It says that two days ago a man in Havana was killed."

Dearborn raised startled eyes and Tribble added, "A Cuban, a member of the Cuban Intelligence. Shot to death. According to the Cuban government, it was your son who killed him."

Dearborn stared at Tribble in disbelief. "Ridiculous!"

"Perhaps, and then again, perhaps not. The Cubans claim that your son was carrying information from a rebel faction in Havana to an anti-Castro group in the United States. The Cuban Intelligence officer confiscated the material and tried to arrest him but he escaped. A little later your son killed the Intelligence officer and recovered the papers. Now he's on the loose somewhere in Cuba."

"I've never heard anything so preposterous in my life!"

"It's happened before. There are a great many Americans who sympathize with the militant anti-Castro refugees. The problem here is that the State Department cannot publicly condone your son's actions."

"Are you mad? Benjamin is no spy. You should know that yourself. It was the State Department that suggested he go to Cuba in the first place. Surely you checked into his background before sending him?"

"It looks like we slipped up. Apparently we didn't check him out as thoroughly as we should have."

"Benjamin," Dearborn said emphatically, "is totally apolitical."

Tribble answered carefully. "Perhaps you don't know as much about your son as you think you do."

"I know that he is a consummate playboy who entertains no interests more profound than women, sports, and fancy automobiles, separately, together, and in any combination."

"Unfortunately the cards are stacked against him."

"Then somebody stacked them. Once Benjamin gets a chance to explain himself you'll see how idiotic this situation really is. The question is what are you going to do to help him?"

"I already told you that publicly . . ."

"Damn 'publicly'!"

"There's not much we can do covertly either. At this point it would not be in the United States' interests to risk supporting any group intent on overthrowing the Cuban government."

"But Benjamin is a United States' citizen. You can't just wash your hands of him."

"We shall issue a formal apology and, of course, request leniency."

"What! I refuse to permit such a sniveling, cowardly response!"

"If and when he's arrested your son will go on trial in Cuba under Cuban law. We can't overlook the fact that all the evidence points to his guilt and that the Cubans don't take kindly to subversives. We shall, however, make a formal appeal to obtain extradition and when they turn us down, which they will, we shall ask permission to send a representative to Cuba to monitor the trial proceedings. Naturally we'll keep you apprised of any and all developments. Beyond that we can't make any promises."

"Then I shall go down to Cuba myself. Immediately."

"You can't get into Cuba without an entry visa," Tribble said patiently, "and you can be sure that Cuba will not issue you one."

"How do you know what they will or will not do?"

"It's our business to know."

"And you refuse to stand up to those Cuban cuckoos?"

"Our advice is to leave well enough alone."

"A peculiar choice of words, Tribble. I fail to divine any 'well enough' in Benjamin's predicament."

"We should prefer that you don't attempt to aggravate an already sensitive situation."

"I'll aggravate you, Tribble, if you don't get out of my apartment by the count of three!"

Tribble rose and started to speak, but seeing Dearborn's fiercely clenched fists, he changed his mind, and permitted himself to be ushered to the front door.

"I am sure that when you've had a chance to think it over, you'll see my point of . . ."

"Out, Tribble!"

"We are, of course, deeply sympathetic. . ."

"Out!"

2

For all his bravado Dearborn was shaken. He retraced his steps to the library, poured himself a brandy and sat down at his desk. If only Benjamin weren't such a lightweight in the brains department he wouldn't be in this pickle now. He'd sashayed off to

Cuba with no more thought than if he were going to Disney World. Painfully, Dearborn recalled the conversation they'd had at the end of January.

"What is it, Benjamin?" Dearborn had asked irritably as Benjamin barged into his bedroom.

"I want to talk with you."

Dearborn, in boxer shorts and clocked silk stockings supported by garters, had been scrutinizing himself in the mirror. Noting his sharp features and plume of lusterless black hair, and squinting at his corded neck and knobby joints, Dearborn thought to himself that although he might have cut a pretty dashing figure at thirty, now at seventy-plus, he resembled nothing so much as a lanky, slightly arthritic crane. It was a rare moment of self-assessment and just the wrong time for Benjamin to prance into the room. "Well, Benjamin, what do you want?"

Benjamin had thrown himself down on the bed and stretched his long legs over the footboard. "I just got back from Washington. I was visiting the State Department."

"What for?"

"Final briefing before I leave for Cuba."

"Cuba? You are going to Cuba?"

"I told you about it a while back. I guess you forgot—or maybe you weren't listening. The Cuban government has invited the United States to send down a basketball team."

"What for?"

"To play an exhibition tournament against their championship team."

Dearborn had slid open the mirrored doors to his closet, selected a shirt, and taken it off the hanger. "You haven't played professional basketball for some time."

"I told you, Dad, it's an exhibition tournament. They want me to assemble the team and act as captain. Besides, my name still carries weight. A lot of weight, it just so happens."

"Benjamin, I'm in a hurry. I have neither the time nor the inclination to discuss your basketball career."

"Okay, okay. So I agreed to go, and yesterday I got a call from the State Department telling me to come to Washington, so I flew down this morning to firm things up."

Dearborn had finished buttoning his shirt and reached into

the closet to rifle among his suits before choosing a tan double-breasted wool tweed, adding to it, after some consideration, a suede vest with leather buttons. "When are you leaving?"

"In a couple of days."

"Benjamin, you are inviting trouble. The Cubans are an impulsive people, quick-tempered, and inevitably prone to violence. Rebellion is in their blood. The situation there is unpredictable and volatile. One never knows when there will be an eruption. If you know what's good for you, you'll change your mind and stay home."

"What makes you such an expert on Cuba?"

"I have been talking with Jaime Villegas."

"Who's Jaime Villegas?"

"My doorman."

"I thought your doorman's name was George.

"There's George and there's Jaime, who was once a millionaria in Cuba . . . "

"A millionaire?"

"How Princeton managed to spew you out without creasing your gray matter is a wonder to me. A millionaria is a sugarcane cutter."

"Come on, Dad. Don't tell me you knew that before you spoke to Jaime."

Dearborn had held up his hand. "Jaime told me that he worked dawn to dusk in Cuba and that he lived on rice and beans because there was no meat to buy, not even for people who could afford it. Ask him if he would risk returning there, even for a day. You might also have a word with Abbott Noble's wife, Alicia, and if my friend Raúl Baki weren't non compos, I'd suggest you get his opinion as well."

"My trip to Cuba is strictly for goodwill purposes."

"There is no such thing as a goodwill trip to Cuba. Not for an American."

"The State Department hopes it'll ease tensions a little," Benjamin had returned with finality.

Dearborn had tried a different tack. "What about the current heartthrob, Benjamin?"

"What heartthrob?"

"Whoever it is who will be languishing here in New York while you're parading around Cuba."

"At the moment I'm between engagements."

Dearborn had regarded his son with faint surprise. "You don't say? Come to think of it, it has been some time since I saw your face gazing up at me from the front page of the *National Enquirer*."

"Watch it, Dad. Your record's not so good in that department either. As a matter of fact, I'm a hell of a lot more worried about what'll happen to you while I'm gone than what'll happen to me."

"Ah. I see. That's it, is it. That's what you're doing here."

Benjamin had gotten that shrewd look around the eyes. "Dad, I was talking to Otto the other day."

Dearborn's mouth had puckered at mention of Otto Rothschild. "I might have guessed it."

"He's going away himself. He'll be in Japan most of February."

"Good riddance. As my lawyer he's a necessary evil. As your friend he is simply a horse's crupper."

"The point is that we'll both be away at the same time."

Dearborn's expression, until then determinedly obdurate, had yielded to a fleeting half-smile. "Both of you, eh." On impulse he had passed over the conservative tie he had been fingering in favor of a red silk embroidered with yellow question marks. "Most of February, you say?"

"I want you to promise me you'll keep a low profile while I'm gone. No fights with the phone company, no stock market fliers, no married ladies."

"I'm not dotty," Dearborn had returned affably. "I don't require a keeper."

"The last time Otto and I were away at the same time, we came back to find you in Doctor's Hospital with a stab wound."

"A nick with a ski pole, as I remember it."

"Administered by the husband of that checkout clerk at Herman's Sporting Goods."

Dearborn had removed a suede jewelry pouch from the top drawer of his bureau, and extracted from it a pair of onyx cuff links. He had then gone to the bedroom door, stuck out his head, and shouted for William.

Benjamin had sat up and swung his legs over the side of the bed. "I take it I'm about to get the bum's rush?"

"Speaking of bums . . . " Dearborn had cast a disparaging eye at Benjamin's rumpled sports jacket and scuffed loafers. "When was the last time you bought yourself a decent suit?"

"Forget the suit. Just promise me you'll behave yourself while I'm gone."

"I'll thank you to remember who is the father and who is the son, Benjamin."

"As if I could ever forget it."

"Did you want me, Mr. Pinch?" a voice had interrupted. William Rhodes, Dearborn's secretary of more than thirty years, had stood in the doorway, plucking aimlessly at his earlobe, his harassed voice drenched in apprehension. "I thought I heard you call."

"Help me with these cuff links, William. Where's my watch?"

"It's there on the night table." William had fetched the watch and Dearborn had slipped it over his wrist.

"Where are my shoes?" Dearborn had asked himself peevishly.

"Dad, listen, I'll be staying at the Novedoso Hotel in Havana. That's Novedoso. N–o–v–e–d–o–s–o."

"Sounds like a nose spray."

"If you need me . . . "

"And if you need me I'll be here at the Grosvenor. That's G–r–o– . . . "

"I've got my car parked downstairs, Dad. I could drive you wherever you're going."

"Where I'm going is no concern of yours."

"So much for an innocent offer."

"You may be goofy, Benjamin, but you are in no way innocent. William, hand me my cane."

Dearborn broke off his reminiscence, downed his brandy, and then poured himself a second drink. There had to be an explanation for it, that is, something short of spying . . . a prank, a dare, some sort of postadolescent foolishness as inane as one would expect from Benjamin.

It was unconscionable that the State Department would refuse to help, farcical that they should credit Benjamin with such

10

devious motives as espionage or terrorism, unthinkable that there was no simple, uncomplicated solution to his son's dilemma. Something could be done. Something must be done. Something would be done.

But Dearborn's brooding thoughts conceded nothing to optimism and hours later he was still sitting at his desk staring off into space.

# 3

Benjamin's troubles had begun with the farewell get-together he arranged in his hotel room at the Novedoso. The party had seemed like an excellent idea, especially since it offered him a final chance with Isabel Quintana. She'd refused the invitation at first, saying, as she'd been saying all along, "Benjamin, it is better if you would forget about me," but he had made up his mind to give it a final try.

Isabel was worth it. A fair-skinned Latin with blond hair, dazzling green eyes, and a great body, she was tall enough to be kissed by a six-foot-four basketball player without having to be lifted off her feet. It was an affair made in heaven, if only she'd cooperate. But no soap. "I am a translator and guide for the Institute," she'd insisted with maddening composure. "I would lose my job if they thought I was fraternizing with one of the visiting athletes."

It rankled. Really rankled. Benjamin's success with women was something he took for granted and it bothered him that she kept saying no even though he could swear she was interested. He'd been working at it since they'd been introduced and still she wouldn't give him a tumble.

"It's your job to entertain us, isn't it, Isabel? So when do you start?"

"I start today. This afternoon I plan to escort the team on a tour of the Castillo del Morro."

That was just the start. He'd had his fill of museums, monuments, and parks and he hadn't even gotten her totally to himself until the day before, when the last die-hard teammate had opted for a nap over the Numismatic Museum.

"The hell with commemorative coins," Benjamin had proposed recklessly. "Let's go somewhere for a drink."

"Benjamin, why will you not take no for an answer?"

"I'm not used to being turned down."

"Yes, I can see that you are very . . . what is the word . . . egotistical."

"I'm leaving tomorrow night, Isabel. You'll be rid of me soon enough. So where's the harm in having a drink with me?"

Finally she'd relented and they'd spent the afternoon in the bar at the Hotel La Habana Libre, where Benjamin had succeeded in warming her up a little, cajoling her into talking about herself, flattering her with his undivided attention, asking dozens of mundane questions, and listening patiently to the answers. She had been brought up in a small town outside of Havana. Her family was large, all of them country people who worked as farm laborers, but literate, and in the case of herself and three of her cousins, college-educated. She lived alone in Old Havana, across the street from the Garbo Café, named not for the famous Swede, as Benjamin had first supposed, but for its architectural style and grace. She had a small circle of friends, she was satisfied with her job, and she was not—at the moment— romantically involved.

This last admission had once again prompted Benjamin to make a pitch, and although Isabel had continued to keep him at arm's length, her refusal was now less vehement. Benjamin attributed her yielding to a combination of things, the romantic atmosphere of the bar, the potent frozen daiquiris, and the buttering up, which was a no-fail strategy. Still, the afternoon had ended with her leaving him high and dry in front of the hotel. And time was running out. Thus the party. To Benjamin's thinking it was the perfect setup with nothing for either of them to lose. A discreet arrangement whereby Isabel would remain behind after the other guests left. A few more drinks, an exchange of ideas, a meeting of the minds, and bam . . . one hell of a farewell party.

The first guest to arrive was Pablo Quesada, the hotel manager, a man in his sixties with a pockmarked face, a crooked nose, a well-muscled body and a doberman pinscher that was like an extension of his right arm. A little later Antonio Olivares, coach of the Cuban basketball team, loped in carrying a basketball autographed by the Cuban team members. Quesada's secretary, Carmen Bonilla, followed. She was a tiny matronly lady with exquisite manners who spoke excellent English and seemed a refugee from another era.

The fourth guest was Patricio Gómez, the hotel security officer. Benjamin wasn't particularly fond of Gómez, with his ramrod posture, his formidable mustachios, and his air of self-importance, but it would have been an insult to exclude him since he had been present in Quesada's office when Benjamin extended the invitations to Quesada and Señora Bonilla.

The fifth and sixth guests were Isabel and her boss at the National Institute for Sports, Physical Education, and Recreation, Nicasio Moya, a mild, innocuous young man who had self-effacingly arranged for the team's hotel accommodations, transportation, and meals, and who began every other sentence with the words, "If you please . . ."

Benjamin had brought in a wheel of cheese from a nearby bodega and provided two bottles each of rum and scotch, along with Cuban cola and soda water. There wasn't any ice but Quesada provided paper cups from the lobby water-cooler and Patricio Gómez used his penknife to cut fat wedges of cheese, which Carmen Bonilla distributed. Isabel looked beautiful. She was carrying her official briefcase but had abandoned the khaki slacks and shapeless jacket she usually wore in favor of a yellow off-the-shoulder blouse and a peasant skirt cinched at the waist with a wide belt. Benjamin was going to find it hard to concentrate on the other guests.

The room was small, and with seven people crowded into it the atmosphere was confused and noisy. Quesada cornered Benjamin between the bureau and the bathroom door to talk politics. Politics wasn't Benjamin's strong suit and he was dubious about the advisability of discussing Cuba's shortcomings, but apparently Quesada had no such qualms. "I tell you Castro pays a high price for the sake of his ego. He has no real power, you know. It is all a pretense. The power lies in the hands of the Kremlin."

"Would you like another drink, Pablo?"

"Nothing would be better for the country than if the United States went to war with Russia."

"Yeah, well . . ."

Tony Olivares interrupted and Quesada drifted away. "Benjamin, I would like to write to you. Will you give me your address?"

Tony was a homely, fun-loving athlete with more privileges permitted him than most Cuban citizens enjoyed, but even he had confided to Benjamin over a mojito, the rum and lime juice cocktail Hemingway immortalized, that he intended to defect to the United States. The possibility made Benjamin wonder whether Tony intended to write him or to show up on his doorstep. He obligingly scribbled down the address and gave it to Tony, then crossed over to Isabel who was engaged in conversation with Carmen Bonilla and Patricio Gómez, the hotel detective.

". . . un enemigo de la Revolución," Señora Bonilla was saying, but she slipped easily into English for Benjamin's benefit. "I was saying that my husband was a newspaper editor, an enemy of the Revolution. He died before a firing squad soon after Castro came to power."

"How terrible," Isabel breathed softly.

"It was terrible for many of us during those first months."

"Terrible," Patricio Gómez pontificated, "yet what hurt the few benefited the many. Do you not agree, Señora Bonilla?"

"I did not think so at the time."

"But now?"

Her cheeks became very pink, and Benjamin grit his teeth waiting for the fur to fly, but before she could respond, Nicasio Moya sidled over to say, "I have brought the Institute car. If you ladies would like, I shall be happy to drive you both home after the party."

Another hairy moment. Señora Bonilla said, "Thank you,

Señor Moya, but no. I have some work to finish for Señor Quesada this evening."

"Isabel?"

Benjamin glanced at Isabel and saw, or thought he saw, a flash of amusement in her eyes. Was he imagining it? No. She continued to look at Benjamin as she answered. "Thank you, Nicasio, but I have another engagement."

Well all right. He'd finally caught the brass ring. No doubt about it. Now it was just a question of a half hour or so of small talk, some gracious goodbyes and, for five of the six guests, the diplomatic heave-ho. Or so Benjamin thought. He hadn't counted on the door bursting open as it did a moment later, admitting three menacing-looking thugs.

"Who the hell are you?"

The one in front tapped the brim of his hat with his forefinger. "Fernando Solís, D.G.I., Cuban Intelligence Service."

He looked like a comic book character, from his polished shoe tips to his jutting jaw, but the pistol on his hip was anything but comical. He was almost six feet tall, shorter than Benjamin but more robust, with pig eyes and a preening swagger. He was accompanied by two hefty underlings dressed in green fatigues who stood pressed in the doorway like Tweedle-dum and Twee-dle-dee, while Solís announced that they were there to search Benjamin's room.

"What for?"

"Routine. Merely routine."

"Routine?" Quesada had protested. "It is not routine for the guests at the Novedoso to be inspected by the D.G.I."

"Nevertheless . . ."

"I think it is disgraceful!" Señora Bonilla exclaimed bravely.

"I am the security officer here at the hotel," Patricio Gómez blustered. "These investigations can be carried out only with my cooperation."

"I suggest then that you cooperate by stepping aside," Solís commanded coolly.

"Wait a minute," Benjamin jumped in angrily, "what am I supposed to have done? I'll be damned if I'll let you search my room without telling me what it is you're looking for!"

"If you resist, then we shall arrest you."

"Benjamin," Isabel said, "don't argue with them."

"If you have nothing to hide," Tony interjected, "then it would be better not to refuse."

"Of course I have nothing to hide!"

Nicasio Moya stepped forward to announce timorously, "Sir, I am the Procedures Director attached to the National Institute for Sports, Physical Education, and Recreation. This gentleman is a guest of the government. He is a member of the American basketball team that . . ."

"I know perfectly well who he is. Now will you kindly let us proceed with our job."

Solís watched with arrogant confidence as his two henchmen searched the room. They worked their way systematically through the bureau and closet before turning the clothes out of the suitcase that Benjamin had packed earlier and which now lay open on the floor.

"This is dumb," Benjamin declared indignantly. "I don't even know what you're after."

One of the men unzipped the plastic toiletry pocket attached to the inside of the suitcase and withdrew a piece of paper that was folded flat and stapled shut. He carried it over to Solís.

"What the hell is that?" Benjamin asked.

Solís pulled out the staple, glanced at the paper, and then held it up for Benjamin's inspection. "You should have guarded this more carefully."

"Guarded it! I don't even know what it is!"

Before he knew what was happening, Benjamin found himself backed against the wall with Solís's gun stuck in his chest. The commotion aroused Quesada's dog, which snarled and strained at his leash, startling Solís into turning his head for a moment. Benjamin, with some vague and stupidly conceived notion of destroying the evidence, grabbed for the piece of paper. He succeeded only in ripping off a corner before Solís cocked the gun he held to Benjamin's chest and Isabel screamed. Benjamin, reacting impulsively, knocked away the gun and leaped for the door.

Fortunately for him, Tweedle-dum and Tweedle-dee fell over each other in their frenzied efforts to reach him and he

16

made it into the hall a second before they arrived. Fortunately too, he knew the layout of the hotel. He ran to the end of the hall, galloped three flights down the back stairs and let himself out the fire-exit door into the alley that lay between the hotel and the building next door. The alley was about sixty feet long with nothing to hide behind, but Benjamin made it out to the sidewalk before his pursuers burst through the door behind him, and by the time they reached the street, he was gone.

# 4

"I don't think so, Mr. Pinch."

"Jaime, you haven't been listening to me. I am offering you a golden opportunity."

They were sitting on a bench in Central Park. Jaime, eyes front, nervously eyed the Sunday strollers as he endured Dearborn's importunate barrage. "I have to go back on duty, Mr. Pinch. Is almost one o'clock."

"How can you pass this up, Jaime? It's a sure thing. You say you have a friend in Miami who has a boat. Well, it means five thousand dollars for each of you. Ten thousand dollars in all. Think of it."

"Suppose they catch us?"

"They will not catch us. At a prearranged signal your friend will pick us up again and take us back to Miami."

"I don't know, Mr. Pinch. I don't think Tomás will do it."

"He'll do it, Jaime. He'll do it when he hears how much money there is in it."

"Tomás, he has to run the charter boat for the fishermans every day."

"It only takes a few hours to make the trip there and back."

"Except if we get caught."

"Didn't you tell me you need money? Didn't you tell me you and Tomás want to open a gas station on Long Island? Didn't you tell me how much Tomás hates the sea?"

"It ain't that he don't like it. He gets seasick all the time."

"Well, here's his chance to cure his mal de mer."

"The gas station gonna cost maybe a hundred thousand dollar, maybe more."

"You're not dealing with a piker, here, Jaime. Fourteen thousand dollars. Fourteen thousand dollars and an opportunity for you and Tomás to be heroes."

This last promise didn't impress Jaime. He shivered and turned up his coat collar. "I don't think is such a good idea. You need someone who knows La Habana. I am from Camagüey province."

"So what?"

"Camagüey is four hundred miles from La Habana. Tomás, he went to live in Cojimar. He's been to La Habana. I ain't never been to La Habana except when I pass through to Mariel when I was comin' here."

Dearborn was momentarily taken aback. "But you do speak Spanish. That's the important point. You will be able to act as interpreter."

Jaime turned to face him. "Sí, but I am a simple man, a millionaria. I cannot talk to important pipples. I have no education. I have no friends in La Habana."

Dearborn realized that the point was well taken. Jaime would be an invaluable aid, language-wise, but when it came to the nitty-gritty of dealing with people, Dearborn might need someone with contacts. "Do you have anyone at all in Havana? Perhaps a member of the family who has . . . not to put too fine a point on it . . . risen above the proletarian level?"

"What's that?"

"Someone with a college education or with connections among the people who count."

"My mother, she works in the mill where they make the guarapo, the sugar syrup. My father, he's dead. I have no brothers. Second cousins, third cousins, yes, but all in Camagüey. Most can read and write. That's all."

"I see. Well, I'll have to give this some thought, Jaime. We

18

may need to expand the landing party a bit. What matters now is that you agree to accompany me. That is the starting point."

Jaime clasped his hands and leaned forward to study the pavement between his feet. "I must think about it, Mr. Pinch."

"It's now or never, Jaime."

"Tomás, he don't like to take chances. Tomás, he don't like nothin'. Mostly he say no to everythin'."

"We can only try."

"Fourteen thousand dollar? I don't know, Mr. Pinch."

"Sixteen thousand dollars for a few days' work. No more, no less. Cash on the line. Take it or leave it."

Once again Jaime lowered his head to stare at the sidewalk.

"Well?"

"Maybe."

"No more opening doors. No more carrying packages. No more dog walking."

"Maybe I will call Tomás."

"That's the spirit!" Dearborn sat back and patted Jaime on the shoulder. "You'll not regret it, Jaime. Wait and see."

Dearborn checked his watch and got up. "It's after one. I have an appointment and you've got to get back to the lobby. Now listen to me. I am planning on a Tuesday departure."

"Next Tuesday?"

"Tomorrow."

"I gotta be ready by tomorrow?"

"That will give you less time to worry about it. Pack your bags and stand by, Jaime."

"I gotta call Tomás."

"Call him tonight, but no matter what he says, we are going, Jaime. If necessary we'll convince him face-to-face."

A few minutes later Dearborn was on his way downtown, his spirits revived, his outlook a little more optimistic. "Try to stop me, will they," he told himself. "No entry visa? Permission from the State Department withheld? They must think they're dealing with a moron. Let's see what they think when I bring Benjamin home."

Dearborn supervised the packing with more than usual care. Everything he was taking would have to go into one suitcase. Besides the basic requirements, he had William pack his sneakers, his sweatsuit, and at the last moment, his bathing trunks and underwater goggles.

William, who usually made all of Dearborn's travel arrangements, was bewildered and slighted by the fact that this time Dearborn had insisted on keeping his plans to himself. He eventually overcame his reticence, however, and suggested bravely, "Mrs. Woolley thought you might be going to Caneel Bay."

"Mrs. Woolley thought wrong."

"I told her you might be going back to La Playa."

"You and Mrs. Woolley are being unusually diligent in your prying, I see."

William bristled but didn't dare give vent to his indignation. With only the slightest edge to his voice, he said, "It's only that I know you vacationed at La Playa last year, Mr. Pinch."

"I went to La Playa to apprehend a murderer, William, not to lounge in the sun.* As a winter playground, La Playa leaves something to be desired. What are you packing? My golfing gloves? Forget the golfing gloves. And I won't need my camera."

William's worry creases deepened. "You're not going to the hospital, are you, Mr. Pinch?"

"Don't be an idiot. Would I take my bathing trunks to the hospital? Now listen, get Mrs. Woolley in here. I wish to talk to you both before I leave."

When William had gone, Dearborn checked to make sure he had the Spanish-English pocket dictionary and the Cuban travel guide he'd bought at Brentano's, as well as the thirty thousand dollars in Swiss francs. The Swiss francs hadn't been easy to come by. First he'd had to deal with the ninny of an officer at his bank. Miss Funk. What a name! And a female at that.

*"Mr. Rothschild usually handles your larger transactions, doesn't he, Mr. Pinch? I see it was only a week ago that you drew a check to Bergdorf Goodman in the sum of eight thousand, two hundred and fifty-seven dollars. It's always wise to leave a substantial cushion for emergencies, don't you think? Or is this an emergency?"*

Prying old harridan. He'd put her in her place. *"The only emergency here is the need for me to find a bank officer who can serve me without coy and altogether unwarranted meddling in my affairs."*

After that ordeal Dearborn had spent the rest of the

---

* *Sneaks,* E. P. Dutton

20

afternoon going from one bank to another to acquire the Swiss francs. First National, Chase, Barclay's Banco Popular, a few thousand dollars from each of a half-dozen different sources. The money filled a large attaché case.

Dearborn removed them now and went into his bathroom for a razor. Slitting the silk lining of the suitcase was simple. After he'd packed the bills, he used Scotch tape to secure the lining snugly under the top rim of the lid, then locked the suitcase, and pocketed the key. He was satisfied. Everything was in order. No loose ends to plague him. Kittie had been most understanding. "Dearie, don't fret about me. I'll keep the home fires burning, if you get my meaning." Marvelous girl, mused Dearborn, magnanimous, indulgent, loyal. A pity he couldn't take her with him.

Dearborn had written Otto Rothschild a note, now lying on the bed, which explained what had happened. Otto was due in Thursday, by which time Dearborn would be long gone. So far the story hadn't broken to the papers, mainly because the State Department had passed the information to the basketball team that Benjamin had been detained in Cuba on official State Department business and because Dearborn had refrained from kicking up a public fuss that would have marred his plans. But according to Dearborn's calculations, the State Department would have to issue a statement sometime within the next couple of days, and when they did, Otto would be prepared to start throwing his weight around.

As to Dearborn's travel arrangements, he felt he had arranged them as well as he could, given his inexperience in such mundane tasks. He hadn't enjoyed paying for the privilege of traveling first class on the plane to Miami, and he could think of more appealing hostelries than the airport motel, but it was peak season and that he'd succeeded in making any arrangements at all was, in his eyes, an accomplishment. He put on his jacket and patted the pocket to make sure he had the tickets.

A moment later William tapped gently on the open door and stood back to admit Mrs. Woolley.

"I am about to leave," Dearborn announced, "and I have a few final instructions."

"What about Mr. Benjamin?" Mrs. Woolley asked.

"What about him? He's not here, is he?"

"What am I supposed to tell him if he comes back while you're away?"

"I have told you before, Mrs. Woolley, and I am telling you again, that Benjamin will not come back before I do."

"There's still Mr. Rothschild. What's he going to say when he finds you've gone off without telling anybody?"

Dearborn picked up the envelope from the bed and handed it to William. "Mr. Rothschild will arrive in New York on Thursday. Call him and tell him you have a letter to deliver. Then take this to him promptly."

"I hope it says in there where you'll be staying in case we need you." Mrs. Woolley persisted. "A man your age going off without rhyme nor reason . . ."

"Before I leave," Dearborn cut in, "there is something you both should know."

William and Mrs. Woolley responded to this announcement with alarm. Instinctively they drew closer together.

"There is apt to be a little excitement around here one of these days."

"What kind of excitement?" Mrs. Woolley demanded.

"You'll see soon enough. The point is that neither of you is to give out any statements."

"Statements to whom?" William murmured timorously.

"The door is to be barred to reporters, photographers, and to anyone else who might pop up asking questions."

"You're in trouble with the police again!" Mrs. Woolley challenged.

"The police are not involved, and once the press realizes that I am not available for comment, they will cease to bother you. In the meantime, keep in touch with Otto, follow whatever instructions he may give you and keep your lips buttoned. Do I make myself clear?"

William deferred to Mrs. Woolley, who answered for them both. "We don't like it, Mr. Pinch. We don't like it one bit."

"I'm not looking for approbation, Mrs. Woolley. Only for cooperation."

# 5

For all its modernity and prosperity, the city of Miami was, in Dearborn's eyes, no longer part of the United States. It was a pastel metropolis run by foreigners, a dazzlingly sunny city where the natives, in gauzy shirts and straw sandals, drove American cars but took their meals in restaurants named La Tropicana and El Pájaro Rojo. It was a far cry from the days when the somnambulant municipality functioned largely as a supply depot for Miami Beach, the luxurious millionaire strip across the canal.

Jaime and Dearborn crossed the canal to Miami Beach. They taxied up Collins Avenue past the picturesque houseboats anchored in the canal and the leviathan hotels that screened the ocean, past Pumpernick's Restaurant, past the Bal Harbour shopping center, arriving finally at the Haulover Beach Park Fishing Pier where they dismissed the cab and set out to look for Tomás. It was six o'clock so he should be in and docked for the night.

"What's the name of his boat?" Dearborn asked, peering around.

"*El Cacahuete.*"

"What's that mean?"

"The peanut. Is a joke, you see."

"One that rather misses the mark, I'd say."

Jaime led Dearborn past a number of boats, and pointed to a small, squat wooden trawler, with peeling paint, that looked as wide fore as aft.

"That's it?" Dearborn observed uncomfortably. "None too prepossessing, is it."

"It runs."

"Yes, well that remains to be seen."

There was no need for a gangplank since the deck was the

23

same height as the dock, and Jaime merely stepped across the narrow gap that separated them, calling out gustily, "Tomás? Ay, chico, dónde estás?"

He was answered by a spate of rapid-fire Spanish as a stocky, toadlike young man dressed in an undershirt, frayed calf-length dungarees, and leather-thonged sandals lumbered out of the cabin. "Ay, Jaime. Is good to see you!"

Watching them embrace, Dearborn suspected that Jaime's friend might be a harder nut to crack than Jaime, and his impression was borne out when the Cuban caught sight of him and swaggered over to shake hands. Dearborn braced himself for the handshake and was rewarded by coming out of it with his fingers more or less intact. "How do you do, Tomás. Pleasure to meet you."

"I told Jaime you should not come, but you came anyway."

"Didn't I told you?" Jaime chimed in. "I told you Tomás said no."

"I certainly did come," Dearborn declared self-confidently, "and I came prepared to pay."

"Ain't no way you can pay me to go back to Cuba," Tomás returned. "Uh-uh. No sir. Not for nothin'."

"May I come aboard?"

"Sure. Why not. But it ain't gonna do you no good."

The interior of the small cabin was furnished with a bunk bed, a built-in table, two wooden chairs, a minute galley and dozens of souvenirs dangling from lengths of colored ribbon strung across the room. For Dearborn, who was at least nine inches taller than Tomás, it necessitated ducking to avoid bumping into the display of beads, paper flowers, rubber animals, and plastic dolls that swayed overhead. He quickly slid onto the bunk bed out of harm's way.

"How you like it?" Tomás asked.

Dearborn hunted for an appropriate adjective. "Cozy."

"Sí, sí, but it would be more cozy on dry land." Tomás smacked Jaime on the shoulder and slipped one burly arm around his neck, hugging him affectionately. "So, Jaime, como estás? I have missed you. We have not seen each other for thirteen, fourteen month."

"Señor Pinch, he pay for the trip."

24

"Too bad he waste his money, but I am glad you are here, Jaime."

"Listen, Tomás," Dearborn interjected, "let's talk about this, shall we?"

"Okay. I ain't against talkin' about it. But first we share a cerveza." Tomás reached out and opened the small refrigerator under a minuscule sink, took out three cans of beer, and distributed them. Then he directed Jaime to sit down at the table and tucked himself in opposite. "Jaime, he told me on the phone they got your son in Cuba. He told me you want I should take you there. He told me you would pay eight thousand dollar before and eight thousand dollar later. Did he told me right?"

"Essentially, yes. Except that my son is not now under arrest. He's on the loose somewhere, probably in or around Havana."

"How you think you gonna find him? Suppose he leaves La Habana? Cuba is seven, eight hundred mile long."

"I'll track him down. I'll make inquiries, seek out advice and help. I'm prepared to pay well for it. You already know that."

"Who you gonna speak to in La Habana?"

"To the authorities. To anyone who might know something about him."

"You know anybody in Cuba?"

"No one."

"You don't know nobody in Cuba, how you gonna keep from gettin' arrested? You start askin' questions, somebody's gonna call the police. The next thing you're in jail."

"I have no intention of permitting myself to be arrested."

"You won't have nothin' to say about it. They come along with a gun. Bam. You're in jail. I know what is like. I was in jail myself two years ago."

Dearborn was startled. "You're a jailbird, Tomás?"

"I ain't no criminal. It was a woman. Her brother, Arturo, he say I cannot marry with her."

"Why not? Why should that have landed you in jail?"

"It was her family. Because the Delgados, they never like me. Maybe because I am from Camagüey. I don't know. But they got me arrested. They say I try to run away with Elena."

"Did you?"

"Yes. We run to Bayamo but Arturo, he came after. She was only seventeen, so that's how they put me in jail. Then they deport me from Mariel."

"Perhaps you would like to see her again, Tomás," Dearborn suggested slyly.

"I am gonna see her again. She is gonna get outta Cuba and come here."

"You can't really be sure of that, can you? Wouldn't it be better to go back yourself and get her?"

"Is too dangerous for me to go back, but I got a friend. He promise me he would find a way to help her to get out. Anyway, right now we are talkin' about your problems. I am sayin' here that you ain't never gonna find your son, not without you know somebody important in Cuba."

"Then I shall find someone, someone who has contacts, who can negotiate with some degree of tact and diplomacy. Have you any suggestions?"

"Not me." Tomás shook his head. "Once I knew somebody in La Habana, an abogado . . . a lawyer . . . by the name Jesús. No more."

"What happened to him?"

Tomás turned a forefinger and thumb into his chest and pulled an imaginary trigger.

"Shot?"

"Shot by God." Tomás thumped his chest with the palm of his hand. "Heart. He drop dead on Obispo Street."

"Regrettable from both our points of view. You don't know anyone else in Havana who could help me?"

"No one."

"You do know people here in Miami though, don't you? Surely one of them has relatives or contacts in Havana."

"No one will wish to put in danger their family or friends."

"I'll pay well. I've already said that."

"You must know someone with the education, someone who knows important pipples. But they will not give you the names of pipples close to them in La Habana. They will not go with you neither. It would be more dangerous than for me to go. The aristocracia . . . you know who I mean . . . ?" Tomás waited for Dearborn's acknowledging nod before going on. "They was the

26

first to leave a long time ago because they fear Castro the most. And now they are here in Miami, they won't go back."

Dearborn was nonplussed. He hadn't come this far to be thwarted. "I shall find someone, I assure you. If it is necessary that I have an intermediary in Havana, I shall have an intermediary in Havana."

Tomás shrugged expressively. "I don't know nobody."

Dearborn pulled the tab off his beer can and downed half the beer, then flipped his handkerchief out of his breast pocket and wiped the foam from his upper lip. He wasn't ordinarily a beer drinker but he needed something to sustain him. "Tomás, am I correct in deducing that you are Jaime's oldest friend?"

"I am."

"Do you feel no sense of responsibility for him?"

"Sure I do."

"Then I think you owe it to him to stand by him. He has agreed to go with me. It wasn't an easy decision and he made it as much for your sake as for his own."

"He don't have to go if he don't want."

"He is a man of honor and he has given me his word. He is also a very brave fellow and deserves to have your support."

Tomás turned to Jaime. "Why you wanna do this thing?"

"Sixteen thousand dollar, Tomás. How we ever gonna save sixteen thousand dollar?"

"Forget the sixteen thousand dollar, Jaime. You gotta be crazy to go back."

"When we got it," Jaime argued, "you'll be glad I done it."

An idea suddenly popped into Dearborn's mind. "What was that you said a minute ago, Tomás?"

Tomás suppressed a belch with the back of his hand. "About what?"

"Someone educated," Dearborn mused. "Someone who grew up in Cuba, someone who is apt to have contacts in Havana, someone willing to go back, someone who is, as you so astutely observed, off his trolley. In short . . . " Dearborn tipped up his beer can, drank deeply, then leaned forward to slap the beer can down on the table," . . . Raúl Baki."

"Who's Raúl Baki?" Tomás asked in a mystified voice.

"Have you never heard of the Baki Distilleries?"

"Yes, but there have been no Baki Distilleries in Cuba for many year."

"True. True. However, there is still a Raúl Baki. I met him last year at La Playa, a resort on the west coast of Florida. We were quite close, in fact so close that when he became ill I arranged for his transfer from the Silver Beach Infirmary to the Tamiami Springs Sanatorium which is only a few miles south of Miami."

"Tamiami Springs!" Tomás declared. "Ain't that a hospital for crazy pipples?"

"That's what we're talking about, isn't it? Tamiami Springs. Their specialty is the chronically insane, and no one is crazier than my friend Raúl. And what was it sent Raúl over the edge, Tomás? I'll tell you. It was the Castro revolution. He lost everything, his distilleries, his house, his bank account. And what is it that obsesses him now, Tomás? It's his determination to return to Cuba to fight Castro on his own ground."

"A crazy mans?"

"What's crazy in Miami might be considered the epitome of good sense in Havana."

"But how you gonna get him outta the bughouse?"

"It won't be easy. He's a ward of the state. He, like you, Tomás, had a little misunderstanding with the authorities. It took all the pull I could muster to get him transferred from the state sanatorium to a private facility, and they aren't apt to let him march out the front door."

"So what will you do?"

"I shall outwit them, of course. Where there's a will, there's a way."

6

On Thursday morning, Dearborn called the sanatorium to alert them to the fact that he would arrive that day to visit Raúl. Then, because the only means of transportation available, aside from a taxi cab, was Tomás's dilapidated pickup truck, Dearborn prevailed upon Tomás to rent him a car.

"I think you must rent it yourself. They must see your license."

"I don't have a license."

"You don't have a license? How can you drive if you don't have a license?"

"It's perfectly all right. I am an accomplished driver with or without a license. I simply don't drive frequently enough to warrant paying the state for the privilege. Just pick up a local map while you're at Hertz."

Forty minutes later Tomás reluctantly turned over to Dearborn the cream-colored Mercury he'd rented. Looking bleak, Jaime settled himself in the passenger seat and unfolded the road map while Dearborn checked out the dashboard and gear shift arrangement. "Park, neutral, drive, reverse, flasher, lights, radio," Dearborn mused aloud. "All in order. Easy as rolling off a log." He started the engine, shifted into drive, then looked around with a perplexed frown. "Something on the blink here."

Tomás stuck his head in the window. "You must release the brake."

"Ah, of course." Dearborn disengaged the emergency brake and the car lurched forward. "We'll return before eight, Tomás," he shouted back. "Don't forget."

Jaime, acting as navigator, directed Dearborn to turn right at a Hundred and Twenty-fifth Street, then to make a left onto Route Ninety-five and from there to head south. "You gotta get on Forty-one west and then switch onto Krome Avenue goin' south." It had begun to rain and Jaime rolled up his window. "You betta take it slow, Mr. Pinch."

Dearborn squinted through the windshield. "Just a sprinkle. Won't last long." He punched one of the buttons on the dashboard. "What's wrong with these windshield wipers?"

"You are pushin' the cigarette lighter."

"Idiots," Dearborn muttered.

The outskirts of Miami were flat and ugly, the highway bordered with fast-food drive-ins, gasoline stations, and discount warehouses. Finally, they turned off into cracker country, the sandy earth dotted with shoestring truck farms haphazardly placed among the coarse bushes and scrub pine. Traffic was light, and even with a wrong turn at Hainlin Mill Drive and a stop so that Jaime could use the men's room at the Monkey Jungle, they arrived at the front gates of Tamiami Springs in less than an hour. They were checked against the visitors' list by the guard who came out of the reception booth to unlock the gate and direct them to the administration building.

The sanatorium was a pleasant change from the stark ugliness of its location. The long curving drive led up to a building with wide columns and a broad veranda surrounded by velvety lawns. The main building had once been part of a private mansion and an effort had been made to retain its gracious Old World atmosphere. The dozen or so dormitories, looking, except for their barred windows, like quaint gardeners' cottages, were placed at wide intervals over the extensive grounds and connected by gravel paths. At one side of the main building were tennis courts, and on the other, a fieldstone wall that surrounded the parking lot.

"Remember, Jaime," Dearborn cautioned, "you are Raúl's nephew. Stick to that story. Say as little as possible and agree with anything I suggest."

"Suppose Señor Baki says I am not his nephew?"

"You may be sure that no one ever pays the slightest attention to anything Raúl says."

It was raining heavily now. Dearborn stuck his face close to the streaming windshield and made an abrupt turn into the parking lot. He swerved toward a row of parked cars. "There's a spot there."

"I don't think . . ." Jaime held his ears, awaiting the loud rasp of metal against metal.

"A little tight," Dearborn noted without concern. He then chose another spot and succeeded in parking without further mishap. He had no sooner switched off the engine than a man wearing a slicker and carrying a king-size umbrella knocked on the back window. He motioned to Dearborn and Jaime to get out of the car and they joined him in a huddled six-legged dash to the door of the administration building. Once inside, the man directed them to an office where a young woman sat typing, then he excused himself.

The young woman rose from her desk. "Mr. Pinch? Dr. Huber's expecting you." She knocked on the door to an inner office, opened it and stood back. "Please go right in." Dearborn remembered Dr. Huber as a bright, motherly woman with a penchant for hyperbole. She justified his recollection by calling out, "Splendid! Marvelous! How good to see you!" She was ensconced behind an antique fruitwood desk in a generously proportioned office that must have been the mansion's main salon. She rose and held out her hand. "How are you, Mr. Pinch?"

"Couldn't be better. And how is my friend Raúl?"

"Unpredictable as ever, I'm afraid. But doing well. Doing very, very well, and quite, quite happy."

"I've brought his nephew, Jaime Villegas, to see him. Thought it might do him some good. Jaime, meet Dr. Huber."

Dr. Huber took Jaime's hand and pumped it energetically. "How do you do, Mr. Villegas. I didn't realize that Señor Baki had relatives here in the United States. Are you from the Miami area?"

Jaime mumbled, "I am from New York."

"That explains why you haven't visited before. It's lovely that you've come now. Absolutely."

Dearborn decided not to waste their precious time on small talk. "Dr. Huber, we thought we'd take Raúl for a little tool around the countryside."

Dr. Huber was equally direct. "Oh no. We cannot permit him to leave the grounds."

"Surely you can bend the rules a bit."

"No, no, certainly not. If we could, we would, but we cannot. I haven't told Señor Baki about your visit. It will be a delightful, delightful surprise. Shall we go find him?"

"I wonder if he'll remember me. I haven't seen him in a year."

"I'm sure he will. He speaks of you often, and with fondness, I think. Of course he still persists in referring to you as Mr. Roycroft."

"He never did get that straight."

"No, poor man. But it's less complicated to let him call you Roycroft than to try to explain that Roycroft was murdered."

31

"To get back to the outing," Dearborn said, gingerly guiding the conversation back to the subject that interested him, "I think Raúl would enjoy a diversion, if only for an hour or two." "Señor Baki's incarceration is my responsibility and I would be held liable if anything were to happen. Frankly, Mr. Pinch, I am not so sure as you that Señor Baki would behave. He associates you with the idea of rescue. After all, he did look upon you as something of an accomplice once. He might try to make a break for it."

"Why should he do that? Didn't you just tell me how happy he is here?"

"Yes, but he continues to insist that it is his duty to return to Cuba. Given the opportunity I'm afraid he would feel obliged to run away. Now, let's not hear any more of it. Come, you'll be very glad to see how well he's doing."

Dr. Huber leaned over the intercom and pressed one of the buttons. "Miss Bing, I think Señor Baki is in the therapeutic games room. Will you check his schedule please." She waited a moment, released the button, then said to Dearborn and Jaime, "Come, I'll take you to see him."

She led them back into the reception hall and from there down a flight of stairs to the basement. They walked past doors marked Art, Shop, Gymnasium, Lecture Hall, and Whirlpool Baths, stopped at a door at the far end of the hall. Dr. Huber opened the door to a room with pastel green walls, pink lights, and groupings of well-worn furniture where fifteen or twenty patients and half a dozen attendants were occupying themselves in a variety of activities. Some were talking, others watching television. A few were playing Scrabble, and one lively foursome was playing dominoes with a tray of graham crackers.

Dr. Huber nodded to two gentlemen playing backgammon at a card table at the far side of the room. One of them was a tall, thin, good-looking gentleman wearing a guayabera and tinted eyeglasses.

"You see how absolutely radiant he's looking?" Dr. Huber gushed. "He has gained ten pounds since he's been with us and he has a beautiful new set of teeth."

"Never mind his teeth," Dearborn said. "How's his English?"

"We've tried giving him English lessons but he isn't interested. Not in the least. He took an immediate dislike to the English teacher. Seems to think Mr. Phlug is a member of the secret police. Won't talk at all in any language when Mr. Phlug's around." Dr. Huber called out cordially, "Señor Baki, here's someone to see you."

Baki recognized Dearborn immediately and, with a happy cry, leaped up from the table and rushed over to embrace him. "Roycrap! My fran, Roycrap!" He held Dearborn at arm's length while he made an effusive speech, the essence of which Dearborn derived from his recognition of the words, "amigo, amable, mucho gusto," and "simpático."

"Here's your nephew, Mr. Villegas, come to see you," Dr. Huber exclaimed, pushing Jaime forward. "Isn't that splendid?"

"Quién es?" Baki demanded, eyeing Jaime suspiciously.

"Surely you remember your nephew Jaime," Dearborn encouraged.

"Quién?"

"Tell him who you are, Jaime."

"Tu sobrino," Jaime murmured, clearing his throat and looking embarrassed.

"Mi sobrino?" Baki repeated, focusing on Jaime, gazing into his face with a concentrated scowl. Finally he asked, "El hijo de Francisco?"

Jaime glanced at Dearborn and Dearborn nodded. "Sí," Jaime answered, "el hijo de Francisco."

"Jaime Velasco?"

"That's the one!" Dearborn interjected heartily, winking at Dr. Huber and muttering in an aside, "Villegas, Velasco . . . poor fellow's as confused as ever."

"Jaime!" Baki exclaimed, crushing Jaime to him. "Sí, sí, es la verdad! Cual el cuervo, tal su huevo!"

"What's he saying?"

"He say," Jaime explained, " 'like the crow, so is the egg.' "

"Charming," Dr. Huber gushed. "Charming. Johnny, water for Señor Baki, please."

One of the attendants brought over a paper cup filled with water and Dr. Huber took a vial out of her pocket and handed Baki a pill from it. He tossed the pill into the air, caught it in his mouth, and swallowed it without calling for the water.

"What's that for?" Dearborn asked.

"Keeps him from becoming overly excited."

"Not apt to put him to sleep, is it?"

"No, no, of course not. At least not for a while. Well, if you'd like, I'll leave you to your visit. I've my rounds to make before tea. Tea will be in the dining room in about twenty minutes. One of the attendants will find you and Señor Baki a table and I'll join you there."

"Don't trouble yourself on our account."

"No trouble at all. I like to chat with our visitors whenever I can. See you in a bit."

Dr. Huber left the room. As soon as she'd gone, Dearborn whispered to Jaime, "Tell Raúl we're going to help him escape."

Jaime relayed the message and Raúl responded with a chortle of delight.

"Tell him to remain cool," Dearborn admonished, with a wary glance at the attendant. "Tell him we have an automobile waiting in the parking lot. Tell him that when the time is ripe, we intend to crash the gate."

"We ain't really goin' to crash the gate?"

"Just tell him."

Again Jaime translated. Raúl immediately threw his arms around Dearborn and shouted, "Viva Cuba! Vivan los Cubanos!"

"Release me, Raúl. You are crushing my cravat. Jaime, tell him to release me."

"Crash the gate," Jaime was murmuring to himself. "I hope we ain't gonna crash no gates."

Dearborn returned from a roundabout trip to the men's room and reseated himself at the dining room table. "Tricky," he whispered to Jaime. "The windows are barred and any doors that aren't bolted are carefully guarded."

"Señor Baki, he is talkin' too much," Jaime informed Dearborn worriedly.

"Falsos testimonios!" Raúl ranted. "La fuerza de sino!"

Dearborn regretted having spilled the beans to Raúl. It was clear that he was in an agitated state of mind.

"Here she come," Jaime warned.

"Quiet him down, Jaime."

"Silencio, por favor," Jaime hissed across the table.

"Nunca silencio!" Raúl returned defiantly, choking on the cookie he was chomping and adding in a gagged voice, "Revolución! Viva la Revolución!"

Dr. Huber hurried up to the table. "Oh my, what has upset him?"

"Viva Cuba!" Raúl shouted. "Vivan los Cubanos!"

"He's not upset," Dearborn said baldly. "Here, Raúl, have another cookie."

"He say now," Jaime whispered in Dearborn's ear, "that the voices tell him to kill Castro."

"What voices?"

"Just voices. The voices."

Dr. Huber sat down between Dearborn and Jaime and sized up the situation. "Perhaps . . . yes, I am sure . . . the excitement of your visit has been too much for him." She reached into her pocket and took out the vial of tranquilizers. "Perhaps I should . . ."

"He's fine!" Dearborn insisted. "Look at him. Nothing on his mind now but the refreshments."

A momentary distraction was provided by the arrival of Dr. Huber's tea and a fresh plateful of cookies. Dr. Huber put the vial on the table, and Dearborn asked casually, "Just where is Raúl's room?"

"He's in C Cottage down near the front gate."

Dearborn exhaled gently. "Near the front gate? Good. That is to say, we shall walk him over there after tea."

"If you wish. I'll send an attendant to accompany you."

"Why should we need an attendant? He can't possibly go over the wall, can he? There are no vulnerable spots, no un-fenced areas, no unlocked gates?"

"No," Dr. Huber replied, "but we cover twenty-three acres, Mr. Pinch. If Señor Baki runs away it might take hours to find him."

Raúl, hearing his name, was stimulated to rise, kick away his chair and call out, "Cuba libre! Cuba siempre!"

"He *is* upset," Dr. Huber exclaimed. "Mr. Pinch, I think perhaps he should go back to C Cottage immediately."

"Whatever you say. But don't worry about the attendant. Jaime and I shall keep a good grip on him. Come on, Jaime."

Dr. Huber's signal was barely perceptible but in seconds it

brought a strapping attendant to her side. "I'm sorry, Mr. Pinch. I simply cannot permit it. As a matter of fact, I think it would be wise to say goodbye to Señor Baki right here and now."

"But we've only been here an hour."

"I know. I *am* sorry. Perhaps you can return another day. Tomorrow perhaps, or the day after. We wouldn't want to risk a relapse, would we?"

"Relapse? The man is already stark ravers. How much more gaga can he get?"

"Nevertheless, you must trust my judgment," Dr. Huber returned with a touch of severity.

She got up and patted Raúl's arm. "No fuss now, Señor Baki."

Dearborn took advantage of her inattention to pick up the vial of pills and pocket them. Then he said, "Tell him to go on, Jaime. Tell him we'll catch up with him later."

Jaime obediently translated, adding that they would see him again soon.

Raúl replied cunningly, "Bueno, Jaime. Entiendo. Das un empujón." This last was a plea to get the ball rolling and was accompanied by a succession of conspiratorial winks.

Dearborn made haste to follow as the attendant marched Raúl away. "We shall take you at your word and return another day, Dr. Huber. Thank you for your courtesy. Delicious tea. No, no, don't bother to accompany us."

Once out of the dining room, Dearborn grabbed Jaime by the arm and rushed him through the hall and out into the pelting rain. He could see Raúl, arm in arm with the attendant, crossing the drive. "Follow me, Jaime." Dearborn got out his car keys and sprinted into the parking lot. He was already turning the key in the ignition when Jaime opened the car door and slid in beside him. "Damn it," Dearborn fumed, "why won't the blasted thing start!" The engine sputtered and finally caught, and Dearborn threw the car into reverse. They bucked their way out of the parking space and Jaime braced himself as Dearborn braked inches from the car behind them, then turned the wheel, and sped forward.

The drive was a wide horseshoe with the main building at its uppermost curve and C Cottage at its base on the far side of the broad lawn. Dearborn cut across the drive and bumped up onto the lawn, careening across the spongy turf toward the two men who had just reached the cottage steps. He honked the horn and both Raúl and the male nurse turned and threw up their arms as the speeding automobile bore down on them.

"Watch out!" Dearborn hailed, sticking his head out the car window. "Up there! Up there!"

The attendant glanced up at the sky, terror-struck, as Dearborn jammed on the brakes a few yards away. "Where?" he screeched. "Where?"

"It's falling!" Dearborn cried out. "Run for it! Get out of the way!"

"Bomba! Bomba!" Raúl joined in, adding to the commotion.

The attendant reacted to the urgency of Dearborn's command by running for cover, first trying to pull Raúl along with him but soon giving up and dashing around the corner of the cottage alone.

Raúl, jubilant, hopped up and down shouting, "Maravilloso! maravilloso!" while Dearborn tried, to no avail, to attract his attention.

"Get in the car, Raúl! Do you hear me! Get in the car!"

Raúl continued to prance around until Dearborn finally ordered Jaime to get him. Jaime flung open the door and dashed after Raúl. He began tugging at Raúl's sleeve but by that time the attendant had poked his head back around the corner of the cottage. "What's going on?" he shouted, "What are you talking about? What's falling? Hey, wait a minute! Leave Baki be! What the hell's coming off here?"

Dearborn glanced up into the rearview mirror. Four burly attendants, led by Dr. Huber, had emerged from the administration building and were flying toward them.

"Shake a leg, Jaime!"

Jaime shoved Raúl toward the car, but by then the attendant had grasped the situation well enough to realize that he'd been duped. He sprang toward Jaime, tackling him around the knees and bringing him down. "No one's taking Baki!"

He was wrong about that. Raúl, with a momentary flash of sense, jumped into the car next to Dearborn and slammed the door shut. Dearborn, his back, at least figuratively speaking, against the wall, gave a last regretful look at poor Jaime helplessly pinned to the ground, then pressed the gas pedal to the floor, and sent the car rocketing back out onto the drive.

# 7

"I shouldn't have come," Benjamin said worriedly.

"I am surprised that you were able to find me," Isabel told him.

"You said you live in Old Havana, across from the Garbo Café. And besides, your name's on the mailbox downstairs. It wasn't hard."

"You didn't know anything about that piece of paper hidden in your suitcase, did you, Benjamin?"

"Of course I didn't. I never saw the damned thing before Solís shoved it in my face."

"Then you should not have run away."

"I could kick myself for it. I panicked, that's all."

"I'm glad you came here."

"I didn't expect a warm reception. I just didn't know where else to go."

"I had made up my mind last night to say yes to you, Benjamin. Surely you knew that."

Benjamin sighed and put his arms around her, burying his face in her hair. "Yeah, I knew that, but that was before I got myself into this mess."

"Well, we must find some way to get you out of this mess." She disengaged herself gently and led him into the apartment. "Come, I'll get you a cup of coffee."

"I assume the team left on schedule?"

"Yes. They took the plane at midnight."

"I figured as much. Well, that leaves me up the proverbial creek."

Isabel turned to face him. "Benjamin, there is something else you should know."

"What is it?"

She shook her head to indicate how little she wished to answer.

"What is it?"

"I thought you might have known, that you might have been hiding somewhere nearby . . ."

"What are you talking about?"

"Solís was murdered last night as he left the hotel."

"Jesus. And they think I did it, right?"

Isabel nodded. "Of course."

Benjamin thought of something in the early hours of the morning and got up to empty his trousers' pockets. Sure enough, he still had the ragged bit of paper he'd ripped out of Solís's hand the night before. He'd stuffed it into his pocket as he ran out of the hotel room, and now here it was, a fragment of typing paper about four inches across.

A perusal of it in the bathroom revealed little beyond what he already knew. It had been torn from a list of typewritten names and addresses and there were three street endings on the piece he held "dra, ano, ata," as well as the name, "Barola," and yesterday's date hastily scribbled in ink. Hell, what good was it now, Benjamin thought despairingly. He tossed the paper into the wastebasket, then leaned down and picked it out again—his eye had caught some fuzzy handwriting on the back.

It looked as if a sheet of carbon paper had lain between the back of the list and whatever someone had been writing on. He could make out the letters, *t–o*, and beneath and to their left, *l–k–l–o*. It was a spidery, indistinct impression but two things stood out. The person who had written the name and date on the front of the sheet had also written the letters on the back. The script was the same. And whoever that person was, he or she had a unique way of forming the letter *K*. It was done with one sweep of the pen, down, up, and down again. ∦ , like a capital *N* written backward, and it was larger than the letters on either side. Here at least was something tangible, something that might prove useful.

Benjamin wished that Isabel would wake up so he could talk with her about his discovery, but it wasn't yet six and she hadn't fallen asleep until after three. He walked across the room to the window. Bending his head slightly, he could see between the wooden slats into the narrow street. The store-fronts were shuttered like so many closed eyelids, a cat was sleeping coiled on the sidewalk in front of the café, hazy daylight filtered through the rooftop clotheslines and filigreed balconies. An old woman appeared in the window opposite, leaned out to study the sky, then withdrew. A moment later a car crawled slowly down the street and Benjamin drew back, watching it until it turned the corner.

"Why are you up?" Isabel asked softly.

He turned to look at her lying in the bed, her face creased from the pillow, her eyes puffy with sleep, but still more beautiful than most women. He walked back and sat down on the edge of the bed. "I've been thinking about what happened last night. Look. I want to show you something." He handed her the scrap of paper.

"What is it?"

"We already agreed that the person who hid that list in my suitcase is the person who killed Solís. Whatever that list is, it's something the murderer didn't want Solís to have. Right?"

"Yes."

"So he killed Solís to get it back."

"Probably."

"Look at this piece of paper."

"What is it?"

"I ripped it out of Solís's hand. It's a piece torn off the list. It has parts of some street addresses printed on it."

Isabel peered at it sleepily. "One cannot tell anything from this. There are a thousand street names that have these endings."

"Look at the back."

Isabel turned the scrap of paper over and examined the writing on the back. "*t–o–l–k–l–o*. What is it?"

"This could have been written by the murderer. See the letter *K*? Did you ever see anyone write a *K* like that? It's a hell of a funny way to make that character. Look, I didn't notice before but it's underlined. See the funny little squiggle under it?"

"Benjamin, what are you saying?"

"That I may be able to find out who put that list in my suitcase and who murdered Solís."

Isabel gave him back the piece of paper and slid out from between the sheets. "I will make us breakfast. Come with me."

Benjamin followed her into the cramped combination living room-kitchen and sat down on the couch while she measured the coffee into a pot. Then she reached into a basket on the counter and lifted out two pieces of an oval, coarse-skinned fruit that she identified as a "sapote," squeezed the juice into a glass, and carried it to Benjamin.

He drank the juice in a single gulp. "I finished packing a couple of minutes before everyone came into my room last night. There wasn't anything in that snap-on pocket but my electric shaver. In other words, somebody in the room planted that list in my suitcase."

"One of your friends."

Benjamin gave a short laugh. "One of my so-called friends."

"Even if it were true . . ."

"It's true all right. It's the only way it could have happened. Which means the murderer was one of five people, Quesada, Gómez, Moya, Olivares, or Carmen Bonilla."

"One of six," Isabel corrected. "I was there too."

"Come on, Isabel, I'm being serious."

"But not entirely unbiased. You want to see which of us writes our *K*s in that peculiar manner, is that right?"

"That's right."

Isabel went back to the stove and turned down the coffee, which had just begun to perk. Then she returned and sat down. "I have two things to say. One is that it is very possible that the handwriting on that slip is not the handwriting of the murderer."

"I'll give you that. But remember that the date on the front, written in the same hand as the stuff on the back, bears yesterday's date. It was scrawled quickly as if it had been an afterthought, done maybe right before the person who wrote it came into my room. All I have to do is check the handwriting of all the people who were in my room last night. If none of their handwriting matches what I've got here, then you're right, it's a dead end. But if one of them did write this, then I've hit the jackpot."

"Which brings me to my second comment," Isabel said. "You are talking about condemning someone who befriended you, someone who is, no doubt, working for the anti-Castro underground, someone who is in all probability a person with whom your government would ordinarily be in sympathy."

"That doesn't make it okay to set me up as a patsy."

"Remember, Benjamin, this person probably did not intend things to turn out the way they have. No doubt it was arranged for someone at the Miami airport to open your suitcase and extract the list before you even knew it was there. What happened to you was an unfortunate accident."

"Unfortunate is right. Don't you realize what the Cuban government is going to make out of this? Espionage? Murder? I won't stand a chance once they get me."

"I think, Benjamin, that you must go to the Swiss Embassy. Give them your slip of paper. Let them do something about it."

"Hell, they can't do anything with a scrap of paper. They need a name, something the State Department can use to lean on Castro."

"I'm afraid for you. I do not want anything to happen to you."

"How do you think I feel? But I'll be damned if I'll take the blame for something I didn't do. I'm going to find out who was responsible. Now, will you help me?"

Isabel sighed and got up. "I would be a fool to say yes." She went to the kitchen counter, pulled open a drawer, and took out a pad and pencil, then scribbled something on the pad and brought it back to Benjamin.

"What's this?"

"Read it."

Benjamin looked at it and smiled. "Idiomatically speaking, you're a little dated."

"We Cubans are out of touch with American slang these days."

She had written in a large firm hand, "It takes a fool to get stuck on a fool." The *K*s were the same size as the other letters, formed with three swift downward strokes of the pencil, no underlining, no idiosyncrasies, nothing like the handwriting on the scrap of paper torn from Solís's hand.

8

It had begun raining an hour before and the storm showed no sign of letting up. Dearborn was nauseated. He might as well have been sealed in a bottle and pitched into the sea as ensconced in the cabin of the *Cacahuete*. And why? Because he had married an exotic dancer who had given birth to a son with no more common sense than she. He had no one to blame for it but himself. It had been he who had permitted Jessamine Moon to bump and grind her way into his heart and he'd been paying for it, in one way or another, ever since.

It didn't help any to watch Raúl's placid progress through the meal Tomás had prepared before their departure from Miami. "'Ropa vieja,' old clothes, an apt name for the stringy concoction," Dearborn thought, "and just about as appetizing." Dearborn had dropped a tranquilizer into Raúl's wine earlier and he'd have liked to take one himself, but there had been only three to begin with in the vial he'd stolen from Dr. Huber and the remaining two were far too precious for such self-indulgence.

If Dearborn was sick, Tomás was even sicker, judging by his gagging groans and curses. But not all of his curses, Dearborn suspected, were directed at the Gods. He had totally failed to comprehend the reason for Dearborn's having left Jaime behind when he fled the sanatorium. "They're gonna arrest him. What's he gonna do?"

43

"Had I remained, Tomás, they would have arrested me as well."

"They should arrest you. You are crazier than Señor Baki."

"Jaime will no doubt prefer jail to Cuba. Besides, I shall see that he is sprung as soon as Benjamin and I return. Now ready the boat, Tomás. The sooner I get there and back, the sooner Jaime will be released."

"Suppose you get shot?"

"I have no intention of getting shot."

"Just in case, you gotta write a letter to the police and tell them Jaime, he didn't know nothin' about no kidnapping. You gotta say it was your idea and the reason you run away from him is because he wasn't no part of it."

"If you insist. Now can we get started?"

That had been hours before. Now Tomás was on deck manning the steering wheel, as they rolled and pitched in the heavy sea. With half-closed eyes, Dearborn watched the wine slosh around in Raúl's wineglass.

"Roycrap, my fran," Raúl declared, putting down the glass and wiping his mouth with his sleeve. "Estaba de Dios que habiamos de marcharnos! Cúmplase la voluntad del cielo!"

"I have no idea what you are talking about, Raúl."

"He say," Tomás translated, staggering in from above, "is the will of God you and him escaped."

Raúl said something else unintelligible to Dearborn.

"He say the voices told him it is time to kill Castro."

Dearborn shook his head and changed the subject. "Let me get this straight, Tomás. Cojimar is only a few miles from Havana. Are you sure of that?"

"I used to live in Cojimar. I worked at cleanin' and packin' fish in the factory in Cojimar. You just gotta start walkin' west and you gonna come to La Habana."

"We should make it in a couple of hours."

"If we don't get shot first."

"I refuse to succumb to your melancholy point of view. Incidentally, what are you doing in here? Is it wise to walk away from the wheel? It seems to me the boat is rocking rather more violently than before."

"That's because I just drop the anchor."

44

"We've arrived?" Dearborn got up onto his knees to look out the porthole over the bunk bed. Nothing was discernible through the salt-streaked glass.

"Sí. We're in the bay at Cojimar. You gotta hurry. We don't suppose to be inside the twelve-mile limit."

"How far are we from the beach?"

"About half a mile. I can bring you about a hundred yards from shore. Then you gotta swim."

"What about my suitcase? I have quite a substantial amount of money in there."

Tomás reached out and opened a cabinet above Dearborn's head. "I got a waterproof bag in here. You could put your money in it."

"Tomás, what's that?"

Tomás cocked his head. "What's what?"

"Didn't you say you turned off the engine? I seem to hear the sound of an engine."

"Ay, Dios!" Tomás turned and plunged back out onto deck.

Seconds later a strange voice, eerily magnified, reverberated throughout the cabin. "Atención *El Cacahuete!*"

"Ataque!" Raúl shouted in response to the voice. "Combate!" He jumped up from the table and darted out the cabin door. Dearborn rushed after him.

The harsh beam of a searchlight played on the deck as a Cuban gunboat approached to the starboardside. The commanding voice persisted, and when the sleek bow of the gunboat dipped into the trough of a wave, Dearborn spotted two fifty-caliber machine guns mounted on the deck.

Tomás had begun tugging frantically at the anchor. "Start the engine!" he cried.

Dearborn pushed Raúl aside and rushed into the cockpit. He turned the key in the ignition, jammed the throttle forward and clutched at the wheel as the boat strained against the anchor, then abruptly lunged free. Dearborn heard a whoop behind him and turned. Raúl had lost his footing on the slippery deck and lay sprawled on his back. Tomás was kneeling at the stern rail with his fishing knife in one hand and all that was left of the anchor line in the other.

45

They were easy targets caught in the glare of the searchlight and Dearborn jerked the wheel sharply to try to elude it. He could see the shadowy shoreline ahead, about a half-mile distant, a jumble of clustered lights marking a village. The searchlight swung around and again fixed on the *Cacahuete*. The megaphoned voice called out something that didn't have to be translated to be understood. They were about to open fire.

Dearborn spun the wheel and the boat swerved as a burst of machine gun fire splattered the deck. He glanced over his shoulder and saw that the patrol boat had swung in close and a couple of seamen carrying rifles were taking aim at him. Tomás bounded forward and pushed Dearborn away from the wheel as a bullet tore into the windshield where Dearborn's head had been a second before. Then Tomás took over the wheel and began steering a tight zigzag course for shore. Bullets sprayed the deck near Raúl who had taken cover behind a wooden tackle barrel, and for a moment it looked to Dearborn as if the huge prow of the gunboat were going to ram them, but Tomás veered skillfully out of its path.

Then suddenly the gap between the two boats widened.

"You're outdistancing them, Tomás!" Dearborn shouted.

"This here is shallow water. They cannot come so close to shore."

"Hallelujah! Hallelu . . ."

Dearborn's cry of triumph was cut short as the *Cacahuete*'s propellers set up a terrible clatter. "My Lord, we're going to run aground!"

"Cuidado!" Tomás warned as the engine began to buck.

Dearborn grabbed the railing with both hands and held on as the boat reared up, shivered violently, then plowed into the sandbar and stopped.

"Come on!" Tomás cried. "We gotta swim!"

"What about my suitcase?"

"What about my boat, you crazy old man!"

Dearborn was weak in the knees by the time the three men crawled up onto the beach. He hadn't swum that far or with such concentrated effort in years. Two or three dozen wooden houses were tucked among the palms and yagrumas on the side of the hill ahead of them, but none showed any signs of life. "Is it possible," Dearborn puffed, "that no one heard the machine guns?"

"People here in Cuba," Tomás said grimly, "they don't come out when they hear guns. They go inside."

Raúl squeezed the water out of his shirt, a pointless exercise since it was raining more heavily than ever, got to his feet, and thumbed his nose at the black waters of the bay.

"They can't see us, Raúl," Dearborn told him, "any more than we can see them."

"We can't see my boat neither," Tomás said bitterly. "And now I ain't ever gonna see it again."

"Buck up. We've eluded them and we're alive."

"God, he has punish me for bein' greedy. I knew I never should of say yes."

Dearborn got to his feet. "Too late to ponder the imponderable, Tomás. We've got to get out of here. Where did you say your friend lives?"

Tomás sighed and rose. He nodded to a house halfway up the hill, a wooden structure raised on stilts, its front door and windows facing the bay. "Come on. We betta hurry."

Dearborn couldn't have hurried if he were being chased by the Loch Ness monster. With a heavy amble he followed Tomás and Raúl and mounted the porch steps behind them.

Tomás pounded on the door while Raúl and Dearborn peered over his shoulder. The door was opened by a small thin man dressed in baggy trousers. Behind him stood four barefoot children dressed in knee-length shirts. He raised his hand to his eyes to wipe away the sleep, then abruptly opened them wide with startled recognition. "Tomás! Eres tú?"

Tomás nodded bleakly. "Sí, José. Oye! I am in trouble." He had spoken in English but corrected himself immediately, and repeated himself in Spanish.

"Con la policía?"

"Sí."

A chubby dark-skinned woman, wearing a shawl over her nightgown, had appeared behind the children. When she saw Tomás she gasped and tightened the shawl around her shoulders, then suddenly let it drop to the floor. "Tomás?"

"Sí, Luisa. Es la verdad."

With a sob she pushed open the door and yanked him inside, then reached out again to haul in Dearborn and Raúl. José stood with the children clinging to him like lampreys. Tomás said urgently, "Tenemos necesitamos refugio."

The woman whispered, "Vengan conmigo," and hurried them into a back bedroom, pushing past to draw the window curtains before switching on a single pale bulb dangling from the ceiling. In a frightened voice she asked, "Que pasó, Tomás?"

Tomás began to explain. When he'd finished, Luisa threw her arms around him. "Tomás, querido Tomás! Ah, ah! Que terrible!"

José shook off the children, grasped Tomás by the shoulders and began talking excitedly.

"What's he saying, Tomás?"

Tomás held up his hand to silence Dearborn and continued to listen. Then he translated. "José say a few days ago another gunboat, she sink a ship carryin' thirteen Cubans a few miles out from La Esperanza on the west coast of Cuba. Twelve men was killed right away and the last one, he confess they was comin' from Florida to get Castro."

"Good God!"

"He say now they are killin' anybody who tries to come or go by boat."

Luisa cut in with a noisy speech in which the words, "pistolas" and "ejecución" figured outstandingly, and once again the three friends fell on one another's necks. Dearborn watched disapprovingly. Overly emotional, these Latins. That was the trouble with them. One could never rely on overly emotional people. "Tomás, please suspend the mawkish sentimentalities," he interjected sternly. "Through no fault of our own we find ourselves in imminent peril. I suggest we pull ourselves together and do something constructive about it."

The look Tomás bestowed on Dearborn left no doubt as to where he thought the fault for their predicament lay. Nonetheless, he broke free of the group and spoke to Luisa, who crossed the room to push aside a curtain that concealed a clothes closet. She rummaged inside, extracted three pairs of baggy trousers made of coarse white cotton and tossed them onto the bed. She added three cotton shirts from a box she pulled out from under the bed, then spoke to Tomás before pushing her family out of the room and closing the door.

"She say we must get rid of our clothes. She say we should dress quick. She don't know if José's pants will fit you or Raúl but you must make the best for now."

They took off their wet clothing and piled it on the floor. Tomás, at about five-feet-four, was the same height as José, and the shirt and pants fit him well, but José's trousers reached only to Dearborn and Raúl's calves.

"What the well dressed fugitive is wearing," Dearborn grumbled ungraciously.

"She say she ain't got shoes," Tomás went on, "but she will get us sandals in the morning."

"Very nice. Very nice, indeed, and my three-hundred-dollar Wildsmiths are lying at the bottom of the bay."

"Excuse me if I don't feel sorry for you," Tomás said under his breath. He suddenly raised his head to stare at the window.

"At least Raúl seems happy," Dearborn remarked, noting Raúl's cheerful, if somewhat soporific, smile.

"Ssh."

"What?"

"Listen."

There were people approaching. They could hear the sound of men's voices coming from the direction of the beach.

9

Tomás made a move to turn off the light, but it was too late. They heard the sound of footsteps on the porch. Dearborn strode to the bedroom door and opened it, but Luisa motioned him back inside. She had already tucked the children into cots behind a screen and whispered something to them before grabbing José's arm and tiptoeing back to the bedroom. Once inside the room Luisa swept up the wet clothes, shoved them into Dearborn's arms and pushed him into the closet, indicating that Raúl and Tomás should get under the bed. Then, before Dearborn had time to close the closet curtain, she pulled her nightgown over her head and dropped it on the spot where the wet clothing had dampened the floorboards.

"Venga, chico," she commanded, and José followed suit, whipping off his trousers to reveal haunches as stringy as Luisa's were pudgy.

They heard, but ignored, the knock on the door. Nor did they turn out the light. Instead, with Luisa directing operations, they jumped onto the bed and proceeded to exercise their connubial privilege, José pumping energetically while Luisa, chunky thighs vibrating, held on for dear life.

There was no second knock. Instead, the front door burst open and through a chink in the curtain Dearborn saw half a dozen armed men in uniforms spill into the dark front room. Immediately the children jumped out of their beds and began prancing around with cries of "Mamá! Papá!" while the men pushed them aside and made for the bedroom.

The leader, a young naval officer with a baby face and spectacles, stopped short in the doorway. Dearborn saw Luisa raise her head over José's shoulder and fix the officer with a dazed, offended stare. "Sin verguenza!" she called out hoarsely, while José, apparently intent on giving a convincing performance, continued to pump away industriously.

The children tried to wriggle past the gaping men but were turned around by the sheepish officer who passed them back through the ranks of snickering sailors.

"Cochino!" Luisa screeched. "Villano!"

"Perdone," the officer said gallantly, while his men strained to get a better look.

"Villano!" Luisa repeated vituperatively.

The officer bowed from the waist, backed out of the room, and closed the door. In another minute he and his men were gone, their boots clattering down the porch steps, their laughter fading in the distance.

"Tell them we must get to Havana," Dearborn told Tomás. "Tell them we need help."

José had sent the children outside to stand watch while the adults ate breakfast, a substantial meal of fresh pineapple, coarse bread, crumbly white cheese, and steaming cups of café con leche. Tomás had just finished detailing their adventure on the high seas and explaining why they were in Cuba. José and Luisa approved of Dearborn, whom they agreed was a gentleman of honor, a superlative father, and a courageous man, but it was Raúl who really impressed them. "Baki? Ah sí, el destilador muy rico! Ronbaki! Ay, chico!"

Raúl responded with uncharacteristic modesty, perhaps the remnants of an earlier sensibility, by murmuring "De nada," and "No es importante," while daintily picking his teeth with the tines of his fork.

Dearborn, drumming restlessly on the table top, waited for Tomás to get on with it. "Well? Are you asking them? What are they saying?"

"Luisa, she know a man with a car. He can drive us but we must pay."

"Fine, fine. Tell her I'll be happy to pay. Tell her I shall pay very generously."

"With what?"

"What?"

"With what?"

Dearborn stared at Tomás in horror, floored by the realization that his thirty thousand dollars was now in the hands of the Cuban Navy.

"We got no money," Tomás said. "Is only four, five mile to La Habana, but now we cannot walk on the road without they see us and shoot us."

"What *can* we do?"

"Don't ask me. You are the one with the ideas. You are the one got me into this. Now, how you gonna get me out of it?"

"Perhaps Raúl. Yes, of course, that's it. It is time to call upon Raúl."

Tomás made a rude sound with his lips. "Raúl? You want I should talk to Raúl? What's Raúl gonna say?"

"We brought him because he is sure to have contacts in Havana."

"*We* didn't bring nobody. *You* brung Raúl. All I done was run the boat."

"Talk to him, Tomás!"

Snorting disdainfully, Tomás did as instructed. Pulling his chair close to Raúl's so that they could converse at close range, he began shouting full into Raúl's face as if the old man were deaf.

Raúl rose gamely to the occasion, offering a list of prominent names that delighted Luisa and José, but that did nothing to advance the situation. Rubio Garrida, sugar magnate, "muerto"; Miguel Enciso, tobacco heir, "muerto"; Fernando Orbe, playboy, "muerto"; Diego Moragas, theater entrepreneur, "en los Estados Unidos"; Estanislao Campos, Bernardo Ruiz, and Alfonso Navarro, "en el cárcel."

Tomás threw out his arms. "What did I tell you? This is gettin' us nowheres."

"Está," Raúl went on, "Clara Ortiz."

Luisa's face lit up. "Conoce a Clara Ortiz? Yo también conozco."

"What's she saying?"

"She say she know Clara Ortiz. Luisa, she been to her house a couple times. Luisa's aunt, she used to be a cook for Clara Ortiz, back in the old days."

"Who is Clara Ortiz?"

"She was a famous actress. Luisa say she lives in Matanzas."

"Is that anywhere near Havana, Tomás?"

"Is in the opposite direction, but Luisa say Señora Ortiz, she know important pipples. Maybe she can help us if we can get there."

"There, you see!" Dearborn exclaimed. "I knew that Raúl would prove invaluable!"

"Yeah, but there still ain't no car."

"Try asking José and Luisa again. Surely they know someone who would agree to help us without expecting to be paid for it."

Tomás turned back to query them. At first they shook their heads, but as he continued to cajole, they began to exchange guilty glances. Finally José said something which caused Tomás to rear back with shock.

"What's the matter?" Dearborn demanded. "Now what's wrong?"

"They're talkin' about Elena."

"Elena who?"

"My Elena." Tomás leaned his elbows on the table and put his face in his hands. "They wasn't gonna tell me. I ask about Elena last night. They lied to me. They say Elena is livin' in La Habana. They say Elena don't come here to Cojimar no more."

"Yes? So? What's wrong? What is it they weren't going to tell you? Has the girl expired?"

Tomás said something in a muffled voice that Dearborn couldn't catch. "What? What? What are you saying?"

"She got marry."

"One of life's little tragedies," Dearborn declared impatiently, "but hardly pertinent to the subject under discussion."

"José, he say that Elena's husband has a car and she know how to drive."

Dearborn's spirits rose again. "You don't say!"

"But she is marry with a man who belongs to the C.D.R. That is the Committee for Defense of the Revolución. He would turn us in like nothin'."

"If he knew, Tomás. If he knew. But Elena would never tell him, would she?"

"She ain't gonna get the chance."

"You couldn't expect the girl to wait forever. That's romantic twaddle. She doesn't love you anymore."

"Maybe she don't," Tomás conceded defiantly, "but if she don't, then she ain't gonna help us."

"We can only hope that conscience will compel her to perform this one last selfless act."

Tomás laughed rancorously. "Oh sure. She's gonna say, 'I broke Tomás's heart so now I gotta save his life.'"

"Obviously José and Luisa think she'll do it. Ask them to go see her, Tomás."

"The hell with her."

"Ask them, Tomás. Just ask them."

Right after breakfast José left for the docks and Luisa left for La Habana de Este, a nearby housing project where Elena lived. She returned before noon to inform them that Elena, upon hearing that Tomás was in Cojimar, had collapsed in a faint on the kitchen floor. Once revived, however, she had listened to Luisa's recital of Tomás's troubles and agreed to drive him, Dearborn, and Raúl to Matanzas.

"Didn't I tell you," Dearborn said smugly. "Shock gave way to conscience."

"She never should of marry. She say she was comin' to Florida."

"Water under the dam, Tomás. Let us not brood about it. Ask Luisa when Elena is coming."

"She already told me. Elena's husband, he work at night at the cannery. He leave for work at ten-thirty, so she's comin' about eleven."

During the afternoon Raúl and Tomás catnapped while Dearborn stood guard and Luisa walked to the store to buy sandals. José came home at eight-thirty, dirty, weary, and smelling of fish, and at nine Luisa served them a meal of ajiaco, a root vegetable stew, with black bread and Cuban beer. Dearborn managed to slip a tranquilizer into Raúl's beer as a safeguard against him becoming too obstreperous later, and after supper José undressed the children, and tucked them into their cots. He then took down a small guitar called a requinto and played while Luisa washed the dishes.

It was just eleven when Elena opened the door and walked into the house.

Tomás leaped to his feet, struggling for composure as she greeted everyone with a loud, and to Dearborn's trained ear, unnatural, "Hola!"

She was a robust young woman who didn't conform to Dearborn's vision of a romantic heroine. She was taller than Tomás, with broad shoulders and no waistline to speak of, fat cheeks and eyes that were set so close together she looked cross-eyed. She did have a mane of beautiful silky black hair, however, and, Dearborn noted generously, a sweet, if somewhat toothy smile.

Luisa introduced her to Raúl, who made an unsuccessful attempt to kiss her hand and to Dearborn, who contented himself with a formal half-bow. Then Luisa brought the two former lovers together, pulling Tomás across the room and literally shoving his hand into Elena's. Their eyes connected in brief agonized recognition and then quickly disengaged. A moment later Tomás was standing once again across the room while Elena remained rooted to the floor just inside the front door.

She mumbled something to Luisa, who turned and repeated it to Tomás.

"What did she say?" Dearborn demanded.

"She say," Tomás repeated, "that her husband will return home at eight in the mornin' and she must be home before he get there. So now we must leave."

Dearborn waited out the effusive farewells between Tomás and his friends, then took Raúl's arm and led him out to the ancient battle-scarred Nash Rambler bearing the official insignia of the C.D.R., which was parked on the road above. Dearborn thought Tomás would get into the passenger seat next to Elena, but instead he climbed with ostentatious deliberation into the back seat. Raúl, who despite having slept all afternoon, was still looking drowsy, elected to share the back seat with Tomás, which left the front seat to Dearborn.

They drove along dark roads between swaying palms, crept through dark villages and saw almost no other cars en route. It was almost one o'clock when they reached Matanzas. They passed through streets of modern two- and three-story cement office buildings built alongside picturesque wooden houses that dated from colonial times. They stopped once to consult the directions Luisa had given them, then proceeded into the center of town, turning right and entering a tranquil neighborhood of tree-lined streets and houses hidden behind tall fences. At first glance it looked like a neighborhood untouched by change but here and there, there were clues to its evolution; a clothesline strung between a tree and the grillwork of a ground-floor window, a basket of fruit on a second-floor window sill, a sagging front gate held in place by makeshift wiring. It took a while to find the street, la calle Estrellita, and a little longer to locate the number, diez y ocho, engraved on a small plaque on the gate.

Elena parked the car and for the first time turned to address herself to Tomás. He listened for a moment, then leaned forward to translate for Dearborn. "She say she must go first. She say is in case Clara Ortiz don't live there no more. Luisa ain't been out here for two, maybe three year."

Elena got out of the car, let herself in the gate and walked up the path to the front door. The house was dark and remained so for long minutes after she rang the bell. Then the door opened a crack and Elena began to talk. They couldn't see who it was she was talking to and the conversation seemed interminable, but finally she returned to the car and indicated to them that all was well.

"Wake up, Raúl," Dearborn instructed, opening the door.

Tomás shook Raúl, who wakened, peered out of the car window and began uttering exclamations of delight, "Estamos aquí! Por fin! Vamos, my frans!"

"Well," Dearborn remarked as Elena drove away a minute later, "he seems to remember the house. Now let us hope that the lady will remember him."

# 10

Dearborn and Tomás entered the dark house. Raúl was standing just inside the door with a woman in kimono and slippers who shut the door behind them and bolted it before she switched on the light. The high-ceilinged foyer was dimly lit by the one bulb in an overhead chandelier that was intended to hold a dozen such bulbs, but it could be considered a kindness, Dearborn thought, since the walls were in need of paint, there were strips of plaster hanging from the ceiling, and the wrapper Clara Ortiz wore was pathetically shabby and faded.

The woman herself was another story. Dearborn judged her to be in her mid-sixties. She was beautiful, with great dark eyes set into a finely chiseled face, white hair, a smooth complexion, and a graceful figure that even the shapeless kimono couldn't hide. She had laced her arm through Raúl's, and he beamed with pleasure as he introduced her to Tomás and then to his good friend "Señor Roycrap."

"Roycroft," Dearborn corrected. "Raúl knows me as Burgess Roycroft."

Despite her affectionate acknowledgment of Raúl, Señora Ortiz was looking bewildered and even a little frightened, though she was doing her best to conceal it. "Roycroft? How do you do, Señor. Welcome to my home."

Dearborn wanted to set her at ease but he wasn't sure just how to go about it. "I know that our unexpected visit must be something of a shock . . . "

"I have not seen Raúl for over twenty years," she conceded, "and I did not comprehend what that young woman was telling me. She said something about the three of you coming here by boat from Miami. Is it true that you were pursued by a gunboat?"

"Mercilessly, Madame."

"It was an attempt to infiltrate?"

"An attempt, not totally successful, I'm afraid." Dearborn glanced into the rooms on either side of the hall. One was a parlor, the other a library with empty bookcases lining the walls. There was barely any furniture in either room and what few pieces there were had seen better days. The floors were bare, there were no curtains at the windows, and both rooms, like the hallway between, were badly in need of repair.

"My apartment is upstairs," Señora Ortiz informed them. "Will you do me the honor of taking coffee with me?"

"At the very least, Madame."

Señora Ortiz kept a tight grip on Raúl as they went up the stairs, drawing him into a conversation that excluded Dearborn and Tomás, but which Tomás translated in a kind of verbal shorthand. "She say how he look. He say how she look. She is askin' is he marry. He say no. He say what he has been doin' all these years . . . livin' in Florida . . . nothin' about the crazy house. . . . She say how she is missin' him. He is askin' her about pipples they know. She is namin' all the pipples who is dead now. He is sayin' for what she is stayin' in Cuba. She is sayin' for why he came here. Uh, oh!"

Dearborn didn't need to ask what the exclamation was

about. Raúl had launched into another tirade against "Castro" and the "communistas." Dearborn heard the word, "revolución."

Señora Ortiz, however, was unperturbed. "Sí," she soothed. "Entiendo. Eres el mismo, Raulito, y yo también. Yo soy la misma."

"She understand," Tomás said in an undertone. "He is the same and so is she."

Their footsteps rang hollow in the long empty upstairs hall and Señora Ortiz twisted her head to look at them as she led them on. "I live on the third floor. One woman alone does not need so much space." She guided them to the back stairs which were entered through a door that required unlocking. Watching her take the key out of her kimono pocket and fit it into the keyhole, Dearborn suddenly became aware of her extreme vulnerability. Living alone in this large house, surrounded by neighbors for whom she was a reminder of past oppression. . . . No wonder she was so fearful.

"Be careful," she cautioned as she opened the attic door and started up the dark steps. "There is no banister."

She and Raúl continued to whisper conspiratorially as they preceded Dearborn and Tomás up the steep steps. When they reached the third-floor landing she clicked on the light and they found themselves in a narrow corridor with worn sisal carpeting and age-splotched walls. She led them into a slant-roofed room on the right that must originally have been the servants' sitting room but was now furnished with pieces that had been brought upstairs from her drawing room: two shabby Queen Anne sofas faced one another across a pink marble coffee table; twin armchairs, upholstered in faded green silk, were flanked by a delicate rosewood desk; and the rest of the room was a treasure house of antiques, hand-tapestried footstools, crystal vases, porcelain figurines, a cloisonné clock, to say nothing of two magnificent paintings, one of which Dearborn suspected might be a Renoir.

Dearborn stood in the doorway with Tomás's warm breath on his neck while Raúl darted around the room running his hands over the inlaid woods and exclaiming over the paintings. He returned to embrace Señora Ortiz and spoke in sentimental tones which she reciprocated with a catch in her voice.

"Señor Baki," Tomás whispered, "he say he give her the paintin'. She say it was when they was in Paris in 1947."

"You don't say. It would appear that their friendship goes a little deeper than I suspected."

"Mira, Raúl," Señora Ortiz declared suddenly. "Te recuerdas de la bata?" With a sweeping gesture she tossed off her kimono and stood revealed in a pink satin peignoir embroidered with ivory rosebuds and seed pearls. Raúl, with an ecstatic cry, seized her hand and covered it with kisses.

"Pity the man is bonkers," Dearborn murmured. "I'll have to break it to her gently."

"You don't have to tell her," Tomás predicted. "She gonna find out all by herself."

Raúl began questioning Señora Ortiz very closely and after she answered him at length she turned back to Dearborn. "Raúl is asking me how I was able to keep my house. I have been telling him that in the beginning, twenty-two, twenty-three years ago, they billeted soldiers here. One of the officers was the son of a friend and close to one of the leaders of Castro's revolution. He promised to get me the papers which would allow me to remain in my house, and he was a gentleman. Many among us believed the revolutionists' promises. It was not until we lost everything that we realized we had traded one tyranny for another."

"Are you safe here? I mean in this neighborhood?"

"There are those neighbors who are friendly. They remember me, or their parents remember me, from the days when I was an actress, but there are many who are not so charitable. They would denounce me if they saw these remnants of my former life."

Raúl interrupted with still more questions which Señora Ortiz answered in Spanish and repeated in English. "He wishes to know how I live. The truth is that I was able to keep my jewels. I sell them, illegally of course and only a few stones at a time, whenever it becomes necessary." She spoke to Raúl and laughed at his reply. "I have asked Raúl why he has still not learned English and he tells me the same how he always told me. 'Spanish is the language of God.' All these years living in the United States and still he doesn't speak English. He is crazy, no?"

"Now that you bring it up," Dearborn returned, "perhaps we should discuss Raúl's mental acuity."

Señora Ortiz looked up into Raúl's face with sweet affection, once again inspiring him to kiss her hand, this time accompanying the kiss with a Prussian click of the heels.

"He has always been impetuous," Señora Ortiz allowed. "When he was a young man he distressed his family by refusing to think or behave like the other young men in his social circle. While the others sailed their boats at the yacht club, he made speeches. When they wrote love poetry, he wrote articles for the university paper. At that time, you know, Raúl believed that in order to overcome the despotic avarice of its dictators, Cuba should become a monarchy. But of course his vision was not met with overwhelming approval. In fact there were some who thought him mentally unstable."

"Speaking of which," Dearborn picked up again, "I think you should know that Raúl has progressed somewhat beyond the sphere of political theory."

"What do you mean?"

"He has come here with some notion of deposing Castro."

"Yes, of course."

Dearborn was startled by her matter-of-fact response. "You don't find the idea bizarre?"

She frowned in puzzlement. "Why should I?"

"I'm not questioning one's right to hold extremist views, Madame. I've been accused of it myself on more than one occasion. But there are practical considerations, don't you agree?"

"Such as?"

"One cannot overthrow a government single-handed."

Her face cleared. "Ah yes, I see. You are waiting for me to acknowledge the existence of a rebel force here in Cuba."

"What rebels?" Tomás blurted out in an alarmed voice.

"Señor Roycroft," Señora Ortiz said reassuringly, "there is no need to approach the subject in so guarded a fashion. Raúl explained to me while we were climbing the stairs that the three of you have come to join us."

"Join you?" Dearborn asked suspiciously.

"Raúl told me you came in answer to the need of The Voice."

"He told you about hearing voices?"

"Naturally I knew he was talking about our branch of El Cuerpo."

"El what?"

"El Cuerpo."

"What about El Cuerpo?" Tomás chimed in fearfully.

"You know El Cuerpo?" Dearborn asked Tomás.

"In Spanish El Cuerpo mean the body. Is a group of people against Castro. The leaders, they are Cuban exiles livin' in Miami."

"Come, come," Señora Ortiz teased coyly, "there is no need to pretend you do not know about El Cuerpo. Surely you were informed that it is I who am the leader of the section known as The Voice."

"Good Lord."

She turned back to Raúl and said a few words to him which inspired him to a brief but impassioned speech.

"She say," Tomás repeated glumly, "that she is glad he have return to join El Cuerpo. He say he pledge himself to her body. He say he has dreamed to be joined to her body."

"A comedy of errors," Dearborn muttered. "An unexpected and appalling development."

# 11

There were two small bedrooms in Clara Ortiz's attic, plus one large bedroom which she had created by knocking down the walls between three adjoining cubicles. In addition there were a good-size bathroom and a small kitchen that once had been a closet. The rooms assigned to Tomás and Dearborn were narrow cells each containing a rope bed and a bureau. Raúl, however, was more fortunate. Picking up where he had left off more than twenty years before, he shared Clara's bed.

The few hours of sleep Dearborn had enjoyed in José and Luisa's house the day before hadn't been enough to overcome the effects of his three-hour immersion in the bay. He fell into a sound sleep and awoke late in the morning when Señora Ortiz arrived with a breakfast tray. "Please forgive me for waking you," she apologized, "but they are coming at twelve o'clock and I know you will wish to dress."

Dearborn bolted upright. "Who is coming?"

Señora Ortiz put the tray on the bureau top and came over to plump up the pillows behind Dearborn's back. "Barrios, Vargas, Mojica, Naranjo, and Asturias, five officers of El Cuerpo."

"Good God! Did you call them or did they call you?"

"Call?"

"On the telephone."

"I have no telephone. I have only a short-wave ham radio with which I contact Miami when it is necessary." She thought for a moment, then added, "I contacted our Miami base last night. I wished to tell them that you had arrived safely."

"Oh?" Dearborn responded warily. "What did they have to say for themselves?"

"It was not a good connection. I could not understand them well, especially since our method of communication involves an intricate code. They seemed surprised to hear that you had arrived safely and that you knew how to contact me. There was a mixup. They thought you were to contact another of our groups in La Esperanza, and I believed that I heard mention of thirteen men, but that may have been the static. Nevertheless, they thought your boat had been sunk off the west coast instead of running aground in Cojimar. I told them they were mistaken, and that you had arrived intact."

"Yes, indeed," Dearborn confirmed. "Three of us and we made it intact. No question about it."

"They say you will be invaluable in serving the transitional government and that you have sworn eternal allegiance to the cause."

"We have? Oh of course, we have. Do or die, that's us."

"Very good, Señor. Now, you asked how I contacted the rest of our little group. El Cuerpo has a verbal relay system for passing messages. It is swift, efficient, and far safer than the telephone."

"A message to Garcia, eh?"

"Except that we employ trucks, bicycles, and private cars instead of horses. Anyway, the others have been informed of your arrival and are on their way here." She put the tray on his lap and went back to the door.

"What time is it?" Dearborn asked.

"Eleven-thirty."

She closed the door and Dearborn listened to the tap of her heels down the corridor. He was still drowsy and confused by the situation. He had hoped that Raúl would lead him to a former acquaintance, a member of the old school who was knowledgeable about the political structure in Cuba and conversant with the possibilities for bribery and/or blackmail—someone who could appreciate his problem and who had no compunctions about defying the authorities. Clara Ortiz certainly fit the bill. But El Cuerpo? An anti-Castro terrorist organization? He hadn't bargained for the possibility of violence and he certainly hadn't intended to commit himself to the overthrow of the Cuban government!

Dearborn became aware of a rumble in the pit of his stomach. For a moment it distracted him from his reflections. He examined his breakfast tray. Smoked fish of some sort, black bread, and a pot of coffee. He picked up his fork and began flaking off bits of the fish and then tentatively popped a forkful into his mouth. Whatever it was, it tasted delicious. He poured himself a cup of coffee and sipped it. The names Señora Ortiz had recited sounded ominous. Or was it only his associations. . . . Barrios, Vargas, Mojica . . . they culled up schoolboy recollections of Pancho Villa and Emiliano Zapata. He had a vision of himself and his companions, blindfolded and barefoot, lined up against a wall. Not pleasant. Not pleasant at all.

He poured himself a second cup of coffee. The stuff was better than a shot of brandy for stiffening the spine. Of course, it was fortunate, that he, Raúl, and Tomás had been mistaken by Clara Ortiz for those poor fellows who had sunk off the west coast of Cuba. And it was true that Dearborn could use the expertise of El Cuerpo. On second thought, perhaps, he was being too fearful. They certainly must be resourceful and they would be prepared to face danger. Stumbling onto them could conceivably be a break in his favor.

63

Dearborn put aside his tray and got out of bed. He'd better talk to Tomás. It took only a minute or two to put on his trousers and shirt and to slip into his sandals. Opening his door he bumped into Tomás, stubble-chinned and sleepy-eyed, already standing on the threshold. "It doesn't look as if you'd slept too well, Tomás," Dearborn greeted his friend.

"Do you know what she say?" Tomás demanded. "She say they gonna make me a sergeant in El Cuerpo. She say Raúl, they gonna make him a major."

"In that case," Dearborn noted dryly, "I shall insist upon being made a colonel."

"This ain't no time for makin' jokes. I am tellin' you, we gotta get outta here."

"Luck has played into our hands, Tomás. Stumbling onto El Cuerpo may have been the best thing that has happened to us. It will be to our advantage to remain."

"Not me. I ain't stayin' here." Tomás dropped his voice to a whisper. "That Señora Ortiz, she is just like Señor Baki. She got dust in the attic." Tomás drew his finger across an imaginary surface and presented the finger for inspection.

"Colorful phrase, that. I would guess that all fanatics could be said to have their share of dust."

"Well, I ain't no fanatic. If Raúl and you wanna stay, okay. But me, I gotta get outta here."

"Don't tell me you are totally apolitical, Tomás. Surely you have some feelings about Castro."

"What do I care about the government. I was a little boy when Castro, he came into power. I don't remember nothin' and for me nothin' ain't changed. I was livin' in a house in Camagüey till I move to Cojimar. My father, he was a sugar worker and me, I work in the factory. No difference."

"One would think you'd harbor some resentment toward a government that deported you."

"And if it was Batista, then maybe I woulda been shot."

"Let me put this another way," Dearborn said patiently. "I beg you to consider the issue of self-preservation. If you walk out of here now, you shall be totally on your own without resource and with no hope of returning to Florida."

"I could go back to Cojimar. José, he ain't got a boat of his own but maybe he could find someone who would take me."

"As an act of charity? No money asked?"

"Maybe I could steal a boat."

"You are being unrealistic, Tomás. The boat would have to be large enough to weather the trip to Miami and I doubt very much that you would find such a vessel unguarded, conveniently berthed, filled with gasoline, and of sufficient horsepower to outrun a gunboat. And you are also overlooking the important point that you will not have earned your sixteen thousand dollars."

Tomás shook his head in frustration and Dearborn was casting around for some way to cheer him up when a bell rang and Señora Ortiz and Raúl emerged from the Señora's bedroom. "On time," Señora Ortiz announced, walking toward the stairs.

"Five of them all at once?" Dearborn asked curiously. "Aren't your neighbors suspicious of such a gang?"

"The neighbors believe they are my relatives," Señora Ortiz assured him over her shoulder. "They come frequently and their faces have become familiar in the neighborhood. You wait here. I shall bring them to you."

"Whatever you say," Dearborn acceded. He led the way into the living room regarding Tomás's sullen face with disapproval. "Buck up, Tomás. I tell you it will all work out."

"Fortitud, fortuna y felicidad!" Raúl cried out enthusiastically. "Ahora trabamos batalla!"

There was only one tranquilizer left in Dearborn's vial but he decided to hold off giving it to Raúl for a while. "Pull yourself together, Raúl. This is no time for a pep rally."

Tomás groaned and raised his eyes heavenward, then stuck his fists into his pockets and leaned forlornly against the door-jamb.

Señora Ortiz returned quickly with the new arrivals, then stepped back to show them off. One of them squealed with delight and rushed forward to embrace Raúl. "Raúl Baki!" she cried. "Eres tu?"

"Alberta!" he returned. "Alberta Barrios! Como estás, mi amiga!"

"Vivo aún, Raúl, vivo aún."

"My fellow members of El Cuerpo," Señora Ortiz broke in, "know that you have been sent to aid us. They know that I have spoken to our Miami headquarters and received assurances as to your loyalty and readiness to die for the cause. Now I introduce with pride, Alberta Barrios, representative of the province of Pinar del Rio, Pablo Asturias from Oriente, Felipe Mojica from Villa Clara Province, Carlos Naranjo of Camagüey, and Enrique Vargas, representative from La Habana."

Dearborn was flabbergasted. These were the Cuban terrorists? Alberta Barrios was a wrinkled old lady who didn't look a day under eighty. Of the four men, one was fat with fleshy wattles and an asthmatic wheeze, one looked like a praying mantis with his small bald head and long brittle arms, the third looked like a doctor in a battered Panama hat and pince-nez, and the fourth—the youngest of the group—resembled a bank clerk, with a slight body and false teeth that clacked like castanets.

# 12

Señora Ortiz served a substantial lunch of bread, cheese and fruit, along with the ever-present pot of thick black coffee. Throwing caution to the winds, Dearborn dropped the last tranquilizer into Raúl's cup. The longer he could prevent them from realizing they were harboring a madman, the better.

During the next hour Dearborn learned more about El Cuerpo and his newly acquired confederates. After the revolution Alberta Barrios had moved from Havana to Pinar del Rio, the westernmost province of Cuba. She lived there with a servant and worked at what had once been her hobby, the craft of pottery-making. "You see, I must care not only for myself but for Maria, my former cook. She is ninety-one and nearly blind. What does she know of equality, of sharing the wealth. She has been with me for sixty-nine years. For fifty-three years she served me and now for sixteen years I have served her. But still she calls me La Señora and so she will until she dies."

Alberta's husband had been a lawyer who worked for the government under Batista. "Gaspar did not approve of Batista," Alberta explained. "But because Batista was what he was, Gaspar could not afford to offend him. 'Little Brother,' Batista called him. Then one day Batista sent his chauffeur for Gaspar and on the way to the presidential palace, Castro's men machinegunned the car. I promised God then that I would not let myself die until I had avenged my husband's murder."

Pablo Asturias had traveled to Matanzas from Santiago de Cuba, the capital of Cuba's easternmost province. He had made the trip by bus, distributing his considerable bulk between two seats and eating his supper from a paper bag.

Pablo lived in Santiago with one of his six sons and a daughter-in-law, in the José Martí housing district just outside the center of the city. He was an artist, but his decadent themes had made him unpopular in the new society. "Nowadays, the canvas must carry a message. It isn't enough to convey sensation or emotion. My work angers some people because they believe it is meaningless and it angers some others because they read into it messages I never intended. When I paint my friend's goat in the field they believe the flowers stand for the Cuban aristocracy and the goat . . . well, you can imagine. When they ask me to paint smiling people working in the fields with Castro's face, like God's, looking down out of the sky, I tell them only the sun and rain can grow sugar. Now I do not paint at all."

With his misshapen Panama hat and old-fashioned pince-nez, Carlos Naranjo still retained an air of elegance. He lived in the city of Camagüey, capital of Camagüey Province, and had been the owner of a large sugar plantation that had been nationalized in 1960. "They said they would pay me the value of the land," he told Dearborn, " but they did not pay me for the cane, for the mill, for the houses that stand on the land, for the machinery, or for the eighty years of love the Naranjo family gave to the land. My father and my grandfather are buried on the land. When Castro took it, he took my future and my past, and I was left with nothing, only debts. I was left to work as a laborer at my own mill. For many years now I have visited my land dreaming of the day when it would be mine again. But lately I have stopped believing the land will be returned to me during my lifetime. Now I dream only of being buried there, where I belong, alongside my father and my grandfather."

Felipe Mojica lived in Santa Clara, about a hundred miles east of Matanzas. Dearborn was not surprised to learn that he was an ornithologist and taught at the Santa Clara University. He not only looked like a professor, with his lean dry-stick appearance, but he spoke like one. "There are fourteen administrative provinces in Cuba, but for us in El Cuerpo there are six. The area in which I work for the cause includes Villa Clara, Cienfuegos, Sancti Spiritus, and Diego de Avila. It is a vast responsibility and I am in constant danger. Unlike my good friends here I enjoy a certain degree of prominence. I teach at the University and therefore my life is open to scrutiny and to criticism. There are my fellow professors and the students, my wife and my children. Then too, I have a mistress. . . ."

At that admission Raúl broke in to extol the virtues of the "acto sexual," squeezing Señora Ortiz's knee for emphasis and receiving a rap with her teaspoon for his trouble.

"To go on," Felipe said, with a censorious look at Raúl, "it is difficult to keep secrets. I am constantly in jeopardy. I am in a position of importance and yet I must take risks, not only for the moral good of my country, but for the sake of my tomaguín."

"Beg pardon?" Dearborn interjected.

"My hummingbird. The hummingbird is my special field of research. I am not permitted to leave Cuba. I do not know what the rest of the world is doing. I do not receive the latest literature. I cannot attend the symposia." Felipe swelled with pride. "It is I who wrote, *The Bird That Flies Backward.* Do you know it?"

Dearborn admitted he did not.

"Now I am working on a catalog of all three hundred and eighty-seven species of hummingbirds but I cannot survive in a vacuum. I must be free to come and go as I like, to invite my peers in the United States and in other countries to visit me, if I wish. Do you understand?"

"Perfectly."

Enrique Vargas was the man who interested Dearborn the most because he was El Cuerpo's man in Havana, or at least, one of El Cuerpo's men in Havana. A slight gentleman in his mid-forties with thinning ginger-colored hair and ill-fitting dentures, he nonetheless seemed the most authentic of the radicals.

Unlikely as it seemed, he had been, by his own admission, a "joven vividor," or playboy, in pre-Castro days. He was of good family, the son of a famous doctor and nephew of one of Batista's vice-treasurers, but he was also the black sheep of his family. "I seduced my first woman when I was fourteen. At sixteen I left school. At seventeen I ran away to France with the wife of my father's assistant. At eighteen I was forced to come home, having squandered my money at the gaming tables and having lost my mistress Florencia to the croupier. When I was twenty my father gave me the apartment building in which I lived. He told me not to ask for more. He would not support my . . . how you say . . . excesses. I celebrated my twenty-first birthday on January 1, 1959, the day Castro and his guerrillas took over Cuba. On January fifth they came to my apartment with machine guns and arrested me."

"What for?" Dearborn asked.

Enrique sipped his coffee calmly. "Because my chauffeur denounced me. He told them who my uncle was, and though I was supposedly the black sheep, it was he, Eusebio Vargas, who deserved the title. He had fled to the United States with money he had stolen from the treasury, money that Castro rightfully believed belonged to the people. Not so rightfully, Castro grabbed the only Vargas he could find."

Enrique used his napkin to dab at the corners of his lips. "They kept me for a month, questioning me, making accusations against me, forcing me to swear to my innocence again and again. They lectured me on the subject of corruption and vice and advised me to swear allegiance to Castro. Then they released me."

"You swore allegiance?"

Enrique smiled. "I am no fool. But that is not why they let me go. It was because I gave the inquisitor my emerald ring and gold wristwatch."

"What is a fool if not a man who allows himself to be compromised," Felipe Mojica commented.

"A man who thinks he cannot be compromised," Enrique answered shortly.

"The student becomes the teacher," Carlos Naranjo remarked.

"And revolution is followed by revolution," Alberta Barrios declared fatalistically.

"My friends," Señora Ortiz said, "I have read the cards and they are in our favor."

"The cards?" Tomás whispered. "Don't tell me she's a fortune-teller."

"Felipe," Señora Ortiz went on, "has brought us a bottle of Bulgarian wine. Uninspired perhaps, but better than no wine. Let us drink to the revolution."

"Here, here!"

"And our friends who have risked their lives to join us."

The Cuban rebels held up their glasses to Dearborn, Raúl, and Tomás.

After they drank, Señora Ortiz proposed that they get down to business. She called on Pablo, who reported that he had recruited two new members, and on Carlos Naranjo, who told how he had brought work to a halt at the mill for three hours simply by removing a critical nut and bolt from a piece of machinery.

Each report was accompanied by extensive comment from all the members and after a few minutes Dearborn stopped attending to the conversational cross fire. Every minute lost here was a minute lost from Benjamin's life. Dearborn felt pressed to act, and eager to cut through the extraneous talk and find some way to help his son.

Felipe Mojica had nothing specific to report but Alberta Barrios was winding up for a speech. "It has to do with our plan. It is something that I know you will all be interested to hear."

Dearborn sensed the onset of another long-winded discussion and decided to plunge in before Alberta got going. "Excuse me," he interrupted. "May I cut in here?"

"Yes, Señor Roycroft?" Señora Ortiz said.

"I have been thinking about how we three can best serve you. It seems to me that we will be most useful in Havana."

"Yes, yes. I know we shall all be interested to hear what you have to say, but I wonder if it might wait until Alberta has given her report."

"I have been contacted by Barola," Alberta obliged.

"It is through Alberta," Señora Ortiz explained to Dearborn, "that all major communication is maintained between our chief in Cuba and the rest of the organization."

"I spoke to Barola," Alberta repeated. "You will be glad to know that Barola has decided to put us in charge of the bombs."

Dearborn regarded her with a stunned expression. "Did you say bombs?"

"Yes, I did."

"We are to be in charge of them?" Carlos Naranjo echoed. "We are to plant them?"

"Exactly."

"Why? We do not belong to the Músculo unit."

"That is why," Alberta answered. "That is precisely why. Of all the units, we are the least known, the least suspected, the least watched. We can enter and leave the Plaza without notice."

"Hold it!" Dearborn interrupted loudly. "Hold it a minute."

"Yes?" Alberta obliged.

"Are you talking about bombs? Bombs that explode?"

"I am."

"What in God's name are you going to do with bombs?"

"We are going to detonate them in the Plaza de la Revolución on Saturday."

"What for?"

"There is to be a celebration there on Saturday during which Castro will speak. We intend to set off a number of bombs . . . small bombs, nothing that will kill anyone, but noisy enough to provide the necessary distraction."

"Necessary for what?" Dearborn asked with foreboding.

"To cover our real objective."

"Which is?"

"To kill Castro, of course. You know that, Señor Roycroft, as well as we do."

# 13

A plot to kill Castro? Here was something beyond Dearborn's reckoning. He was thoroughly discomposed.

"Finally we are ready," Señora Ortiz declared. "For so long we were too few, a hundred members or less. But as time went on our numbers increased until now. . . ."

"We are strong," Pablo picked up. "We are almost five thousand here in Cuba alone. We have members trained in intelligence, communications, and warfare. By Saturday evening the government shall be in the hands of El Cuerpo."

"By Saturday evening?" Dearborn echoed.

"Surely you know all about it."

"I don't know all the details," Dearborn murmured. "They thought it would be safer to withhold them. In case we were picked up, you know."

"A wise precaution," Señora Ortiz allowed. "Well, it is planned for Saturday, February twenty-fourth, which is the anniversary of the start of the 1895 Revolution. Castro is a great admirer of José Martí and it will be an all-day celebration during which Castro will address the people. Thousands of spectators will be there, among them our people—ready to attack when the signal is given."

"We gotta get outta here," Tomás whispered.

"It will be difficult to subdue Castro," Enrique continued. "He must be struck with the fatal shot immediately."

"He is a tiger," Alberta agreed.

"And a little mad," Pablo added. "I have nightmare visions of him, like Rasputin, remaining on his feet after his body has been riddled with bullets."

"The assassin must have a clear shot," Señora Ortiz commented.

"That is precisely why," Alberta declared with assurance, "the bombs are such a brilliant strategy. Can you picture it when they go off, one after the other? Mayhem, hysteria, panic!"

"Perfecto," Carlos exclaimed. "The decoys have done their work. The assassin steps out of the crowd, raises the rifle, takes aim . . ."

"Perfect," Pablo agreed. "It will be a moment of glory, a moment of triumph!"

"And we shall all be there to see it," Enrique said ecstatically.

"Not me," Tomás said under his breath.

"The moment of retribution will have arrived!"

"When do we place the bombs?" Pablo asked, tugging at his trousers where they cut into the massive flesh of his thighs.

72

"On Friday evening," Alberta replied.

"Do you know anything about bombs?" Dearborn asked.

"They are timed devices," Alberta explained. "Enrique will go to Guanabacoa on Friday afternoon to pick them up. There will be ten of them, each one set to go off in twenty-four hours at ten-second intervals."

"How can you be certain they won't kill anyone?" Dearborn insisted on knowing.

"We shall be careful where we place them," Alberta said. "They should cause no destruction beyond a radius of a few feet."

"Perfectly harmless," Señora Ortiz said reassuringly. "Only noisy."

"We shall choose the appropriate spots when the time comes," Alberta went on. "Suggestions have been made, for instance, underneath the stage, beneath the television scaffolding, and inside a telephone kiosk."

"There will be risk to us," Señora Ortiz commented.

"There is always some risk, but we shall be cautious."

"Who has been chosen to eliminate Castro?" Pablo asked. "Did Barola say?"

"As usual," Carlos suggested, "it will be a member of Los Dedos."

"Of course," Señora Ortiz said impatiently. "And as usual, no one will know who that person is."

Dearborn was following the conversation as best he could. For his benefit, everyone except Raúl was speaking in English, with only occasional lapses into excited Spanish. However, at this point he found it necessary to ask for clarification. "What is Los Dedos?"

"I am sorry, Señor Roycroft," Señora Ortiz answered. "I suppose you know the various divisions by their English titles. We are one segment of the unit called La Voz, or as you know it, The Voice. We are the direct contact between the Miami base, called El Cerebro or, if you will, The Brain, and all the Cuban chapters. It is our primary function to collect and disseminate information. Los Músculos are the fighters, those members who are trained for combat."

"And Los Dedos?"

"Los Dedos means The Fingers, which is, as you know, the section which handles eliminations."

"As in the case of Fernando Solís," Pablo elucidated.

"Who is . . .?"

"Was . . ." Felipe corrected.

"He was a member of the Cuban Intelligence, the D.G.I.," Señora Ortiz explained. "He was eliminated here in Cuba by one of Los Dedos."

"Shocking," Dearborn said without thinking. "Bloodthirsty business."

Silence fell on the members of the group, who stared at Dearborn as if he had made an unspeakable faux pas. Finally, Felipe said in a remonstrative tone, "There is no war without killing."

Another suspicion had taken hold of Dearborn and he attempted to couch his next question more delicately. "You say a Cuban Intelligence official was . . . um . . . dispatched. When was this?"

"Nine or ten days ago," Señora Ortiz informed him. "The official had uncovered information that was in the process of being relayed to El Cerebro in Miami. It was necessary for our agent to kill him in order to get it back."

"What happened to your agent?" Dearborn asked, his suspicions growing.

"Nothing," Enrique confirmed. "The information in question had been hidden in the suitcase of an American visitor . . ."

Dearborn sat up straighter and Tomás, aware of what was being revealed, nudged him warningly.

". . . who very foolishly ran away. When Solís was murdered a few minutes later, the blame fell quite naturally on the American."

"What happened to him?"

"He succeeded in escaping."

Dearborn clasped his hands between his knees, pressing them together until his knuckles whitened.

"He escaped," Felipe picked up, "but he will be caught. Immediately after the murder, the police blockaded all the roads leading out of the city. He has not a chance to get away."

"You're gonna let this guy get blamed?" Tomás broke in indignantly.

"Every war has its share of innocent victims," Señora Ortiz

said defensively. "One must reconcile oneself to the thought that sometimes their sacrifice aids a noble cause."

"An immoral point of view," Dearborn couldn't keep himself from saying.

"Too bad about the American," Alberta said, "but such are the fortunes of war."

"If the American can manage to elude the police for a few more days," Enrique added, "it will help us immeasurably. So long as the police are occupied with the manhunt they are less aware of our activities."

"That is indeed important," Alberta confirmed. "Barola told me that there are two more eliminations arranged. The American, no doubt, will be assigned responsibility for those as well."

Dearborn began to get up but Tomás restrained him. "Don't say nothin'," he whispered.

"You still have not told us who is to be the assassin," Pablo asked.

"As Clara said, we do not know the name. No one ever knows the name. But it will be the same person who eliminated Solís. It was a daring murder and was carried off smoothly. Obviously it is that kind of expert who should be assigned to Castro's assassination."

"An excellent decision," Señora Ortiz proclaimed, while the others, with nods and exclamations of approval, concurred.

Dearborn couldn't trust himself to speak. How could these mature, well-bred, seemingly civilized people speak with such equanimity of anarchy and murder?

"If the police should see this American," Carlos said thoughtfully, "they would probably not bother to arrest him. They would probably shoot him dead."

"Let us hope so," Alberta promptly responded. "It would simplify the situation. No further suspicions. No further investigations. Case closed."

"What!" Dearborn cried out in a strangled voice. "How can you . . ."

"Enough of this," Señora Ortiz broke in loudly. "Let us not waste time on such speculation. Enrique will drive back to La Habana on Monday morning. Señor Roycroft, I agree with you that you will be most useful in the city. Besides, you run a risk staying here where your presence might be noticed. In La Habana, where everyone is a stranger, you will attract no attention. That is to your liking, is it not?"

Dearborn nodded mutely, afraid to trust himself with words. To his liking? Is that what she said? As if there were anything in this God-forsaken world that could be to his liking.

# 14

The murder was still front-page news. Each day, *Juventud Rebelde* included the same candid photograph of Benjamin standing at the sidelines during one of the basketball games, fists clenched and face screwed up with frustration at a missed shot. Beneath the photo the caption read, "Murder in his heart!" The headline in *Granma*, the official organ of the Communist party, announced, "Murder, American-style!" and proceeded to describe how Solís had been shot in the back of the head as he opened his car door, how the bullet had penetrated his brain to emerge beneath his right eye, and how American it was to shoot a man without giving him a chance to see his enemy.

The consensus was that the United States was taking a hands-off position on the subject of Benjamin, an attitude characterized by the Cuban press as suspicious and one that did little to bolster Benjamin's morale. The papers reported that the State Department had chosen to disassociate itself from Benjamin's plight in order not to call attention to the fact that he was a C.I.A. agent who had been trying to smuggle into the United States a list of Cuban subversives. His "assassination" of Solís was termed "bestial and sadistic."

Benjamin and Isabel were lying in the dark looking up at the ceiling, their bodies barely touching. "It stinks," Benjamin summed up. "It really stinks."

"A representative from the D.G.I., the Cuban Intelligence Service, came to the office again today," Isabel told him. "He wanted to ask me more questions."

"About what?"

"About how well I know you. He asked me if I had seen you socially as well as in my capacity as government translator."

"What did you tell him?"

"That we had spent a number of afternoons together sight-seeing . . . along with all the other members of the team."

"Not that you've fallen in love with me?"

"I do not recall telling you that I have fallen in love with you."

"You have though, haven't you? Admit it."

"Benjamin, be sensible. I am talking about something important."

"What could be more important than your falling in love with me. Unless it's my falling in love with you. But then I've already told you that a couple of dozen times."

"I think," Isabel persisted worriedly, "that someone may have told him that I was friendlier to you than to the others."

"It would make sense," Benjamin said thoughtfully. "Whoever killed Solís would like to see me take the blame."

"How can you say that? It would be such a cold-blooded thing to do."

"These people *are* cold-blooded."

"These people? Please remember that I am one of these people."

"No, you're not. You're intelligent, principled and very beautiful."

"I am a Cuban, Benjamin."

"Yeah, there's the rub. How am I going to Americanize you?"

"Benjamin, stop it. You're in trouble. Please listen to me. You should seek the protection of the Swiss Embassy. You'll be safe there."

"And stuck, too. It's bad enough I'm cooped up here in

your apartment. I should be out looking for the bastard who got me into this mess."

Isabel said in a strained voice, "It is too dangerous to go out into the streets. The Cuban police could not touch you if you were in the Embassy."

"And the State Department would leave me there to rot. They've as much as given the Cubans carte blanche to throw me in the slammer or stand me up against a wall. And besides, even if they *were* willing to save me, how could they do it? Land a helicopter on the roof? Send in the paratroopers? Forget it. Look, I've been turning this thing over in my mind again. Take Tony Olivares, the basketball player, for instance. He told me he hates it here. He doesn't like Castro and he's even more down on the Russians. In short, he wants out. Of course, he never talked about changing the system, only escaping from it. Still . . ."

"Olivares may complain," Isabel remarked, "but he is one of the more fortunate Cubans. He is respected as a celebrity, well paid for what he does, and he enjoys special privileges. I wonder if he doesn't assume his cynical posture because it carries with it a certain glamour."

"He's taking chances knocking the establishment."

"A calculated risk. He knows how important he is and he knows that so long as it remains just talk he is in no danger of being arrested."

"Then there's Quesada, the hotel manager. He's another one who's always bad-mouthing Castro."

"Have you ever heard him say anything that leads you to think he would advocate a coup d'etat? From what I know of him he is a conservative reformer. He would like to bring about change, but gradually and without violence."

"Or so he pretends."

Isabel conceded the point with a nod.

"Okay," Benjamin went on. "How about Carmen Bonilla, Quesada's secretary?"

"You think it might have been a woman?"

"Why not? She's an aristocrat, an innocent bystander who was hurt by the revolution. There must be plenty of hostility bottled up inside of her."

"Señora Bonilla grew up in different times, Benjamin. In

the old days, Cuban women were brought up to be dependent upon their men, with no reason to think for themselves and no knowledge of politics. It is a passivity difficult to overcome."

"Still, she's learned how to take care of herself, hasn't she?"

"I think it is her only accomplishment."

"What about Patricio Gómez?" Benjamin went on.

"The hotel security officer? Yes, I know him. A sweet man but a fool. He told me one day that his father had been a street cleaner. He considers himself very fortunate to have attained the exalted position of hotel detective. I don't think you will discover that Señor Gómez is engaged in subversive activities."

"Aren't you being naïve?" Benjamin returned. "What better cover than the pretense of being unambitious, loyal to the government and slightly stupid?"

"You believe that poor Patricio Gómez may be an anti-Castro radical and you have been sending me to look for evidence in Nicasio Moya's desk. It is all so useless."

"Why? Do you think that just because Moya is somebody at the Sports Institute he can't be a subversive?"

"Nicasio is unimaginative, subservient, dull, and cowardly. In other words, he is typical of the bureaucratic underlings who inevitably succeed in government."

"Do I detect a touch of the rebel in you?"

"Yes, all right. I am aware of the imperfections of our system. But it is that knowledge which makes me sure that Nicasio is as far from being an anarchist as anyone could possibly be. However, Benjamin, there are anarchists here in Cuba. There is a group called El Cuerpo and I think it is El Cuerpo you are dealing with."

"El Cuerpo?"

"It is an organization of anti-Castro terrorists who have their headquarters in Miami and a large network of members in Cuba. It is possible . . . no, probable . . . that it was one of them who was attempting to smuggle out that list in your suitcase. If so, then you are in terrible danger from them."

"Why? They don't know where I am any more than the police do."

"They would know soon enough if you were to begin seeking them out."

"Hell, I can't just hole up here forever. I've got to do something to help myself."

"I am helping you, Benjamin. Or trying to."

"Yeah, but so far with no luck."

"Nicasio dictates his letters and he locks his desk at night."

"Couldn't you get him to write something down for you?"

"What? The letter *K* is not common in the Spanish language. I cannot ask him to jot down in kilometers the distance between Kenya and Kuwait."

Benjamin laughed, but Isabel went on earnestly, "If only you could escape from the island. There are those who would take you for a price."

"What price?"

"They say the refugee runners are asking as much as ten thousand pesos."

"I've got about five hundred dollars in American travelers' checks that I can't cash and about two hundred dollars' worth of pesos that I was going to change back into dollars' at the airport."

Isabel put her head down on his chest. "What shall we do, Benjamin?"

Benjamin stroked her back and laid his cheek against the top of her head. "It's still early. We could fool around a little."

She raised her head in surprise. "How can you think about sex at a time like this?"

He bent his head to kiss her, then slid his arms under her body and drew her to him. "It's my saving grace, or so they tell me."

# 15

Isabel had left for the Institute and Benjamin, sitting over his fourth cup of coffee, gazed at his photograph in the morning's newspaper and at the headline above it which read, "American Sought for Second Murder!"

After twelve days he was still news, still Cuban Enemy Number One, still tops on the Most Wanted list. And now, on top of it all, he stood accused of killing a second government bigwig, this one the commander of the La Habana Guard, a squadron of crack soldiers assigned to protect Castro. It was beginning to look as if he were going to be the scapegoat for every crime committed on the island.

"You were right," he had told Isabel. "It's that group . . . who'd you call them? El Cuerpo? They've found the perfect patsy. I've got to get out of here and begin doing something to clear my name."

That proposal had set her off again. "Benjamin, all you will be doing is placing yourself in greater danger, danger from the D.G.I., from the police, from El Cuerpo."

"Let's stop arguing about it. I'm in trouble no matter what I do. At least let me try to help myself the way I think best."

"Benjamin, I have been thinking again about the refugee runners. I have some jewelry, a ring, and a wristwatch. My family lives in Puerto Padre. I can get in touch with them. They may be able to lend me something."

"Come on, Isabel. You told me it would take five to ten thousand pesos to hire someone with a boat. You couldn't come up with anything like that. Even if you could, I wouldn't be able to return it."

"I don't care about getting the money back."

"Will you go back to the United States with me?"

Isabel had looked startled, then said, "I do not wish to leave Cuba. I have family here, friends, my life."

"I'm asking you to marry me." Benjamin had surprised himself saying it, but he knew he meant it, that it was what he'd wanted to say from the beginning.

"No," she had answered. "It would not work out."

"If you think I can just say, 'So long, Isabel, it was a swell couple of weeks,' you're nuts."

"There is nothing more to say, Benjamin."

"Damn it, why do you have to be so pigheaded!"

"I ask you the same. You will never find the murderer but you insist on trying."

"God damn it, I will find him!"

It had been in the heat of the discussion that followed that Benjamin had found out about Nicasio Moya.

"The more people you prove innocent," Isabel had been arguing, "the closer you will get to being killed."

"Is that why you haven't knocked yourself out to get the goods on Moya?"

"What if I get a sample of his handwriting, and what if it turned out that he is innocent. Then what? It would send you looking for more trouble!"

"Did you get it? Damn it, you did get it, didn't you?"

"Yes, yes, I got it."

She had taken a piece of paper out of her handbag. "There is to be a Cuban cultural celebration during March. The Sports Institute will be working out a program with the Conjunto Folklórico Nacionál. I asked him to write down the name and address on a slip of paper."

Benjamin took the slip she handed him. The handwriting was small and cramped and in no way resembled the handwriting on the scrap of paper he'd torn out of Fernando Solís's hand. The letter K fit smoothly between the two ls in Folklórico.

"Now, of course, you are angry."

"How long have you been carrying this around?"

"Since Thursday."

"And today's Monday. Damn it, you know how important this is to me."

"I only know how important you are!" she had returned. "I knew from the first that Nicasio was innocent. It was in the papers. Solís was alone when he went out to his car. Nicasio had stopped Solís's men to speak to them. He could not have murdered Solís."

"And you kept it from me?"

"I did not want you to go on with it. The situation is hopeless."

"I've got to go on with it."

"Oh, Benjamin, why must you go on with it? Why? Why?"

"If you don't want to help me, then I'll go it alone."

She had left then, without saying when she would return and without saying goodbye.

Benjamin was angry at her for holding out on him, angry at her for rejecting him, angrier still at himself for letting her get to him so badly. "The hell with it!" he declared to himself finally. Then he got up and went into the bedroom.

He was already dressed except for his shoes and socks and it took only a minute to put them on. He then took his wallet from the dresser drawer and checked to make sure it contained his credit cards. They weren't designed for what he had in mind but they would serve. He rummaged around, found a pair of Isabel's sunglasses and put them on, then went into the bathroom and took a nail file out of the medicine cabinet and put it in his pocket. It was the next best thing to a pocket knife. As an afterthought he found a pencil and a piece of paper and jotted down Isabel's phone number. Then he left the apartment, closing the door firmly behind him.

The building had no elevator and Isabel's apartment was on the third floor. Benjamin looked down the stairwell and, seeing no one below, ran down the stairs and slipped out the front door into the narrow busy street. He realized that because of his appearance he stood out in the crowd, and this worried him. He decided that it would be necessary to alter his looks and although he couldn't do much about his height, he could change his clothes. He found a clothing store a block farther north. In front, hanging from a clothesline strung across the plate-glass window were a dozen or so men's shirts. Some were of colored fabric, some were white, all were versions of the guayabera, a four-pocketed, pleated shirt which amounted to the national costume of Cuba. Benjamin picked out a shirt and carried it into the shop, emerging a few minutes later wearing the guayabera and carrying his own shirt in a paper parcel.

He turned in a westerly direction, which, if he was correct, would bring him to the section of Havana known as the Vedado and eventually to the Novedoso, the hotel in which he and the basketball team had been billeted. He hadn't gone more than a few blocks when he recognized Monserrate Avenue. The Floridita Restaurant was on Monserrate and he had been there once with Antonio Olivares. Now he had his bearings. He turned north on Agramonte and west again through Central Park, his confidence increasing as he noted some familiar landmarks on the far side of the park, the Paseo del Prado and the dome of the Academy of Sciences.

Havana was divided into three sections: Old Havana, where Isabel lived, decaying but romantic, with its narrow streets no wider than the carriages that had once transported the gentry; central Havana, the busy commercial hub of the city, distinguished by the famous Malecón, or embankment, that forms Havana's seawall and the Prado, a broad boulevard graced by laurel trees; and the Vedado, the tourist area in west Havana, with its hotels and restaurants. The Novedoso was in the Vedado section. If he were to turn south again Benjamin would hit Simón Bolívar Avenue and the Avenue of Salvador Allende, at the end of which would be the Novedoso's pink and white facade.

His mind was perfectly clear as to what he must do. He had thought about it often during his enforced seclusion. Now that Nicasio Moya had been cleared there were only four suspects left to investigate: Pablo Quesada, the hotel manager; Patricio Gómez, the hotel detective; Antonio Olivares, the captain of the Cuban basketball team; and Carmen Bonilla, Quesada's secretary. Three of the four were at the hotel, which would make that the logical place to begin.

He would start with Quesada, the rough-necked but likable hotel manager, with his amiable regard for everything American, his outspoken political opinions, and his faithful doberman. However, getting into Quesada's office undetected would take some doing. The office was in the lobby, and even when Carmen Bonilla was absent from her desk in the anteroom, there were frequent visits from employees and guests. Patricio Gómez's office would be even harder to penetrate since he shared a cubicle in the basement with the housekeeper, a formidable lady whose presence, according to Gómez, was something akin to an enemy occupation. "I do not think she eats or sleeps," Gómez had once confided to Benjamin, "and I swear to you that I have never seen her enter or leave the ladies' restroom."

Under the circumstances, Benjamin decided it would be best to start easy with Quesada's apartment on the top floor of the hotel, which he believed would be fairly simple to enter. After that initial practice run he would be ready for the more complicated task of breaking into and entering Quesada's office and Gómez's inner sanctum.

But before he reached the hotel he had to walk halfway across the city, no mean feat for a man whose face was plastered daily on the front pages of both Havana newspapers. He dumped the parcel containing his shirt into a waste bin near the Central Park entrance. He had no sooner entered the park when he spotted two guardsmen walking toward him and he was forced to take refuge among a grove of poinciana trees. After they passed, he reemerged and continued across the grass toward the west exit. He picked up speed when a couple of Cuban businessmen, carrying briefcases, cut short a conversation to eye him and to make some sort of comment as he passed. He knew it could have been his imagination, but he was taking no chances. He began to jog, loosely so as not to call attention to himself, but purposefully, covering the distance to the exit in a matter of seconds.

A few minutes later on the Prado he dodged two policemen by crossing the street and ducking behind the statue of a bronze lion. Then, as if those encounters hadn't been enough to unnerve him, something even more disconcerting happened. As he crossed the Avenida Belascoain, a dilapidated taxi drew up at the intersection, slowed down, then speeded up and shot by as Benjamin began to cross, passing so close that Benjamin barely missed having his toes run over.

It wasn't the near-miss that startled him. Nor was it the driver, a thin man bent over the steering wheel with a look of fanatical concentration. It was the nearest of the three passengers in the rear seat who drew his attention, a man who looked exactly like the crazy Cuban Raúl Baki. It was an uncanny resemblance and if Benjamin hadn't known that Baki was the star boarder at a funny farm in Florida he'd have sworn that it was he staring giddily out the taxi window, smiling and nodding familiarly to Benjamin.

"There can't be two of him, can there?" Benjamin asked himself. "Oh hell, this is Cuba, isn't it? The place is full of Latins with big chins and a lot of teeth." Nonetheless it took a while to convince himself that forceful chins, piercing black eyes, and daffy smiles were a dime a dozen, even in Havana.

85

# 16

Benjamin forgot about Raúl Baki when he reached the Novedoso. Now that he was within striking distance he was feeling a little less sure of himself and decided to go over his plan again. During the week he had stayed at the Novedoso he had been in the habit of sleeping late and leaving for his sightseeing excursions at noon. On four of the seven days, Monday through Thursday, he had met Señora Quesada on her way through the lobby carrying her string marketing bag. This was Monday. He checked his watch. Ten to twelve. According to his calculations she should be coming out of the hotel any minute.

Lunch for most Cubans was at two or even later, so Pablo would be busy in his office until then. Although Benjamin had never been present to clock in Mrs. Quesada at the completion of her shopping chores, he was sure she'd stay away for at least an hour. Judging by the ration lines he'd observed in front of the butcher shop, it might take as long as an hour and a half. He stationed himself on a bench across from the Novedoso, picked up an abandoned newspaper and pretended to read, glancing frequently over the top to watch the comings and goings from the hotel.

He was rewarded after a few minutes by the sight of Mrs. Quesada, string bag slung over her arm, emerging from the lobby. He waited until she turned left onto Menocal Avenue, then tucked the paper under his arm, strolled across the street, and walked up to the double doors leading into the hotel. There were a few people inside, none of whom looked familiar. The front desk was to his right, facing the elevator, so that the clerk had his back to the door. The switchboard operator, who ordinarily faced the door, had her back turned and was pouring sugar into a container of coffee.

Benjamin crossed the lobby self-consciously, the back of his neck prickling with apprehension. A circle of plastic-covered seats surrounded a tall potted palm in the center of the room. He slipped behind the palm and sat down facing the elevator, afraid to make himself conspicuous by standing directly in front of it. Again he used the newspaper as a shield while he watched the elevator. The floor indicator was sweeping downward from the sixth floor. It stopped at three and again at two. When the doors opened a group of people emerged and walked toward the desk. Now using them as a screen, Benjamin slipped into the elevator and pushed the unnumbered button for the top floor.

The elevator rose, stopping on the fourth floor to admit two American women who greeted Benjamin in their best high-school Spanish. "Buenos diás, Señor."

Benjamin acknowledged their greeting with a cordial nod. When the elevator carried them up to the top floor, one of the woman said, "Es usted un relativo del manejo?"

Benjamin nodded agreeably as he stepped out of the elevator.

"El hijo?"

"Sí," Benjamin offered accommodatingly as the doors closed behind him.

The small square hallway contained only two doors, one of heavy metal that led to the fire stairs and the other an apartment door with a wooden knocker and Quesada's name in the card slot. Benjamin put his ear to the door and listened, then put his hand on the knob and turned it cautiously. Locked, of course. He checked beneath a straw mat on the floor, then sensibly, though fruitlessly, ran his hands across the top of the door-frame. There was no key conveniently waiting for him, but still, circumstances were in his favor. Just as he'd hoped, Quesada's door was no different from the hotel-room doors on the floors below, having one simple lock requiring the most basic burglar tools, namely his credit card and the nail file. It took only a minute to release the lock and open the door. He stepped into the foyer and closed the door behind him.

Directly before him the foyer opened into a sunny living room furnished in cheap blond laminate and bamboo like the hotel rooms below. The hall to his left, he thought, must lead to the bedrooms and bath and he decided to start his search with the master bedroom. He found it easily enough and began looking around. He peered under the four-poster bed and underneath the bedclothes, opened dresser drawers and rifled through the two closets. The only thing he found that even remotely resembled what he was looking for was a thick plastic autograph book of the sort one could buy in any ten-cent store in the United States. It was lying in a drawer of the night table and Benjamin hoped it might contain, at the very least, a sample of Quesada's handwriting. Instead it turned out to be just what it purported to be, a book filled with celebrity autographs, his own included. He remembered then that Quesada had asked him to sign it a few days after Benjamin and the team had checked into the hotel.

He replaced the autograph book and went into the second bedroom which was more sparsely furnished than the first, with only a bed and a ladderback chair. It didn't look promising but he knelt to look under the bed and slid his hand under the bed sheets just in case. He was rummaging around in the closet when he was brought up short by an ominous clicking sound on the polished floor in the hall. He poked his head out just as Quesada's sleek black doberman appeared in the doorway. Mutual shock was replaced by mutual action. The doberman sprang and Benjamin fell backward into the closet and slammed the door. A second later the door vibrated with the force of the dog's weight, and Benjamin jumped back, hitting his head on the clothes bar, raining hangers around his feet and twisting his back on the rebound. He knew the dog couldn't turn the knob but he held onto it for dear life, his heart pounding, his mouth dry with panic.

Quesada's voice, when it finally came, wasn't reassuring but Benjamin greeted it with relief. He maintained his grip on the doorknob until Quesada's imperative commands halted the dog's frenzied attack. Then he heard Quesada shout, "Venga! Arriba las manos!" Benjamin opened the door and raised his arms over his head. Quesada had snapped a leash onto the dog's collar and had the strap wound around one of his hands. He held a gun in the other and was staring at Benjamin in amazement. "Benjamin Pinch?"

"Hello, Pablo."

Quesada said inanely, "The police are searching for you."

"Don't I know it."

The dog was pulling at the leash, standing on his hind legs and pawing the air in his effort to get at Benjamin. "Look, I haven't got a weapon and I'm not going anywhere. Do you think you could call off the dog?"

"What are you doing here?"

"It's a little hard to explain, especially while I'm staring into that set of fangs."

"I was shocked when I learned about the murders," Quesada said. "I found it hard to believe that you would kill anyone."

"I didn't have anything to do with either murder."

"Not that I mourned their passing, you understand. They are men without conscience, sin conciencia, as we say, hard men, bullies. But you have sealed your fate, my friend. Sooner or later they are sure to find you and the punishment for killing these men will be severe."

"I can't say I'm looking forward to it."

"You still have not answered my question, Benjamin. What are you doing here?"

"I've been looking for Solís's killer."

The dog made another lunge and Quesada jerked him back. "In my clothes closet?"

"To tell you the truth, I thought you might have done it."

Quesada actually lowered the gun for a moment, not that Benjamin could have taken advantage of it even if he'd wanted, not with the hound of the Baskervilles salivating over him. "You think I killed Solís? Are you joking with me?"

"You don't see me laughing, do you?"

"How could you think that?"

"Tie up the dog and I'll tell you."

Quesada hesitated, then nodded curtly. He unwound the leash and slipped the strap over one of the bedposts but he didn't put away the gun. "Come. Let us go inside."

Benjamin wasn't sure the dog wouldn't pull the whole bed after him in his eagerness to rip Benjamin to shreds and he was glad when Quesada closed the bedroom door behind them. He was curious about something. "What made you come upstairs, Pablo?"

"I met one of my guests in the lobby. She informed me that

she had just met a member of my family on his way up to the seventh floor. She said he told her he is my son. Surprising news to a man who has only daughters."

"Damn. Is that what she asked me? I had to get smart with one of the only two Spanish words I know. The wrong one."

"The hotel has been robbed more than once. The crime rate in La Habana is high. Of course, I did not expect to find *you* hiding in my closet."

They entered the living room and Quesada motioned with the gun to one of the chairs. Benjamin sat down while Quesada remained standing. "So now, what is this about, my friend?"

Benjamin took a deep breath. "I didn't kill Solís, but I figure that someone in my hotel room that night did. I had just packed my suitcase before everyone walked in, and there wasn't any list hidden in it then. The suitcase was lying open on the bed. The room was small and crowded. We were all moving around, drinking, talking, bumping into one another. Someone must have zipped open the plastic pocket and slipped in the list. And whoever did that must have followed Solís downstairs and shot him as he was getting into his car."

"And for some reason you thought it was me. What was that reason?"

"No, not exactly. I just picked on you first because I thought I could get in to search your apartment without too much trouble."

"Expecting to find what?"

"I don't think I'd better tell you that."

"I look upon you as a friend, Benjamin. I thought you felt the same about me."

Benjamin was embarrassed. Here he was holding a civil conversation with the man and at the same time accusing him of murder. His back hurt and he wasn't feeling relaxed enough to lean back against the chair cushions. Instead he crossed his arms and rested them on his knees. "It's a hell of a situation. I like you, Pablo. I don't want it to be you, believe me. But you do qualify, even down to having a gun."

"If I had killed Solís with this gun, do you think I would still keep it? I would have thrown it to the sharks long ago."

"You're not a fan of Castro's, Pablo, God knows, you've

made no bones about that. Who's to say you're not working for El Cuerpo?"

"What do you know about El Cuerpo?"

"I've heard about it."

"And you think I may have committed murder in the name of El Cuerpo?"

"You thought I did, didn't you?"

Quesada shook his head. "You are mistaken, both about El Cuerpo and about my ability to kill, even in the name of freedom. Much as I object to the present government, I do not believe it can be toppled by acts of open defiance. I believe it will erode, bit by bit, until finally it disintegrates. That is fine. That is the only way. That is the way I support. Not random violence."

Benjamin wanted to believe him, and chanced testing him, hoping he'd come through. "Listen, Pablo, will you take me down to your office? Get rid of Señora Bonilla, lock the door and give me a chance to look around?"

"Without even knowing what it is you are looking for?"

"I'm only asking you to let me prove you didn't do it."

"What for? I know I did not do it."

"Let me see for myself. If it's true, then it's another name cleared."

"Another?" Quesada asked warily. "I thought I was Suspect Number One."

"I already found out Nicasio Moya is in the clear."

"Oh? Let me see. According to my calculations that leaves Antonio Olivares, Isabel Quintana, Patricio Gómez, and my secretary, Señora Bonilla."

"I may be able to clear you and Señora Bonilla when I examine your office."

"If so, then there will be only three suspects remaining, Olivares, Señorita Quintana, and my security guard, Patricio."

Benjamin had been honest with Quesada up to that point but he didn't want to talk about Isabel. Better, he thought, not to single her out. "That's right. Three."

"You are blowing smoke rings, Benjamin. Puff, a suspect. Puff, a trail of smoke."

"Maybe, but I don't think so. Anyway, I'm asking you to give me a hand. Will you?"

"What choice have I? If I refuse, you will assume the worst. Besides, although I have not yet convinced you that I am innocent, you have convinced me that you are. And since we are friends, I must help, is that not right?"

# 17

It was unexpected luck that Monday was Carmen Bonilla's day off, so no excuse was needed to send her out of the office. Quesada brought Benjamin down the fire stairs and they slipped into the manager's office. Quesada then locked the door of the anteroom, led Benjamin into his own inner office and, with an expansive gesture, waved at the clutter of papers on his desk. "There it is, Benjamin. I have nothing to hide. Open the drawers if you wish."

Benjamin was acutely embarrassed. He wished Quesada would leave the room or at least turn his back, but Quesada simply crossed his arms and leaned against the doorjamb watching. Benjamin began by leafing through some of the typewritten letters, then moved to Quesada's memo pad and riffled the pages. He couldn't tell much from the handwriting. It was bland enough to match the equally undistinguished *l*s and *o*s on the scrap of paper in his pocket but he could find nothing bearing the letter *K*. He went through the desk drawers with no better luck.

"Nothing?" Quesada asked when it became evident that Benjamin had stopped searching.

"Nothing for and nothing against," Benjamin answered with some chagrin.

"Would it help to examine my safe?"

"Maybe."

"Well, let us try." Quesada, with a patient smile, crossed the room to the old-fashioned steel safe and knelt in front of it. Discreetly, feeling the consummate fool, Benjamin put himself conspicuously out of reading range of the combination.

"All right," Quesada announced, swinging the door open.

Benjamin saw the stacks of neatly banded bills on one of the safe shelves. He reached for the rubber-banded envelopes on another shelf and for the three big ledgers lying on the safe floor, then sat down cross-legged to examine them. The ledgers were the Novedoso's account books. Benjamin flipped through them, running his finger down page after page of expenses until he came to one for "Keroseno." The K didn't match the one in his pocket but then the K came at the beginning of the word, which might make a difference. "Did you write this?" he asked Quesada, pointing to the entry.

"No. Señora Bonilla keeps the books. She wrote it."

There was nothing else of interest in the ledgers. Benjamin pulled the rubber bands off the envelopes. Inside one were personal papers belonging to Carmen Bonilla, her birth certificate, an expired passport, and something marked "testamento" that he assumed was her will. The will bore her signature which proved nothing. Inside the second envelope were sales receipts, in the third a folded sheaf of official-looking papers that might be insurance documents. These bore the neat, uninteresting signature of Pablo Quesada, which also proved nothing. Benjamin put everything back into the safe and got up.

Only one fact seemed to be of even speculative interest and that was that Benjamin hadn't uncovered anything that might indicate subversive connections, not that they couldn't exist and not that Quesada would be careless enough to leave dangerous material around.

"Could I look at Carmen Bonilla's desk?"

"If you wish."

Quesada followed Benjamin into the anteroom and stood by while Benjamin searched. Benjamin found nothing of significance on top of the desk and nothing in the center drawer, but in the second drawer down he found a memorandum with the name "Kika" penciled on top. Neither K was similar to the scrap which he carried in his pocket. "Did Señora Bonilla write this?" he asked Quesada, holding out the sheet of paper and pointing to the scrawled name.

"No. Patricio Gómez wrote it, I think. Yes, that is his handwriting."

Bull's-eye, Benjamin thought. Gómez was in the clear. No trip to the dungeon in the basement would be necessary.

"Have you finished?" Quesada asked.

"I guess so."

"And?"

Benjamin shrugged noncommittally.

"You do not read Spanish, Benjamin. How do you know what it is you are looking for?" Quesada took the memorandum out of Benjamin's hand. "This, for instance, is a request from Security for a daily list of occupied and unoccupied rooms. Of what possible interest could that be to you?"

"It isn't."

"Are you looking for microfilms or spy plans or secret codes? How would you know them if you saw them? I want to help you, Benjamin, if only you will tell me how."

Benjamin had an idea. "There's one way you can help me. I want some addresses. Señora Bonilla's home address, for instance."

"Yes, I see. You want the addresses of everyone who was in your hotel room on the night of the murder. Señora Bonilla, Patricio, Isabel Quintana, and who else?"

Benjamin no longer needed Patricio Gómez's address but he couldn't tell Quesada that. "Antonio Olivares."

"I have Señora Bonilla's and Patricio's addresses. It will take me only a minute to find the others." He wrote down the first two addresses on a sheet of Novedoso letterhead, then looked up Olivares's and Isabel's addresses in the phone book. Benjamin noticed that he copied the wrong house number for Isabel and hoped he'd gotten the others straight. Before Quesada put down his pen, Benjamin said, as if it were an afterthought, "Kika. What is that?"

"Señora Bonilla is known by her friends among the staff as Kika. It is a . . . what you call a nickname."

"Would you mind jotting it down for me?"

"You think that name has significance?"

"It might."

"But you will not tell me what." Quesada shook his head with amused tolerance while he scribbled the name Kika next to Señora Bonilla's name.

Benjamin studied what he'd written for a chagrined moment before saying, "Pablo, you can take a poke at me if you want."

"For which of your many sins?"

"For any one of them that appeals to you.

It wasn't Quesada's handwriting on the scrap of paper Benjamin was carrying any more than it was Patricio Gómez's. That narrowed the list of suspects to two, Carmen Bonilla, Quesada's aristocratic secretary, and Antonio Olivares, the easygoing coach of the Cuban basketball team. Of those two, it seemed more likely to be Tony. He was young, energetic, passionately pro-American and defiantly anti-Castro. But Benjamin didn't want it to turn out to be Tony, who of all the people he'd met was seemingly the least calculating and in some ways the most softhearted. Nevertheless, he couldn't ignore the logic of it.

Tony had told Benjamin enough about his habits for Benjamin to feel certain he'd find the apartment empty that afternoon. On three mornings of the week, Monday, Wednesday, and Friday, Tony taught basketball at the University of Havana. On those days he went straight from the University to the Sports Arena for professional team practice and he didn't get home until seven if there was no game, or until midnight if there was one. This being Monday, Benjamin should have the place pretty much to himself, with little likelihood of Tony popping up unexpectedly.

But whether he would find what he was looking for and whether it would be enough to take to the Swiss Embassy, was another question. Benjamin had thought it through before—the problem of actually pinning the murder on the guilty party—and he knew it wouldn't be as simple as finding out how the culprit made his *Ks*. He'd been taking it one step at a time until now, but with the real possibility that Antonio Olivares might be the man he was looking for, he had to face the fact that he couldn't limit himself to searching for a sample of Tony's handwriting. It would prove Tony put that list into Benjamin's suitcase but it wouldn't prove that he'd killed Solís. Benjamin was going to have to find better evidence than that, a gun perhaps, or something that indicated that Tony was connected with El Cuerpo.

Tony's apartment was near the university, on Espada Street, a good half-hour walk from the Novedoso. Benjamin left by the same alley door he'd escaped through on the night of the murder and, following Quesada's directions, started to walk north along Menocal Avenue. It was almost three-thirty and the streets were filling up with the after-lunch crowd, which meant that Benjamin would be a little less conspicuous than he might have been an hour before. Nevertheless, a man six-feet-four-inches tall towered over the run-of-the-mill Cuban and had to attract some attention. He moved along quickly on the theory that he shouldn't give any one person too good a look.

He was within viewing distance of Espada when he suddenly felt a hand slapped on his shoulder and turned to find himself face-to-face with one of the Cuban basketball players he'd met during the tournament. Benjamin felt the blood leave his face and for a terrible moment Benjamin found himself light-headed and weak in the knees. He had nothing to say and didn't even try. He couldn't even remember the fellow's name.

"Pinch!" the fellow shouted, but the tone wasn't hail-fellow-well-met, although he'd obviously acted from impulse and had no idea what to do with Benjamin now that he'd stopped him. He began looking around trying to locate someone to appeal to while Benjamin, recovering his senses, attempted to jerk his arm away.

Physical resistance triggered the man into action. He called for help as he began struggling with Benjamin. Benjamin threw a badly aimed punch that grazed the side of the man's head and a second later took a right to the eye that staggered him. People were stopping and Benjamin heard someone else shout his name. He shoved his adversary away, broke free, and began running.

A few people took up the chase but Benjamin's height and general fitness gave him an advantage they couldn't match. He had outdistanced them before he had even turned the corner and by the time he heard the sound of a police siren he was loping up the front walk to Tony's building with no one behind him. He knew the neighborhood would be teeming with police in a few minutes, which was going to make getting into Tony's apartment a lot easier than getting out. But for now it would provide a safe refuge and he bolted into the foyer and back through the hall to Tony's door. Pulling out his nail file, Benjamin quickly set to work, feeling for the tumbler, breathing a sigh of relief when it shifted, entering quickly, and slamming the door behind him

# 18

Enrique's car was a 1950 Ford with bald tires and a hand-brush paint job the color of dried blood. It had an awesome number of dents, scratches, and scrapes, not surprising, considering his harrowing driving technique, which kept Dearborn and Tomás tensely alert as Enrique zigzagged along Central Highway at breakneck speed.

Enrique was in an instructive mood and entertained his passengers by pointing out scenic landmarks along the route, using his elbows to steer while he waved his hands descriptively. Raúl, serene in the front seat, oohed and aahed and made ebullient comments each time they passed a spot he recognized. Tomás, on the other hand, winced with each sickening swerve, and when Dearborn whispered, "Perhaps I should take the wheel," he responded with a sob, barely audible but eloquent.

Enrique had been right about the police. There were blockades at all the intersections on the outskirts of Havana, but the police, busily stopping cars traveling north, south, and east, showed no interest at all in cars entering the city and Enrique breezed through without attracting a second glance. Once within Havana's city limits he explained that he lived in Old Havana and that was where he was taking them.

Dearborn hadn't visited Havana in more than forty years. The Capitol building looked vaguely familiar and he thought he remembered the National Museum of Art, but except for those landmarks everything was strange to him. Only the atmosphere was familiar, the sparkling light, the tropical warmth, and the graceful palm trees. But in the old days daytime Havana had been an easygoing, leisurely city. Now the streets were crowded and the pace was much faster. The pedestrians were as well dressed but the police, although a peaceable-looking lot (notwithstanding the gun handles protruding from their leather holsters), were numerous, far more numerous than he could recall.

Enrique drove his car into the old section of the city, passing streets that finally began to strike a familiar chord. Dearborn remembered the names Obispo and O'Reilly. The shabby houses, soft hued and dilapidated, the narrow alleys and the musty scent of antiquity stimulated his recollections. He was particularly affected by the sight of the Cathedral of Havana. There had been a restaurant across the street where he had eaten roast pork and black beans in company with a voluptuous girl named . . . he tried hard to recall her name and couldn't . . . but he did remember that she had possessed an affectionate nature and that her dueña had drunk too much wine and had fallen asleep in the taxi going home. Where was she now, that lovely whats-her-name with her pouting mouth, her round hips, her prodigious breasts?

"We are here," Enrique announced, the right wheels of the car bouncing up onto the sidewalk just before he jammed on the brakes. Dearborn noticed that two other cars were similarly parked along the narrow street and decided that Enrique's lopsided placement was a deliberate strategy intended to allow for passing traffic. Enrique removed his car keys from the ignition and motioned to them to join him on the sidewalk. "This is where I live," he pointed out. "Numero Ocho, Cabrahigo."

The building was painted a sickly aquamarine and had a pair of handleless wooden doors at its entrance which opened onto a mosaic-tile hallway. Enrique led them to a second door which opened out into a bare courtyard strung with clotheslines. From there he guided them up a flight of stairs to the third floor. "Mi casa es su casa," he announced graciously as he opened the door. "My house is yours."

Señora Ortiz's mode of living had already reconciled Dearborn to touches of luxury in the midst of poverty. He noted the silver desk set on the scarred pine table, the carved antique triptych edged in gold leaf hanging on the water-stained wall, and the handsome Oriental screen standing in the far corner of the room. But he was more interested in the fact that there was no bed in the room. There was only a dresser, an armless couch pushed against a corner wall, a table with two rickety kitchen chairs tucked under it and a nondescript armchair. It wasn't the most comfortable setup for one occupant, much less four, and he wasn't encouraged by the thought that before the end of the week their ranks would swell to nine.

"There is only one room," Enrique told them, "and unfortunately, only one window. The bathroom is through that door. There is no bathtub and hot water only in the morning and evening."

"Where's the telephone?" Dearborn asked.

"I do not have a telephone."

"Señora Ortiz doesn't have one either. How do you all keep in touch?"

"With a system of scheduled communications using notes, public phones, and meetings in public places. It is complicated but far safer than the telephone."

Raúl, who had been eyeing the couch longingly, strolled over and stretched out. He crossed his arms behind his head and asked Enrique a question which Tomás translated. "Señor Baki, he ask when will we get guns. Señor Vargas, he say in a few days."

Enrique now addressed himself to Tomás, which caused the latter to recoil with horror. He shook his head. "No, chico! Impossible!"

"Es necessario," Enrique insisted, and when Tomás objected again Raúl joined the argument, adding his bass voice to Enrique's excited vibrato.

"What's the matter?" Dearborn asked.

"They think I should carry a machine gun."

"Say yes, Tomás. Don't argue with the man. This is certainly no time for argument."

"Not me. I ain't goin' to carry no machine gun. I don't like guns. I'm tellin' you these pipples, they scare me."

Dearborn turned his face away from Enrique but let Tomás see his wink. "We are members of El Cuerpo now, Tomás. We must do as ordered."

Tomás refrained from saying more and let his blighting squint and tightly compressed lips speak for him.

"Tengo hambre," Raúl suddenly declared, abandoning the subject of guns in favor of the more practical consideration of food.

"He say he's hungry," Tomás repeated. "He want his breakfast."

Dearborn, welcoming a change of subject, said affably, "Not a bad idea. How about it, Enrique?"

"I do not have a kitchen," Enrique informed him, "but there is a cabinet and sink behind the screen and in the cabinet you will find dried papaya, a box of crackers, and a tin of coffee. The coffeepot and a hot plate are under the sink. Be sure, before you plug in the hot plate, that you turn off the light. I shall return before nine and when I come I shall bring food for our supper. Is there anything else you wish?"

"I could do with a shave," Dearborn said, "and a change of clothes."

"I cannot help you with clothes but there is a razor in the table drawer. Take what you need from the dresser. Goodbye, my friends. Until this evening."

He went out, shutting the door behind him. As soon as he'd left Tomás busied himself behind the screen. The meal he prepared was no banquet but the sweet papaya cut their appetites and the coffee revived their spirits. After they had eaten Raúl rose and began to pace. Until now he had been relatively docile, the cumulative result of the tranquilizers Dearborn had fed him. But there had been no drugs for a while, and Raúl was starting to show signs of renewed cantankerousness. Dearborn watched him warily.

"Roycrap," Raúl said when he noticed Dearborn's eyes on him. "Estoy impaciente. Estoy un gallo de pelea."

"What's he saying?"

"He say," Tomás translated obligingly, "that he is a fightin' cock."

"No argument there."

"Roycrap, vamos a comprar pistolas."

"What?"

"Gons! Gons! Vamos a comprar."

"Good Lord, is he talking about guns again?"

"He say we must buy some guns."

Dearborn shook his head. "No guns, Raúl! Forget the guns!"

Raúl understood Dearborn's tone of voice, if not the actual words, and was moved to answer with an impassioned speech which Tomás made no attempt to translate except for a relevant word here or there, like "castrate" and "behead."

"No violence, Raúl!" Dearborn commanded. "No rough stuff!"

But Raúl had already begun charging toward the door and only Tomás's quick reflexes kept him from running out.

"Money!" Dearborn declared. "Tell him we haven't any money, Tomás!"

Tomás did as Dearborn suggested but Raúl was not to be deterred. "Al contrario," he announced, "hay mucho dinero."

"He says there is money."

"Show him your pockets, Tomás." Dearborn pulled his pockets inside out and Tomás followed suit.

Raúl remained unimpressed. "*Yo* tengo dinero," he revised. "Mucho dinero."

"Where?" Tomás asked in Spanish.

"En el jardín de mi casa en Marianao. Enterrado en mi jardín en Marianao."

"He say," Tomás repeated, "that he have money buried in his garden in Marianao."

Dearborn became instantly alert. "Where is Marianao?"

"Is a suburb of La Habana," Tomás answered.

"Tengo mucho dinero," Raúl informed them again.

"How mucho?" Dearborn demanded.

101

"Veinte y cinco mil pesos."

Tomás translated. "He say twenty-five thousand pesos."

"Twenty-five thous . . . !" Dearborn was incredulous. "What is that in dollars?"

"About thirty thousand dollar."

"I think he's telling the truth, Tomás. Ask him again."

Raúl said again, "Veinte y cinco mil pesos." He seemed slightly offended that they doubted him. "Es la verdad," he declared adamantly.

"Is possible," Tomás verified. "Castro, he don't let nobody leave Cuba with no money."

"This may be an answer to a prayer, Tomás."

"But is many years since Señor Baki, he been here in Cuba. Maybe they dig up his garden. A lotta rich pipples bury money twenty, twenty-five year ago."

"There's only one way to find out."

"You mean we gotta go there?"

"Exactly."

"How we gonna do that?"

"We'll talk to Enrique when he gets home."

"What you gonna tell Señor Vargas?"

"I shall tell him the money is needed for El Cuerpo. He needn't know anything else."

"It will be dangerous to try to dig up somebody's garden."

"We're equal to it."

"Maybe you are equal to it."

"We're going to need money, Tomás. Getting it is worth any amount of risk."

"The whole reason I am here is because I was tired bein' seasick. I must have been nuts."

"Now listen, tell Raúl we're going after his money as soon as it's feasible. That should quiet him down for a while."

Dearborn was right. The news satisfied Raúl, who abandoned his break for freedom in favor of another nap on the couch.

Dearborn looked around the room. "Is there a radio here, Tomás? Take a look. They must have news broadcasts during the day."

Tomás, rummaging behind the screen, at last uncovered a radio that they left on for most of the day, switching stations now and then to catch whatever news was sandwiched in between the pervasive musical programs. But it was evening before Dearborn finally heard Benjamin's name broadcast. He stood over the radio, straining to make sense out of the Spanish, while Tomás, in staccato sentences, interpreted. "He is in La Habana. He was seen. Two men seen him. Central Park. This mornin'. They seen him again this afternoon. Near the Universidad. Someone try and stop him. Fistfight. He run."

"Did they catch him?"

"No. He got away."

"Thank God."

Tomás held up his hand and went on listening. Then he began shaking his head.

"What's wrong? They *didn't* catch him, did they?"

"No, but there was someone else killed. Yesterday mornin'. The head of the La Habana Guard."

"And?"

"They are sayin' it was Benjamin Pinch who done it."

Dearborn walked over to the armchair and sat down. He put his head in his hands. "El Cuerpo."

"Must be."

"We're going to get that money tonight, Tomás. And tomorrow I'm going after Benjamin."

# 19

They weren't sure until they got to Marianao whether or not Raúl's house was still there, but indeed, the sprawling hacienda remained standing. According to Raúl, it had once been the center of a nine-acre estate, but was now simply a large house set on a relatively small plot of land. Enrique explained that many government officials lived in Marianao, saying bitterly, "The citi-

zens are called upon to make sacrifices in the name of the social-
ist state while the so-called socialists live like capitalists."

They parked the car in a shadowed spot at an oblique angle
to the front door. The grounds weren't fenced in and according
to plan, Tomás reconnoitered the house, returning to report
that he had seen six occupants. "They are sittin' in the dinin'
room, two men, a woman and three hijos, two boys and a girl.
Too many pipples," He added worriedly.

"Not ideal," Dearborn agreed. "On the other hand, so long
as they are together the number doesn't really matter. Enrique,
are you ready to do your bit?"

"I am ready," he declared confidently.

"Remember now, you don't know Tomás's name nor he
yours. When you introduce yourselves you'll say that you're
Señor López and he'll tell them that his name is Juan Blanco.
You're clear on how to signal if you discover you've worn out
your welcome?"

"I shall ask Tomás to fetch my address book which I think I
have dropped in the taxi. He will come out to the car and sound
the horn. After he returns with the address book I shall pretend
to make a telephone call, offer my excuses, and then we shall
take our leave." Enrique slipped his hand into his pocket, took
out a small notebook and tossed it onto the back seat.

"You're sure you can carry it off?" Dearborn asked.

"I am a member of El Cuerpo, Señor. I have undertaken
dangerous missions before. And you? Are you equanimous?"

"Perfectly."

"We don't know how long it will take to dig up the money,"
Tomás broke in nervously.

They had tried to question Raúl about the matter, but his
repeated declarations that he would find the money if it took all
night had done nothing to reassure them.

"I think," Dearborn decided, "that we must limit the time to
forty minutes. Anything beyond that would place too great a
burden on the two of you. If we find the money before the forty
minutes is up, we'll return to the car to wait. Otherwise we shall
give it no more than forty minutes before we return. Starting
now, that will make it . . ." He tapped his bare wrist and Enrique
consulted his watch.

"Ten-forty," Enrique said.

"Ten-forty will be the deadline. You'd better give me your watch, Enrique. I'll need it more than you."

Enrique took off the watch and handed it to Dearborn. "I shall put the car keys into the glove compartment. That is where they will be just in case."

"Just in case what?" Tomás demanded.

Dearborn said impatiently, "If there should be trouble, Tomás, we will depend on you to apply strong-arm tactics. But I am talking firmness, Tomás, not violence. Ask Raúl if he's set."

"Señor Baki, está listo?"

"Sí," Raúl replied boldly. "Siempre!"

Tomás shook his head gloomily. "I am prayin' he don't start singin' or makin' no speeches while you're in the garden."

"If you must pray, Tomás, pray he remembers where he buried the money."

"Come," Enrique said. "We have talked enough. Now it is time to act."

Dearborn watched Tomás and Enrique as they got out of the car and walked up the path to the front door. They rang the bell and Tomás put his arm around Enrique as if to support him. After a minute a woman opened the door, and although Dearborn couldn't hear what was being said, he knew that Tomás was telling her the story he'd rehearsed, that he was a taxi driver and Enrique, his passenger, had suffered a dizzy attack and required emergency aid.

Apparently the ruse succeeded. Dearborn saw the woman wave them into the house and he immediately got out of the car, beckoned to Raúl, then removed the two shovels from the floor in back. Raúl slid out of the back seat, and before Dearborn could hand him a shovel, he sprinted across the dark lawn and disappeared around the side of the house. Dearborn rushed after him, and found him standing in the shadow of a boxwood hedge studying the backyard. "Dónde está la fuente?" Raúl murmured, "y los rosales?"

There was no fountain and there were no roses. Instead, there was a flagstone terrace just outside the back door, a grape arbor near the far corner of the house, a luxuriant vegetable garden taking up most of the yard, and a clump of palmetto palms bordering the back of the property. Dearborn feared that Raúl would be too disoriented to find the spot where he'd buried the money, but after a moment Raúl crossed the patio and, with one arm outstretched, approached the house. For a terrible instant Dearborn thought he might knock on the back door, but he merely touched a spot on the doorjamb, pivoted to the right, counted off a certain number of steps, then turned right again to face the vegetable garden. Dearborn heard him mumbling some sort of rhyme and concluded that it was a set of directions he'd committed to memory.

"Cuantos pasos, veinte y tres,
Y cerca de la fuente, seis,
Diez y siete entre las palmas,
Y cinco pasos más."

He paced off the width of the patio and made a beeline for the garden, wading through a strawberry patch and pausing to pull up a tomato stake. Then after taking a fix on the trees at the back of the property, Raúl moved between them, out of Dearborn's sight. Anxiously Dearborn hurried to join him. He was standing in a secluded spot behind the grape arbor, pushing the tomato stake into the soft earth.

"Is this it?" Dearborn whispered.

"Aquí! Aquí!" Raúl replied cheerfully.

"Ssh, ssh, keep it down, Raúl." Dearborn handed him one of the shovels and Raúl indicated the scope of the job by drawing the heel of his sandal along a rectangular patch roughly three feet by five.

"That big a hole?" Dearborn questioned in a low voice. "What did you bury it in? A steamer trunk?"

Raúl put his foot on his shovel and jammed it into the earth and Dearborn followed suit. For twenty-five minutes they worked side by side, alternating the thrust of their shovels. By the time they had dug a trench almost four feet deep, Dearborn was beginning to despair of finding anything. Then, with what seemed like his four hundredth thrust into the hard ground, he felt the shovel strike something that gave off a dull clunk. "Here's something," he whispered.

Raúl was gleeful. "Espliego!" he hissed, tossing away his shovel and swooping down to brush away the dirt.

Dearborn tried to see what it was Raúl was uncovering. He stooped down and squinted at it. He expected to see a crate or a container of some sort. Instead, revealed inch by inch, was a neatly intersticed set of bleached bones. "What in God's name is that?" Dearborn asked in a shocked undertone.

"Espliego," Raúl whispered. "Ah, pobre Espliego, un compañero muy fino, muy hermoso, muy agradable."

Dearborn bent down closer. "That is a dog, is it not?"

"Dog, Dog. Sí. Mi perro pastor."

Dearborn flopped down at the edge of the grave and leaned on his shovel. "This is what we came here to disinter?" He regarded Raúl from over the top of the shovel. "You see before you a disappointed man, Raúl."

"Pobre Espliego," Raúl said sadly.

"Never mind Espliego. What about the twenty-five thousand pesos? You are not only a madman, Raúl, you are a failure."

"Levantáte," Raúl suggested, indicating that Dearborn should rise. "Date prisa!"

"It is fortunate," Dearborn murmured wearily, "that I am a man of infinite self-control. "You have dealt me a blow, Raúl, a blow below the belt."

Suddenly, the car horn blasted, and with a startled grunt Dearborn let go of the shovel and jumped to his feet. Raúl, who had begun to pick up the bones and place them on the grass at the side of the grave, seemed oblivious to the signal. "Come on, Raúl," Dearborn commanded. "Time is up."

Raúl showed no inclination to leave. He was humming to himself and lining up the bones on the verge of grass.

"Cease that," Dearborn whispered exasperatedly. He took hold of Raúl's arm and tried to pull him away but Raúl resisted and Dearborn realized that nothing short of knocking him over the head with the shovel would move him. But he persisted nonetheless, demonstrating the extent of their peril by pressing the trigger of an imaginary gun to Raúl's temple and jabbing at him with an imaginary knife.

"Ha, ha," Raúl responded with good humor, but without suspending his activities.

Somewhere behind them a door opened. A second later the

patio was flooded with light. Dearborn made one last attempt to pull Raúl out of the trench but his friend refused to budge. There was nothing to do but leave him. Dearborn slipped behind the grape arbor and made his way along the outskirts of the garden toward the house. When he poked his head out from behind the shrubbery he saw a man standing on the patio. All hope for Raúl faded when he saw that the man was carrying a knife, and with a sick feeling of helplessness Dearborn ducked down and made his own way to safety.

He got back into the car and slid behind the wheel, removed the key from the glove compartment, and inserted it into the ignition. Then he leaned forward to watch the front door. There were no sounds of conflict issuing from the backyard but if Tomás and Enrique didn't hurry, they'd still be there when it erupted. He checked the time. Ten-forty-two. Where were they? By now they should be coming out of the house. What was going on out back? Dearborn tried to visualize the silent struggle between Raúl and the man with the knife and was swept by a wave of remorse. Maniac or not, the fellow was Dearborn's responsibility. At that instant only the thought of his obligation to Benjamin kept Dearborn from leaping out of the car and rushing back to help Raúl. He hardened himself with the reminder that Raúl had promised him pesos and delivered dog.

He glanced at his watch again. Ten-forty-three. Sticking his head out the car window, he looked up and down the street. No police cars yet. The neighborhood was still calm.

Ten-forty-four. Still no sounds of conflict and no sign of Tomás and Enrique either. How long should he wait? How long was it safe to sit there? What would happen if a neighbor saw him and decided to investigate?

He was beginning to think he should start the car and try circling the block when Tomás and Enrique emerged from the house. Dearborn didn't see who let them out but the pleasant "Hasta luego" gave him a shock. Was everything all right then? And if everything was all right in the house, what was happening in the garden? He waited until they reached the sidewalk, then started up the engine. Enrique opened the back door for Tomás, who was burdened with a large paper bag, then climbed into the front seat next to Dearborn. "Where is Raúl?"

Dearborn eased the car away from the curb. "In the garden. We were digging in the back of the garden, out of view of the house, when a man came out carrying a knife. I tried to make Raúl leave but he refused. It was that simple."

"The knife was to cut vegetables," Enrique explained. "Señora Ruiz insisted that her husband give me some vegetables from their garden!"

Dearborn stopped the car. "Good Lord! He didn't even know we were out there?" Dearborn stepped on the gas and drove the car around the next corner.

"By now maybe they found him," Tomás suggested. "You betta be careful."

Dearborn drove around the next three corners at breakneck speed and screeched to a halt in front of the house. He began to open the car door. "Come on, Tomás!"

"What are we suppose to do?"

"Tackle him. Carry him out bodily. Whatever we have to do."

"Wait," Enrique called out. "Who's that?" He put his hand on Dearborn's arm and pointed to someone a half-block distant, walking away from them.

"Raúl," Dearborn confirmed. He started the car and inched forward.

"He lost his shirt," Tomás noted.

"He is carrying something in it," Enrique corrected.

"That something," Dearborn explained dryly, "is all that's left of Espliego."

"Espliego? What is Espliego?"

"Well you may ask."

They pulled the car alongside Raúl who looked up interestedly, then crossed to the car with a whoop of joy, pulled open the back door and jumped in next to Tomás. He threw himself back against the car cushions and began saying something in an animated voice.

"What's he saying?" Dearborn demanded.

"He say he has found it," Tomás answered excitedly.

"To be sure, to be sure. I know he's found it. The question is what are we to do with it."

"What are you sayin'?" Tomás asked in bewilderment. "He

say he found the money. He say he had bury it under the body of his dog so in case somebody was diggin' aroun', they wouldn't dig no deeper."

"What?"

"Sí," Raúl said happily. "Yo lo tengo!" He leaned over the front seat to drop the bundle into Enrique's lap and as it unrolled, bills spilled out over Enrique's knees and fell into the seat between him and Dearborn, cascading to the floor like confetti.

# 20

Benjamin's search was inconclusive, but confirmed his belief that Olivares was a champion of everything American: his bookcase revealed an eclectic taste, but Twain, Poe, Hemingway, and Fitzgerald dominated, and what seemed to Benjamin to be a fine cityscape of New York hung over his bed.

On the bedside Benjamin found a pocket-size notebook filled with American names and addresses, included among them Benjamin's name with a red-penciled star next to it. When he flipped through the rest of the notebook he saw other names starred in a like manner, and although there was no way of telling what the stars meant . . . perhaps his name had been starred to indicate that he was carrying the list of agents to Miami . . . he was sure they held some significance to El Cuerpo. When he looked farther and found in the drawer a pile of newspaper clippings about Solís's murder with his own face scowling out of the photograph, he was all but convinced.

He felt rotten. Tony wasn't only a damned good basketball player, he was a nice guy. Benjamin had sensed this from the first. They thought alike and they shared similar tastes. Everything from the beer bottles in Tony's refrigerator to the old 78 rpm records with their disproportionate emphasis on Bach and jazz gave Benjamin a revulsion for what he had come there to do. What kind of world was it anyway when survival came down to good guy versus good guy. They'd spent a few happy hours together. Tony tended to be a cutup, something of a joker, somebody who laughed a lot. He hadn't struck Benjamin as the killer type. On the other hand, what was the killer type? Even Dillinger must have been good for an occasional laugh.

It didn't help that nothing in the apartment was locked up. Benjamin felt as ashamed of going through Tony's effects as he'd felt in Quesada's office, only more so. He was careful not to disarrange the clothes closet or the dresser drawers and he replaced everything exactly as it had been on the desk in the living room. There was plenty to look at, from letters to photographs to diagrammed basketball plays scribbled onto sheets of paper and tacked up on a board in the kitchen, but there was nothing Tony had written that included the letter $K$—no gun, nothing at all that could incriminate him. Benjamin was at a loss. Tony seemed to be his man but Benjamin didn't know how to prove it. The only thing he could think of to do was to follow Tony everywhere, hoping he'd lead Benjamin to El Cuerpo. But this was a difficult assignment to begin with, and even more so with the entire Havana police force on Benjamin's tail.

He had finished searching the apartment and was standing in the living room wondering how safe it would be to go back into the street when he heard Tony's key in the lock. He turned to dash through the bedroom to the back window, but had barely taken a step when he heard Tony's voice behind him.

"Ben! God damn! You are here!"

Benjamin turned around to see Tony's plain friendly face regarding him from the foyer.

"I have been coming home every day hoping you would be here. How did you get into the apartment? Did you find the key? I have been leaving it under the doormat."

Benjamin mumbled something about the credit card and the nail file.

Tony laughed. "I thought the . . . what do you call it, the tools of your trade . . . were a little more sophisticated."

"What do you mean, tools of the trade?"

"The C.I.A."

"I don't have a damned thing to do with the C.I.A."

Olivares walked over to Benjamin, put one hand on his shoulder, and held out the other to shake hands. "It is good to see you, Ben. I have been worried about you."

"Nice of you to say so," Benjamin said stiffly.

"You should have come here immediately. I would have found some way to help you. Where have you been hiding?"

"Around."

"Sit down. What would you like? Are you hungry? Would you like a cup of coffee?"

"No thanks."

"Well, sit down then." Olivares lowered himself onto the couch, spread his arms out along the back, and nodded to the armchair opposite. "How long have you been here?"

"About an hour."

"You are lucky you were not picked up. The streets are filled with police."

"They're looking for me. One of the guys on your team spotted me on the way here and came after me."

"He didn't see you come into my building?"

"No. No one saw me turn into your street."

"Good. Then you are safe. You will stay here until I find some way to get you out of Cuba."

"El Cuerpo should be able to arrange it."

Olivares raised his eyebrows. "El Cuerpo? So the C.I.A. is working with El Cuerpo?"

"No, damn it," Benjamin said wretchedly. "*You're* working with El Cuerpo."

"I?"

Benjamin was impressed with Tony's ingenuous look of surprise. "Come off it, Tony. It didn't take any brilliant deduction to figure out who stuck that list in my suitcase."

The look of surprise increased. "Are you telling me that you know nothing about that list?"

"Of course I don't. How many times have you pulled it off before? What's it called? Con the visiting 'Yanqui'?"

Olivares slid forward onto the edge of his seat. "Did you kill Solís, Ben? Tell me the truth."

"Damn it!" Benjamin got up, circled the chair, then threw himself back down. "*You* killed Solís, you son-of-a-bitch!"

The hurt expression that flashed across Olivares's face seemed genuine. "You came here because you thought I was responsible for the trouble you are in. You are looking for a confession."

"I came looking for something."

"Are you satisfied that you found it?"

"You've saved every story that was written about the murder. You've got a notebook filled with American names and addresses. My name's in there with a nice fat star next to it. All you ever talked to me about was getting out of Cuba and how much you hate the Cuban government."

"You cannot conceive that I kept the newspaper clippings because they concern a friend? That is the reason, Ben, the only reason. As for the notebook, those are the names of people I have met here in Cuba, people I hope will help me if I ever succeed in getting to the United States. Your name is starred because you are a particular friend."

Benjamin told himself that he'd been deceived once and that he wouldn't be again, but he was having a hard time looking Olivares straight in the eye.

"As for my wanting to get out of Cuba, I do not deny it. But ask yourself this. If I were a member of El Cuerpo, would I wish to leave, or talk so openly about leaving? Would I be so frustrated by my inability to get out? Does that sound to you like I am an underground radical?"

"Shit."

"I think we have both been wrong about one another, Ben. You are not working for the C.I.A. You were not smuggling information into the United States and you did not murder Fernando Solís. On the other hand, I am not working for El Cuerpo. I have never had anything to do with El Cuerpo. I have never been engaged in any subversive activities and I have never murdered a man. But there is a difference between us, Ben. Even when I believed you were guilty I wanted to help you."

Benjamin rallied to his own defense. "You aren't a hunted man. Nobody's going to gun you down in the street. Hell, another guy's been murdered, and they've pinned that one on me too."

"Why have you not gone to the Swiss Embassy?"

"For what? To be locked up there with no way of getting out? If I prove I didn't do it, they'll have to let me leave Cuba."

"You take a very naïve view of our police system. Believe me, you would be best off at the embassy."

"You sound like Pablo Quesada."

"You have seen Señor Quesada?"

"The same way I saw you. He walked in on me while I was searching his apartment."

"You found nothing incriminating?"

"He didn't have a notebook full of names if that's what you mean."

"My notebook is hardly conclusive evidence of any wrongdoing," Olivares said. "It does not prove that I murdered Solís any more than it proves you did not."

"I was looking for a gun."

"I have no gun."

"Or a sample of your handwriting."

"Of my what?" Olivares asked. "But you saw my handwriting in that notebook."

"Yeah, but I couldn't find the right set of letters."

"What are you talking about?"

"Look, are you willing to write something down if I dictate it to you?"

Olivares got up promptly and crossed to his desk. "Tell me what you want me to write." He picked up a pad and pencil.

"Hickory, dickory, dock, the mouse ran up the clock."

Olivares regarded Benjamin quizzically. "Hickory, dickory, dock?"

"You heard me."

"The murderer is addicted to nursery rhymes?"

"Don't worry about it. Just write it."

Olivares picked up the pad and dashed off the sentence, pausing to ask, "Is dickory spelled with an *o* or an *e*?"

"It doesn't matter."

"Here." Olivares handed the pad to Benjamin and watched as Benjamin looked it over. "Well?"

A fresh wave of self-loathing washed over Benjamin. "You've been giving it to me straight, Tony."

"If you mean I've been telling the truth, you are absolutely right."

Benjamin suddenly threw the pad across the room. He jumped to his feet. "I'm sorry. Hell I'm sorry. I'll get out of your hair now." He started into the hall.

"Hey, wait a minute, chico. Don't go."

"I've got to go, Tony. Look, forget you ever knew me."

Benjamin opened the door and rushed out into the hall. He didn't stop running until he reached Belascoain Avenue and saw a couple of policemen half a block in front of him. Then he forced himself to an amble. Tony had been telling him the truth. Tony had accepted Benjamin's suspicions, forgiven him his mistrust, returned meanness with generosity, all of which made Benjamin feel more like a bastard than ever. This spy stuff wasn't up his alley. How could anybody live with it? All Benjamin wanted now was a ticket out, to show them he was innocent and make them believe him.

He turned the corner onto Avenida Manglar. A few minutes later he spotted the monument to José Martí in the Plaza de la Revolución, the enormous square where, traditionally, crowds gathered by the thousands to listen to Castro speak. Apparently a political or cultural happening was imminent because there were workmen hammering away at a wooden platform close to the masonry stage that dominated the center of the Plaza, getting ready to mount huge amplifiers and television cables that other workmen were unloading from a truck.

Benjamin started to walk away. Then he thought again. The Plaza was probably the last place anyone would look for him. As a matter of fact he didn't see a policeman anywhere and who would expect to find a fugitive hiding out under Castro's nose? A young girl walked by and Benjamin chanced stopping her. "Excuse me. Do you speak English?"

She shrugged noncommittally.

"Is Castro going to speak?"

"Castro? Sí."

"When? Cúando? Is that it? Cúando?"

"Sábado."

"Saturday?"

"Sí. Está el aniversario de la Revolución de Martí."

115

"Thanks. Thanks a lot. Gracias."

So Castro would speak on Saturday. Four days off. In the meantime there was all the paraphernalia and confusion, as well as that intriguing television platform. Castro might have done him a favor.

He wandered among the workmen, assuming the casual interest of a tourist, but by the time he'd circled the square he'd mentally tagged the television scaffold for his own. The workmen had constructed it less than three feet from the stage and it was boxed on top and bottom to provide buttress against the surging crowds. By removing one or two nails from an inconspicuous board at its inside base, that is, between it and the stage, Benjamin could provide himself with a handy, well hidden entrance and exit to its hollow interior. It wouldn't allow him to sit up, but the base was about twelve feet long, giving him more than enough space to stretch out.

Not perfect, in other words, but adequate. However, he needed a tool of some sort, a hammer or something else that could be used to pry up the nails. Something stronger than his nail file. A few more minutes of studious investigation rewarded him with a mislaid monkey wrench which he slipped under his belt and hid beneath the loose-fitting guayabera. All that remained was to find a place where he could eat his supper and wash up. Next on the agenda, an out-of-the-way restaurant with a clean toilet, a sink with hot water, and a bar of soap.

# 21

It had taken Dearborn a while to recollect the name of the hotel Benjamin had told him about. "What was it? Something medicinal. A dose of something. Nose spray. Nose dose. No, not nose.

Nove. Ah yes, the Novedoso." Finding the hotel itself didn't worry him. He would merely have to find a public phone and look it up in the directory.

Getting Raúl to part with his money had been another matter. Raúl had balked. Until such time as he decided how it would be spent, no one was welcome to dip in. According to Raúl the money would be used to further the cause of freedom, with perhaps a few pesos set aside for cigars. The two hundred pesos Dearborn eventually cajoled on the pretext that it was to buy arms was woefully inadequate but at least it bought him some clothes and left him with sixty-two pesos spending money.

He took a bus to the hotel, getting out across the street. The more he saw of Havana, the more he regretted what it had become. There was a sharp contrast between the splendid wide boulevards and the new blockhouse-type architecture, the rococo fountains and the squat bus pavilions, the casual stroller who used to meander down the streets and the businesslike crowds which bustled through them now. The Novedoso was small, neat, and modestly vulgar with its cheap tile and plastic lobby furniture, but he noticed that the guests were an international mix. He heard Russian spoken, as well as Swedish, and from two brown-skinned gentlemen in turbans, fluent French. When he stepped up to the desk, the desk clerk appraised his plaid slacks, red blazer, and sports shirt, then asked in stilted English, "American teachers' tour, Sir?"

"I am not a guest at this hotel. However, I would like to see the manager."

"You wish to see Señor Quesada?"

"If that's who he is."

"And what is you name, Sir?"

"Roycroft."

"Un momento, please." The clerk came out from behind the counter, crossed the lobby and disappeared down a hallway next to the bank of elevators. He was back in a minute. "Come with me, Sir." He led Dearborn to Quesada's offfice, tapped on the door lightly, then walked away.

"Enter," a voice called out.

Dearborn opened the door, cast a leery eye on the alert doberman standing in the middle of the room, and closed it again.

He heard Quesada speak to the dog and then call out again, "Enter, please. It is quite all right. The dog will not harm you."

Dearborn stuck his head around the doorframe. The dog had dropped back onto its haunches but was still glaring at him with slavering anticipation.

Pablo Quesada rose, coming out from behind the desk to extend his hand. "Come in. Come in. I promise you that you are quite safe."

Quesada was a burly man, shorter than Dearborn and about ten years younger. He looked more like a boxer than a hotel manager, but his manner was cordial enough. "How do you do. . . . Señor Roycroft, is it?"

"That's right."

"What may I do for you?"

"Mind if I sit down?"

"Not at all. Please do." Quesada returned to his chair. "You are an American. Where are you staying?"

"On the other side of town."

"You are in La Habana with a tour group?"

"Do I look like a tourist?"

"The only Americans I meet, Señor Roycroft, are tourists."

"Is that so."

Quesada frowned and looked at him queryingly.

"I'm here," Dearborn said, "to ask about an American who stayed here at your hotel recently, a basketball player, a fellow who was down here to participate in a basketball competition."

"Who is that, Sir?"

"Benjamin Pinch."

Quesada asked sharply, "What interest have you in Benjamin Pinch? He left the hotel almost two weeks ago."

"The hotel, but not the country."

Quesada snapped his fingers and the dog stretched, rose, and moved next to his chair. He put his hand on the dog's head. "Do you know that the police are looking for Benjamin Pinch?"

Dearborn inclined his head.

"He has been missing since February seventh. This is February twentieth. No one has seen him. No one has any idea where he is."

"A man doesn't vanish in a strange city unless he finds someone to help him," Dearborn noted.

"That may be, but what has it to do with me?"

"He stayed at this hotel, Quesada. You must have a pretty good idea of what your guests are up to. I'm sure you routinely report their comings and goings to the police."

"Please explain yourself more clearly, Señor Roycroft. I do not understand what you want from me."

"I want some information about Benjamin Pinch."

"Who are you?"

Dearborn reached into his pocket and took out the cheap wallet he'd bought that morning. It was bulging with bills. Dearborn had utilized an old trick by wrapping a twenty-peso note around forty-two one-peso bills. He flashed the roll with the élan of someone able to meet any price. "How about it, Quesada? Can we do business?"

Quesada took his time answering. He said brusquely, "I am not so naïve as you think. You are a member of the D.G.I., the Cuban Intelligence organization, are you not?"

If Dearborn had been carrying his cane he would have banged it on the desk. As it was he declared irately, "Cuban Intelligence? How can an American be a member of the Cuban Intelligence? Have you lost your marbles?"

"Come now, do you suppose I am fooled because you speak such perfect English? You are actually a Russian, are you not?"

"I am most certainly not."

Quesada remained unconvinced. "The police have not succeeded in finding Benjamin Pinch and so the D.G.I. has decided to take a hand. You have heard stories about me, that I question the government, that I question Castro who supports communism but will not relinquish his dictatorship." Quesada pointed a finger at Dearborn. "That may be true, yet I am a loyal Cuban and as a loyal Cuban I resent you coming here pretending to be who you are not, attempting to trick me into admitting that I am harboring a man accused of being a foreign agent, of practicing upon me a deception unworthy of us both. What's more, there is no one I dislike more than a Russian, a Russian in any guise."

Dearborn was thoroughly put off by Quesada's anger. Who did he think he was, to get angry at Dearborn? "Do not accuse me again of being a Russian, Quesada. I will say it once more, and only once more. I am not a Russian."

"Then what are you doing here?"

"I am looking for my . . ."

Quesada tilted his head forward. "You are looking for your. . . ?"

"Now see here, did you know Benjamin Pinch? Did you ever get a chance to talk with him?"

"I told you that I am not in the habit of answering the questions of strangers."

"If you *did* know him, then you realize that he is simplicity personified. He is trustful, uncritical, hopelessly impractical, and totally incapable of duplicity or subterfuge."

"Are you suggesting that you think Pinch is innocent?"

"Suggesting? I am insisting! I know the boy well. He's an amiable ass. Bright enough, but a thoroughgoing blunderhead. I daresay that even if he wanted to join the C.I.A., they probably wouldn't have him."

Quesada sat back in his chair and gazed at Dearborn with an intent, slightly bewildered air. "You have never been to Russia?"

"I never said that. I was in Leningrad in 1934. Remarkable city, but too far from Paris to rate a second visit. Don't suppose it's the same anymore."

Quesada narrowed his eyes suspiciously. "Only Americans who are members of tour groups are granted entry visas. You say you are not here as part of a tour?"

"I don't recall saying that."

"Are you here on a tour, Señor?"

"No."

"Then are you a guest of the government?"

Dearborn took a deep breath and plunged in. "I'm not going to pussyfoot around anymore, Quesada. I landed in Camagüey a couple of days ago. Swam ashore after the Cuban Navy confiscated my boat."

Quesada was startled. He didn't know whether to believe Dearborn or not. "Are you telling me that *you* are an American agent?"

"I am *not* an American agent. Look, Quesada, answer me this. Yes or no. Plain and simple. Are you for or against the boy?"

Quesada stroked the dog's head without taking his eyes off Dearborn's face.

"Well?"

"For," he answered finally. "Now, who are you?"

"I am Dearborn Pinch, Benjamin's father."

Quesada was astounded, but his decision had been made and he didn't retreat. "I may have . . . as you suggested a moment ago . . . lost my marbles, but I believe you. I suppose it is the resemblance between you and Benjamin."

"I suppose we do look somewhat alike."

"I was thinking more that you are both fools. Devoted, I have no doubt, but fools nonetheless."

Dearborn didn't take offense. He was too glad to have discovered an ally. "I've got to get to him before the police do."

"You should have come here yesterday."

"Why?"

"He was here. I told him to go to the Swiss Embassy but he has some theory about the man who killed Solís. He is looking for the murderer."

"Boob!" Dearborn burst out. "Idiot! What good will that do? Does he think the police will believe him? What does the D.G.I. care for his half-baked theories?"

"The theory is shaky but not completely unsound. It is only that he has very little chance of proving it. He has a sample of handwriting which he speculates was written by the murderer. It is not much, just three or four letters, part of a word, but it shows certain idiosyncrasies . . ."

"Three or four letters? And he only *theorizes* that it was written by the murderer? Typical. Tell me, Quesada, what are the letters?"

"Only one matters. The *K* which was written in a peculiar manner. Here, let me show you. . . ."

# 22

Dearborn left the hotel carrying a map of Havana and a list of three names and addresses supplied by Quesada. The names

121

were Antonio Olivares, Isabel Quintana, and Carmen Bonilla. According to Quesada, Nicasio Moya, the Procedures Director at the National Institute for Sports, had been speaking to Solís's henchmen in the lobby when Solís was killed, which eliminated Moya as a suspect. Patricio Gómez's handwriting hadn't included the eccentric *K*, which eliminated him as well.

Benjamin was a fool, but judging by what Quesada had told Dearborn, his reasoning in regard to the probable killer had some merit. It was even conceivable that if his luck held, Benjamin might actually learn the identity of the killer. The problem was that, succeed or fail, he hadn't the slightest chance of extricating himself from the mess he'd gotten into. Quesada had put it succinctly: "The government of Cuba wishes to believe that your son is an American spy and even with proof to the contrary they will continue to insist that he is a spy." There was a flaw in the boy, Dearborn mused, a defect of some sort inherited from his mother. A lack of perspective, an illogical determination to bend the end to suit his means. But there was no point in dwelling on his son's shortcomings. Benjamin had to be saved, as much from himself as from Fidel Castro.

Quesada had said that Benjamin intended to go to Antonio Olivares's apartment first and apparently he'd carried out his intention since the news reports had placed him near Espada Street when he'd been seen the previous afternoon. Dearborn made this his first stop, but it was a fruitless visit. Olivares, Dearborn decided, was probably off somewhere practicing that idiot game which occupied so much of Benjamin's time. Basketball. If it hadn't been for basketball Benjamin wouldn't be in his present fix. Neither would Dearborn, for that matter.

An investigation of the building, including a visit to the backyard where Dearborn peered into Olivares's bedroom window, gave no hint as to whether Benjamin had ever made it to the apartment. He certainly wasn't there now and the apartment showed no sign of having been searched. Dearborn prepared to move on.

Señora Bonilla, Pablo Quesada's secretary, lived in Siboney, a community on the outskirts of Havana. After failing to find a taxi, Dearborn was again faced with taking the bus, a complicated undertaking requiring noisy inquiries and elaborate sign language. After a number of false starts and considerable confusion over which bus he should take, where he should transfer, and where he should get off, he succeeded in making his way on the *F* bus to Kirov Street, making a mental note of the street name which might soon prove useful. From Kirov Street he walked to Jade Street and located the small house belonging to Carmen Bonilla.

There was no sign of activity in the house but there was a car parked in front and Dearborn assumed that Señora Bonilla must be at home. He smoothed his hair, straightened his shoulders, and rang the bell. The woman who opened the door was small and pretty, with gray-streaked hair, an aristocratic bearing and a pleasant manner.

"Señora Villegas?"

"Perdoneme?"

"I am looking for Mr. Jaime Villegas."

Señora Bonilla shook her head. "No vive aquí."

"I beg your pardon?"

"You are an American?" she asked, switching into English.

"I am. I am looking for the friend of a friend. Name of Jaime Villegas."

"There is no one here by that name. My name is Bonilla. You must have the wrong address."

Dearborn had perused the street signs on his way from the bus stop and was prepared for the second phase of his operation. He made a show of pulling a scrap of paper out of his pocket and consulting it before holding it out to her.

She pointed to the address. "I cannot read the number very well, but this reads Japon Street. You are on Jade Street." She pointed back the way he'd come. "Japon Street is two streets east of here."

Dearborn took back the piece of paper and studied it. "I believe you are right. How stupid of me." She seemed on the verge of closing the door so he added quickly, "Pardon me, Madame, would it be presumptuous of me to ask a favor?"

She waited politely for him to explain.

"I am staying at the . . . er . . . Nacionál Hotel." It was the only hotel Dearborn knew besides the Novedoso and he hoped it was still in business. She nodded slightly so he assumed it was. "I had rather a difficult time finding my way here. I had to take two buses and I'm not quite sure which they were." His excuse had the ring of sincerity because it was the truth.

"Please wait here. I shall write down the directions for you."

"Also . . . " Dearborn added hastily, "there are no public facilities hereabouts."

"Public facilities?"

"Bathrooms, Madame." Dearborn smiled ingratiatingly, trying to appear as unthreatening as possible. He was prepared for her natural hesitation at admitting a stranger to her house. But he wasn't prepared for the imposing man who suddenly loomed up behind her. He was dressed in civilian clothes but Dearborn's eyes were drawn to the telltale bulge under his suit jacket. Dearborn said heartily, perhaps a little more heartily than he'd intended, "How do you do, Sir. Sorry to bother you. I seem to have come to the wrong address. I was just asking your wife here if I might . . . "

"Come in," the man said. It sounded more like an order than an invitation.

"Thank you. Very kind of you." Dearborn permitted himself to be ushered through the foyer to a small bathroom in the back hall. When he got there, he didn't hear the sound of retreating footsteps and therefore was glad that he was actually in need of the toilet. Damned indelicate to stand there listening to a man relieve himself.

Now what? Quesada had told Dearborn that Carmen Bonilla lived alone. Dearborn had been sure he could wangle his way into the house and then charm some information out of her, but he hadn't expected to have to charm the sinister-looking Mr. X as well. A decision was called for. Should he stay or should he go? If he went, he couldn't come back. If he stayed, he might put himself in jeopardy. Who was the fellow anyway? Did every Cuban carry a weapon? How much trouble was Dearborn in?

He flushed the toilet, washed his hands at the basin, peered at his face in the mirror, and made up his mind. When he reemerged he said authoritatively, "I should like to have a word with Señora Bonilla, if you don't mind."

The man made no acknowledgment, but led Dearborn to the parlor where Señora Bonilla sat at a desk, her back to them, sorting through a jumble of papers. He spoke to her in Spanish and she turned. "Yes? May I be of further assistance?"

"Yes you can. You can tell me if Benjamin Pinch has been here."

"Benjamin Pinch? The C.I.A. agent? The man who killed Solís?"

They reacted with shock, but where the woman evidenced only surprise, the man displayed something more, the just-as-I-thought attitude of a person trained to be suspicious. "Who are you?" the man demanded.

Dearborn thought quickly. "I am with the Special Interests Department of the Swiss Embassy. I am making inquiries on behalf of the United States government."

"Can you prove it?"

"Must I prove it in order for you to answer my questions?" Dearborn asked sharply. "Have you something to hide?"

The man became immediately defensive. "We don't know nothing about Pinch."

"I have reason to believe he might have been here yesterday, that he might even have tried to enter the house surreptitiously."

"It was Pinch?" Señora Bonilla blurted out. "A thief broke into my home during the night. I called Patricio . . . Señor Gómez . . . I never guessed that it was Benjamin Pinch."

Gómez? Dearborn knew the name. The man was the house detective at the Novedoso. "You are the Novedoso's security officer, are you not?" Dearborn asked.

"You know who I am?"

"Of course."

"I do not understand," Señora Bonilla said in a puzzled voice. "Patricio and I were acquainted with Benjamin Pinch, but I can think of no reason for him to break into my home."

"Did you call the police?"

"They were here this morning. But there was little satisfaction from them. They say that since nothing was stolen . . . "

"Nothing was stolen? Nothing at all?"

Señora Bonilla pointed to the mess of papers on her desk. "He went through my papers. You can see for yourself. He opened the drawers in here and in the kitchen. I found pieces of paper all over the floor. But he took nothing."

"Where were you when this was happening?"

"I was asleep in my bedroom. I did not hear anything. This morning I found the kitchen window had been pried open. There was a broken nail file on the kitchen floor."

"When you say that nothing was taken," Dearborn pursued, "do you mean that nothing of value was taken? That is to say, did you notice whether or not any of your papers were missing?"

"The only papers I have that are of value I keep in the safe at the hotel. There are not many. My birth certificate, my will, my passport, which has long ago expired."

"Señor . . . er . . . what is your name?" Gómez interjected.

"Roycroft."

"Señor Roycroft, what could Benjamin Pinch want from Señora Bonilla?"

Dearborn folded his arms and pursed his lips. "I wonder if Señora Bonilla can answer that."

"I cannot answer it," she declared. "I have no idea at all what Benjamin Pinch might want of mine. I have nothing that could interest him."

"The name El Cuerpo doesn't ring a bell?"

She and Gómez exchanged startled glances. "What has this to do with El Cuerpo?"

Dearborn decided to try intimidation. "Is it possible that you are a member of El Cuerpo, Señora Bonilla?"

She denied it strenuously. "How can you say such a thing! How dare you accuse me of such a thing!"

Patricio Gómez's mustachios quivered. "Do you not know what trouble you could make to say she belongs to El Cuerpo? She could get arrested if the police hear about it!"

"Patricio," Señora Bonilla said anxiously. She rose from her chair and walked to his side, putting her arms around him and looking up into his face. "Do not lose your temper, Patricio mine."

"Maybe you would like to talk to the police yourself," Gómez shouted. "Maybe you would like to show them the identification that you refused to show me!"

"The whole day," Señora Bonilla sobbed, "it has been terrible! I do not understand what is going on."

Dearborn decided that the time had come to withdraw, but first he had one more thing to do. "I wonder if you will tell me . . . "

"Oh no!" Gómez warned. "She is not going to tell you nothing more."

"It is only that . . . "

"She will answer you nothing!"

"What is it?" Señora Bonilla broke in tensely. "Ask it and then get out."

"It has to do with my getting back to Havana. I came by bus. My car broke down yesterday. . . . Ah, well, I am simply not sure which bus . . ."

"Take the *F* bus on Kirov Street," Señora Bonilla interrupted.

"I must change, must I not? The *F* bus doesn't go all the way to the Embassy. I wonder if you can write out the directions for me."

Señora Bonilla snorted with exasperation but she walked back to the desk, wrote something down on a piece of paper, and thrust it into his hand. "Here. Now please go."

Once outside, Dearborn read what she had scrawled and gave a deep sigh of satisfaction before sticking the piece of paper into his pocket and starting down the block.

# 23

Quesada had given Dearborn Isabel Quintana's home address, but since it was late afternoon and she was probably still at work, Dearborn decided to visit her at the Sports Institute. His success at passing himself off to Carmen Bonilla and Patricio Gómez as an Embassy official, plus the fact that Pablo Quesada had mistaken him for a member of the D.G.I., gave him the courage to believe he could deceive Isabel Quintana as well.

He had already discovered that the taxis in Havana did not cruise but instead were stationed at strategic points around the city. Fortunately he found a taxi stand near the bus stop on the Avenida de la Independencia and was able to engage it almost as soon as he got off the Siboney bus. It turned out that the Sports Institute was only a block from the bus stop and he'd barely gotten into the cab before the driver braked in front of a building and announced dramatically, "Instituto Nacionál de Deportes Educación Física y Recreación!"

"Crooks," Dearborn murmured as soon as he got out of the cab. "Every mother's son of 'em."

He slammed the door and stood looking up at the building. Imposing, official, impersonal, and therefore not too hard a nut to crack. He entered into a capacious lobby through a revolving door, but found his way to the elevators blocked by a receptionist's desk behind which sat a uniformed guard.

Dearborn regretted his attire, the sports jacket and ridiculous slacks he'd bought in a shop specializing in fashions for the *turista*. He would have felt vastly better able to cope in pinstripes and spats and sighed audibly as he thought of his ebony cane, confiscated, along with his suitcase and money, by the Cuban Navy. But one carried on as best one could under adverse circumstances. That was one of the rules he lived by. "My good man," he announced, striding up to the desk. "I am here to see Miss Isabel Quintana."

The guard took his time scrutinizing Dearborn, then picked up the phone and asked for the "Oficina de Relaciones Públicas. While waiting for the connection, he allowed his eyes to drift down from Dearborn's stony countenance to his sleazy outfit. It was damned irritating to be so minutely inspected and Dearborn returned the guard's familiarity with a sharp stare of his own.

"Whasjorbeeznez?" the guard asked, putting his hand over the mouthpiece.

"I shall state my business to Miss Quintana in person," Dearborn returned irritably. He transferred his gaze to a wall poster depicting a Latin-looking sprinter carrying the ribbon across the finish line.

"Jumostatjorbeeznez," the guard insisted.

Dearborn sighed, and, taking his cue from the travel poster, replied, "Foot races."

"Whajusay?"

"An international running meet. Hands across the sea, etcetera."

The guard relayed the message, saying something that sounded to Dearborn like, "Four aces for Hans Crosby," but apparently it was understood because he then said to Dearborn, "Che say ju chud see Jorge Jiménez."

"If I wished to see Jorge Jiménez I would have requested an

interview with Jorge Jiménez. Tell the young lady that it is she I wish to see."

The guard passed on the message, then began to relay dutifully, "Che say . . ."

"Never mind all that 'she say' business. I have an appointment at the Government Palace at five-thirty. Tell her it is imperative that I see her now."

Mention of the Government Palace turned the trick. After a few more mumbled words the guard pointed to the elevator and said, "Esecon floor, okay?"

The guard continued his blank-eyed stare as Dearborn walked toward the bank of elevators. Dearborn rode the elevator to the second floor and stepped out into a foyer where a skinny woman behind the desk was methodically gluing stamps to a towering pile of envelopes. "Miss Quintana please."

The receptionist said in desultory fashion, "Un momento. Espera, por favor." Taking a stamp off the tip of her tongue, she popped it onto the envelope and pounded it home with the side of her fist.

Dearborn waited a moment, then asked irascibly, "Do you intend to have me wait until you have completed that banal task before I am attended to?"

"La Señorita viene," the receptionist responded in a bored voice.

"What? La Señorita what? Can't you speak English? What has this country come to? Last time I was here everyone spoke English!"

"Yet you do not speak Spanish, Sir?" a soft voice behind him asked.

It was a verbal slap, gently administered. Dearborn turned and said tartly, "I do speak French, Madame."

"And I do speak English, Señor."

The young lady addressing him was a stunning green-eyed blonde, slender but curvaceous, and obviously equal to any situation. "No offense intended," Dearborn said, backing down with equanimity.

"I forgive you your thoughtlessness. I am Isabel Quintana. What is it you wish?"

"I'd like to have a word with you in private."

"I understand it concerns an international running event. I am only an interpreter with the Institute. I am not directly concerned with sports activities. I think perhaps you should see Jorge . . ."

"Not that Jiménez fellow again. You're the one I'm here to see."

She cocked her head. "Really? Well then, what is it, Señor?"

"Where can we talk?"

She turned and led him down to a large open room where a dozen women sat typing. She stopped to pick up a notebook and pen at her desk, then motioned to Dearborn to follow her into a glass-enclosed cubicle. The lettered name on the office door read, "Nicasio Moya."

"Señor Moya has left for the day," she said. "We can talk in here. Now what is it you want of me?"

Dearborn went right to the attack. "Can't you guess?"

"I have not the least idea."

"It has to do with an American here in Havana."

"You are seeking an English-speaking guide? If so, I must tell you that I work only for the Institute. My job here occupies all my time. I have no time left to work for private individuals or tour groups."

"I am not here to hire you, Miss Quintana. I am seeking information."

Isabel frowned. "Who are you?"

"I am with the secret police."

"The D.G.I.? But you are an American."

"Quite so."

"A member of the D.G.I. who does not speak Spanish?"

"I do speak Spanish," he returned promptly. "However, since I am most comfortable in English and since you are as fluent as I in the language, I prefer to conduct our interview in my native tongue."

"What is it you want?"

"I want to talk about Benjamin Pinch."

Isabel backed up a step. "I have been visited by the D.G.I. on two occasions since Fernando Solís was murdered. I have already told all I know about Benjamin Pinch. I have not seen him since the murder. I had no idea that he was an American agent until it was revealed to me by one of your people."

Dearborn said reassuringly, "Of course. We know that. You are not under suspicion."

"Then what is it you want from me?"

"We have reason to think that Pinch may try to contact you."

"Why should he do that?"

"He has attempted to contact some of the others who were in his hotel room on the night of Solís's murder."

"Why?"

"We believe he is looking for protection."

Isabel shrugged. "He has not attempted to contact me, but if he does I shall call you immediately."

"That is precisely what we do not wish you to do," Dearborn told her. "You cannot hold him by force. He will merely slip out of our grasp again. What you must do is agree to hide him."

"You wish me to help him?"

"Precisely. It won't be easy. He may be skittish . . ."

"What is skittish?"

"Quick to run. But if he comes to you, you must keep him from leaving. He's a pushover for the ladies, especially for ladies as beautiful as you, Miss Quintana."

Isabel said in a controlled voice, "Are you suggesting that I seduce him?"

"I am suggesting that you captivate him. There is evidence that in the hands of a seductive woman Pinch tends to become addled."

"What?"

"Fizzle-brained. Insipid. Irresolute. In other words, tractable."

"I do not think he is so easily handled as you think. What's more, I do not think he will try to contact me."

"The man is desperate."

"He is not a fool. He knows I would turn him in."

Dearborn wondered if she were sincere or simply very clever. "You aren't holding anything back from me, are you, Miss Quintana?"

"Even though I told everything I knew after the murder, I have continued to be questioned and harassed. Just when I believe I am to be left in peace, I am again bothered. I know nothing about Benjamin Pinch, except that he did not seem to me to be a criminal. He has not contacted me and I do not believe he will."

"Still, if he were to do so, I would like you to tell him that you were visited by an American C.I.A. agent. Say that the agent sought you out because he knew that you and Pinch had been friendly. Tell him that the agency wants to help him and that the agent has promised to call on you again."

"He might not believe it."

"Mention the name Roycroft. Burgess Roycroft. It is the name of someone he once knew."

Isabel said in a hostile voice, "You want me to lead him to you so that you can place him under arrest. No. The answer is no."

"It is your patriotic duty to help us."

"It is not my duty to lead a man to prison."

Dearborn found her indignation suspicious. One would think she would agree to anything just to be rid of him. "I'm rather surprised at your reluctance to cooperate," he said.

"That is because you are accustomed to dealing in subterfuge and deceit. I am a good Cuban, loyal to my country, willing to work for the common good, proud of my heritage. But I am also a person of honor. I do not denounce people or trick them or lie to them. I do not work for the D.G.I. You cannot ask me to go against my conscience."

Dearborn continued to protest for another moment in order to lend authority to his impersonation, then as he walked toward the door he said, "I fear you misjudge me, Miss Quintana. I am not the bloodthirsty man you think I am."

She pulled the door open for him and said in a hostile whisper as he passed, "It might profit you to reflect upon your own conscience before you make that claim with such confidence."

# 24

She might know where Benjamin was. Dearborn wasn't sure of it, not sure enough to confide in her, but there were strong arguments in favor of it. For one thing she had not displayed the docility one would expect from an innocent person confronted by the police. For another, her answers, if not rehearsed, had been calculated and evasive. And if those points weren't enough, the strongest argument of all was her physical attractiveness. The young woman was a beauty. What little common sense Benjamin had invariably evaporated at the sight of a beautiful woman. He'd made a pitch for her. Dearborn didn't doubt it. And he was willing to bet she'd fallen for him. If Dearborn stuck to the Quintana woman long enough she might lead him to Benjamin.

The prospect exhilarated him and he lay in wait for her with anticipation. There were no restaurants within sight of the entrance to the Sports Institute so he made do with soft ice cream purchased from a street stand which advertised "Coppelia Deliciosa!" and with an orange he bought from a passing vendor.

It was after seven when Isabel finally came out of the Institute. Dearborn followed, hanging back when she stopped under a crowded *Pare* sign, waiting out of sight while two buses went by. She boarded the third bus along with a dozen or so others, and Dearborn dashed forward at the last minute to squeeze through the bus doors and drop his five centavos into the coin box.

The mass of standees shielded him from Isabel while permitting him to keep his eye on her, but the trip was long and when Isabel finally got out of the bus on the corner of Teniente Rey and La Habana in Old Havana, there were far fewer passengers and no one standing in the aisle. Fortunately, Dearborn had by then succeeded in situating himself next to a portly gentleman reading a newspaper that screened Dearborn from Isabel. His luck held until she exited by the back door, allowing him time to leave from the front and resume his surveillance. He followed her to her building on San Ignacio Street and after she had gone inside he followed her into the narrow hallway to look for her name on one of the dozen tin mailboxes. It was there. *Isabel Quintana. 3A.*

He was, he figured, only a few blocks from Enrique's apartment on Cabrahigo Street and he thought of it longingly but without hope as he took up a stance on the sidewalk opposite her building. For the next two hours he relieved the boredom by reciting poetry to himself, starting with "The Village Blacksmith," moving on to "The Charge of the Light Brigade," and encoring with selections from "The Rime of the Ancient Mariner."

It was almost ten when she finally emerged from her building and walked up the block. It was dark by then and Dearborn had no trouble following her, but he realized that if she planned to take another bus he wouldn't have the rush hour commuters to screen him. He waited to see which bus stop she chose, then looked around for a taxi stand. There were none nearby but he reasoned that there should be one near the east entrance to Central Park. It was a six or seven block walk but the lumbering buses moved slowly, so with a head start he might be able to find a taxi before the bus disappeared.

Dearborn walked as far as Aguacate before crossing the street and watched from a distance until Isabel boarded a bus marked *Vedado*. Then he turned and hurried toward the park, his long legs carrying him forward rapidly enough so that the bus was still visible when he turned onto Zulueta and sighted the taxi stand. There was a cab at the curb, and Dearborn hailed it. He began to get in but ran into difficulties when the cab driver explained with extravagant gestures that the cab was on call. The issue was settled when Dearborn pressed a ten-peso tip into his hand, promised an additional ten pesos over and above the regular fare, and, to forestall further argument, leaped into the back seat and locked both doors. There was further confusion a moment later when Dearborn insisted that the driver make a U-turn and proceed west on Teniente Rey behind the lumbering Vedado bus.

"Dónde? Por dónde?" the taxi driver demanded.

"Behind the bus. Follow that bus."

"Qué?"

"The Vedado bus-o!"

"El autobús? Ah, sí. Quiere ir al Vedado."

"No, no. What are you doing?"

The driver had stepped on the gas, come abreast of the bus at the Paseo del Prado and streaked past.

"Whoa!" Dearborn cried. "Don't pass el bus-o!"

"Ah, El Paseo," the driver responded obligingly. "Quiere El Paseo." He swung around the corner onto the Prado.

"Not El Paseo, you fool! Turn this damned car around!"

The driver scowled at Dearborn in the rear-view mirror but swerved into another wide U-turn. "Qué quiere? Dragones?"

"Right! Turn right!" Dearborn leaned over the front seat to point out the direction, then fell back as the taxi swerved around the corner onto Dragones.

The bus had disappeared around a curve in the road and Dearborn urged the driver to step on it. Again they caught up with the bus and whipped by.

"Blast! What are you doing? Don't pass it, you damned fool!"

The driver again misunderstood and turned onto Belascoain, causing further fulmination and resulting in another tumultuous about-face that carried them back onto Dragones. The bus had just reached the intersection.

"Right!" Dearborn commanded as the bus crossed their path. "Reduce speed!"

The phonetic proximity of "reduce speed," to "reduce la velocidad," as well as Dearborn's forceful delivery, turned the trick. The driver slowed down, though not enough to prevent them from once again cruising past the bus. Dearborn soon found himself in the position of tracking the bus from in front, twisting his neck to watch it through the rear window, calling out for further reductions in speed whenever the bus halted to discharge a passenger.

It was inevitable that the cab driver would finally realize what he was being asked to do. It hit him at a point where the road swept into a particularly wide curve, and the bus was lost to view. Once again Dearborn began crying for him to slow down. "Ah! El autobús!" the driver suddenly exclaimed. "Ah, sí! Okay, okay!" He pulled onto a grassy triangle to wait for the bus and when it failed to catch up with them, he whipped the taxi around and sped back the way they'd come. "Un trapillo, eh?" he declared enthusiastically. "Su mujer y un otro hombre?"

"What? What?"

"Hanksy-pank?"

"Turn here. Make a left."

The taxi shot across the road and entered G Street near the campus of the University of Havana. Dearborn leaned forward over the back of the front seat. "Damn it, where is it? Wait a minute. There! There it is! See it up ahead?"

The bus was just turning left onto Twenty-third Street and the cab driver speeded up in order to overtake it. It turned left again onto an avenue identified by a white concrete road marker as Paseo, and left again a few blocks farther on. Something was wrong here. Dearborn looked around in bewilderment, then with sudden horrified recognition. The bus had started its return run. "Step on it!" he shouted. "Go, go! Pass the bus! Pass it!"

As the taxi pulled abreast of the bus Dearborn poked his head out the window to peer through the bus windows. There were three passengers, none of them Isabel Quintana. Dearborn smacked the back of the seat with his fist. "Gone! She got away!"

"Las mujeres," the driver soothed, "no valen la pena. No warth the troble."

"He followed me, Benjamin. He was waiting for me when I came out of my apartment building. He didn't get on the bus with me but he was standing on the sidewalk as the bus went by. I got off the bus at Zulueta and waited. After a minute I saw him come along and get into a taxi. He gave directions to the driver to follow the bus."

"And then you hopped a cab yourself."

"Yes."

"It looks like we've got trouble all right."

"He didn't suspect me at first, but I gave myself away. I behaved stupidly. I became flustered when he said he was from the D.G.I."

"I don't know. It sounds kind of fishy, especially the part about him being an American."

"Why? He explained it plausibly. After all, there was a large American population in Cuba before the Revolución and many of them chose to remain because they believed in Castro. They are men conversant with both cultures who are ardently anti-American despite their background."

They were sitting hunched over a wooden table in a dark

corner of the tiny restaurant, finishing a meal that consisted of chicken with rice and fried banana. The beer was warm and they drank it from unmatched coffee mugs. There were no other customers, only the proprietor who sat on a high stool behind the counter reading a magazine.

"What have I gotten you into, Isabel? I must be nuts."

"Never mind me. By the time you called me last night I was sick with fright, worrying about you. You must give up this reckless idea of looking for Solís's killer."

"Now? When I'm so close?"

"How close are you?"

"I think it must be Carmen Bonilla, but damn it, I turned that house upside down without finding any evidence against her."

"No samples of her handwriting?"

"Oh yeah. Plenty. But none that signify. Of all the damned letters of the alphabet, it has to be the *K* that's got the personality."

Isabel said gently, "You must resign yourself. There is no more you can do."

"I know, I know, but you can understand how I feel. I'm so damned close!"

"I understand your desire to prove your innocence, but I know my country and my countrymen. There can be no satisfaction for you in any case. You must get to the Embassy before it is too late."

Benjamin used his fork to push his half-eaten food around his plate. "And leave you behind? How am I supposed to do that."

"Do not bring up that subject again."

"There's nothing here for you. What the hell kind of country is this anyway? An impoverished island, headed by a dictator and run by ignorant, uneducated bullies, with half the population ratting on the other half, and nobody sure when or where the ax will fall!"

"You are unfair, you know. You make it seem far more hopeless than it is."

"When was the last time you bought a new dress? When was the last time you ate a decent steak?"

"There are more important things than pretty clothes or fancy food."

"There isn't anything more important than personal freedom," he argued, aware of how banal he must sound but desperate to jar her out of her complacency.

"I disagree. There is dedication to an ideal."

"Bullshit."

"Benjamin," Isabel said impatiently, "please. I do not want you to wait any longer to go to the Embassy."

"I thought I'd try following Carmen Bonilla for a day or two. See where it leads."

"No. You should not. That D.G.I. man, he said that they know you have been searching out those who were in your hotel room that night. If the D.G.I. is watching me, they will be watching the others."

"I'll be careful."

"I cannot bear it. You must not. You have so much to fear, not only from the D.G.I., but from El Cuerpo."

"Suppose I promise to give it to the end of the week, say Saturday, then chuck it in."

"Where will you stay until the end of the week? Will you come back to my apartment?"

"You know I can't do that. But it's okay. I found a place."

"Where?"

"I won't tell you. It's better if you don't know. But take my word for it. It's watertight, snug, and safe."

"A room somewhere? But suppose someone recognizes you?"

"It isn't going to happen."

"Oh God, Benjamin, if you had any pity for me you wouldn't take such terrible risks."

"And if you have any pity for me you'll come live with me and be my wife." Benjamin squeezed her hand. "Promise me you'll think about it?"

"If you promise to go to the Embassy tomorrow."

"Saturday."

"Friday. Here, I will write down my phone number and my extension at the Institute. I share this extension number with Nicasio Moya. If he answers simply tell him that you are with the

Canadian mission and are calling about the Conjunto Folklórico Nacionál."

"Say what?"

"A project I am working on. Nicasio won't question it and will call me to the phone immediately."

"You drive a hard bargain, but okay. Look, are you finished with your coffee?"

She nodded and put down the coffee cup.

"Then we'd better split. It's not safe to spend too much time in any one place."

"Oh God, Benjamin."

"By Saturday it'll be over one way or the other. Okay? Just be patient, stop worrying and hang in there."

# 25

It was after midnight when Dearborn got back to the apartment on Cabrahigo Street. The lights were still on and Enrique opened the door. "Hello, Vargas. How's tricks?"

"You are back? We have been wondering where you were. Are you all right?"

Judging by the fact that Tomás was nowhere in sight and that Raúl was fast asleep on the couch, Dearborn decided that the "we" was mere politesse. He stepped inside and closed the door. "I am not all right, Enrique. I am in a state of advanced exhaustion."

"Raúl said that you went out to purchase a gun. Do you not know that we have our weapon sources in El Cuerpo? It is true that we of the La Voz section do not ordinarily carry firearms, but we shall, of course, be armed on Saturday. That I promise you."

139

"I thought of that myself after I'd left so I skipped buying the gun and got myself some clothes instead. Figured I might have to pass myself off as a tourist and I wanted to look the part. What do you think?"

Enrique took in the red jacket and plaid trousers and said pointedly, "Surely it did not take you all day to shop for them?"

"All day?"

"You have been gone for twelve or thirteen hours. I was beginning to think you were lost."

Dearborn picked up the cue. "Precisely. I *was* lost. I had a devil of a time finding my way back here. Kept jumping on and off buses. Unnerving experience."

"La Habana is not so large a city that you could be lost for an entire day."

"True," Dearborn conceded, groping for a reasonable explanation, "but I fell asleep on one of those damned buses and woke up somewhere in the suburbs, in a place called Siboney. Then I had a difficult time finding someone who spoke English and could point me back to Havana proper. Thought I'd be out in the hinterlands forever. It has been . . ." He interrupted himself to look around and ask, "Where is Tomás?"

"He has gone to Matanzas."

"He has done what?"

"He has gone to Matanzas to get Señora Ortiz. In a few hours the others will also arrive."

"But this is only Tuesday."

"Wednesday," Enrique corrected.

"Still a little early to assemble the troops, isn't it?"

"There are only three days left in which to arrange all the details, coordinate activities, and prepare ourselves for Saturday's coup."

Dearborn was exhausted and Enrique's news was the final irritant to his already jangled nerves. "Last night I slept on the floor," he declared exasperatedly. "I have not slept on the floor since Chubby Hardwicke, under the influence, locked me in the fraternity broom closet. I have never slept four to a room. Now you are proposing to increase the tenancy of this squirrel cage by another six persons? Impossible!"

"We in El Cuerpo must bear our hardships stoically. Remember, we may soon face greater discomforts than these."

"And another thing," Dearborn went on contentiously, "Why did you send Tomás to Matanzas? Why didn't you go yourself? Suppose he's stopped? Suppose someone asks him for identification? Suppose someone reports a stranger going into Clara Ortiz's house? Suppose the car breaks down?"

"He insisted."

"He what? Since when is Tomás so gung ho?" Dearborn was rattled by a sudden unpleasant thought. "When did he leave?"

"I arrived home at six. That is earlier than usual, but I wished to get an early start to Matanzas. Tomás offered to go in my place. He insisted that since I had driven all day I should remain here and rest."

"When did he leave?"

"Sometime after six."

"It's almost one in the morning," Dearborn pointed out. "It doesn't take seven hours to drive there and back."

"Perhaps Señora Ortiz was not yet ready to leave."

"And perhaps Tomás has been picked up by the police."

"No," Enrique objected. "I am sure that nothing has happened."

"Then where is he?"

"As I said a moment ago . . ."

"How long could it take for Señora Ortiz to throw a couple of things in a suitcase? Havana's not the south of France. She wasn't planning on bringing a steamer trunk, was she?"

Enrique's composure was beginning to crumble, "Do you really think it is possible that something has gone wrong?"

"Of course I think it's possible. What do you think I'm saying!"

Enrique tottered to a chair. "The car. I am the only one of us who owns a car."

"That's all you can think about? Your car?"

"The car is central to our plans."

"And Tomás is central to mine. You never should have sent him off like that."

"I told you, Señor, that I did not send him. He insisted."

Across the room Raúl stirred, opened his eyes, and propped himself up on one elbow. "Bombas!" he announced portentiously. "Es necesario comprar las bombas!"

"Is he talking about bombs?"

"Yes. He is saying we must buy the bombs." Enrique spoke to Raúl and then translated. "I told him we do not have to buy the bombs. It is only necessary that we pick them up in Guanabacoa."

"We have enough to worry us without Raúl. Tell him to forget the bombs, Enrique."

"I am to pick up the bombs in Guanabacoa," Enrique explained morosely. "How can I tell him that without a car there will be no bombs."

"Don't tell him any of that. He wouldn't know what you were talking about. Simply tell him to go back to sleep."

Enrique spoke to Raúl in an authoritative tone and Raúl nodded that he understood. He stretched, rubbed his belly, then rose and answered Enrique while he was buckling on his belt and buttoning his shirt.

"I told him it is too late to go but he insists."

"Can't you see the man's a lunatic?"

"All great men are fanatics," Enrique said calmly. "It is the source of their great strength."

"Enrique, if he starts to leave the apartment we'll have to stop him."

By then Raúl had trotted into the bathroom and begun splashing water on his face.

"Lock the door," Dearborn instructed.

"I shall talk with him. I am sure that he will listen to reason."

Raúl, refreshed, came out of the bathroom and returned to pull the couch away from the wall. Behind it was a burlap rice sack containing his money. He had tied a piece of rope around the neck of the sack and now he picked it up, wound the rope around his waist and secured it. "Vamos, Enrique."

Dearborn placed himself in front of the door. "Wait a minute, Raúl. Let's talk about this."

"Vamos my fran, Roycrap."

"I'm afraid you're going to have to tackle him, Enrique."

"I am going to tell him about the car," Enrique proposed. "Raúl, escucháme!"

Raúl said politely, "Perdoneme," and began shouldering Dearborn to one side. Dearborn attempted to put his arm around Raúl's shoulders but Raúl shrugged him off. Then Dearborn grabbed the back of his shirt but he yanked himself free.

"Raúl," Enrique said, "estamos en un apuro."

"What are you telling him?"

"That we have problems."

"Forget the problems! Find something to hit him with!"

"Escucháme, Raúl," Enrique persisted.

Dearborn grabbed him around the chest in a bear hug and Raúl promptly dragged Dearborn out the door onto the landing.

"Don't just stand there, Vargas!"

"El coche, Raúl. Quiero hablar del coche."

"Forget the coachy! Go for his knees!"

Dearborn and Raúl were now struggling at the top of the stairs. Suddenly, from below, a soft voice called up, "Raúl, querido, estoy aquí."

With Dearborn still clinging to his back, Raúl leaned over the stair rail. "Clara? Dónde estás?"

Señora Ortiz, with Tomás behind her, was already halfway up the stairs. "Ah, my friends," she whispered breathlessly, "here we are. We have finally arrived."

"Clara, mi amor," Raúl exclaimed, wrestling free from Dearborn and lifting her hand to his lips.

"Ssh," Señora Ortiz cautioned, pointing to the dark windows above and below. "Callàte, Raúl."

"Señor Roycroft," Enrique declared triumphantly, "you were wrong. You see! I told you nothing had happened."

Dearborn had talked himself into believing that Tomás had met with a terrible fate. He was astounded and relieved to find that he had been mistaken. Once inside the door, however, he demanded an explanation. "Did something happen to the car, Tomás?"

"No, nothin'."

"You didn't run into any kind of trouble?"

"No trouble. Why should there be trouble?"

"You've been gone for eight hours."

"That's how long it takes."

"That's how long it takes by foot, not by car." Dearborn edged closer and sniffed Tomás's breath. "Do I smell liquor?"

"No, you don't."

"Then what is it? Out with it. Where were you?"

"I been to see Elena."

"Good Lord!" Dearborn was shaken. That Tomás might wish to renew his acquaintance with the homely and phlegmatic Elena was disconcerting enough. That he might elect to do so knowing she was married, and to a man immersed in loyalist activities, was more than disconcerting. It was frightening. "Why would you take such a chance? The woman did you wrong, Tomás!"

Tomás looked sheepish. "She say that her brother told her I was dead. He told her the police, they shot me while I was in jail."

"And she believed him?"

"Why not? Before they put me on the boat at Mariel I spoke to a friend of mine. My friend, he was suppose to get outta jail. I ask him to tell her how they sent me to Florida. I ask him to find a way to help her to escape from Cuba. Elena and me, we used to talk plenty about going to Florida. But my friend, he never told her. Maybe he never got outta jail. I don't know."

"That's too bad, Tomás. Nevertheless, it's too late now. The lady is married."

"She is still in love with me and I am still in love with her."

"Yes, well that may be, but it doesn't make the situation any less hopeless."

"I told her I would go back for her."

"What? You what? Out of the question, Tomás."

"Tut, tut," Señora Ortiz interposed. "Tomás and I have talked it over. I read the cards for him before we left Matanzas. It will be perfectly all right. The fates are in his favor."

Dearborn started to object, but to forestall any further discussion Señora Ortiz raised her voice a bit and talked over him. "I have also determined that the signs are favorable for our success on Saturday."

"There is much to be done," Enrique declared.

"Yes," Señora Ortiz agreed briskly. "For one thing, we must choose the person who will martyr himself."

Dearborn was instantly alert. "What's that?" he asked with foreboding. "What are you talking about? Why must someone martyr himself?"

"The word has been passed to me. It is not enough to issue statements and distribute pamphlets. Someone must reach the ears of the people and it has been decided that the honor will fall to one of La Voz. There will be, perhaps, a million people in the Plaza on Saturday. One of us will capture the microphone and hold it long enough to deliver the message. I shall write the speech."

Dearborn was regarding her with an expression of sheer stupefaction.

"It must be a compelling cry for freedom," Señora Ortiz said, "a rallying call to all of Cuba to unite. It will set forth the aims of El Cuerpo and ask for support. It will be inspiring. It will be . . ."

"Suicide," Dearborn supplied flatly. "Out and out suicide."

# 26

On the following morning, after shrugging off Raúl's unceasing attentions, Clara began drafting the martyrdom speech. Everyone else left the apartment early, Enrique to go to his job, and the others to gather and disseminate information in accordance with their function as the "voice" of El Cuerpo. Dearborn, looking for an excuse to absent himself as well, suggested that it would be wise for him and Tomás to familiarize themselves with the city, a suggestion that Clara approved of and that Raúl, once apprised of their intentions, greeted with delight. "Estar a solas con mi querida Clara. Qué buena fortuna!"

"What's he saying?"

"They want to be alone."

Dearborn and Tomás left the apartment and strolled toward the waterfront, Dearborn using their time alone to fill in Tomás on what he had found out thus far. "I think I have located someone who may know where Benjamin is. I have begun watching her in the hope that she will lead me to him."

"She? She is a woman?"

"She's a translator at the Sports Institute."

"What make you think she know where he is at?"

"I have a sixth sense when it comes to these things."

"You did not tell her who you are?"

"No," Dearborn answered. "First I want to make sure I'm not wrong about her."

"Listen, I think we gotta get outta here pretty soon. This El Cuerpo, they're crazy pipples. They ain't gonna be happy until they kill themselves and us too."

"I'm in complete agreement. It's time to make arrangements to get out of Cuba. We're going to need a boat."

"We can't buy a boat. There ain't no boats for sale in Cuba. No cars and no boats. We gotta hire somebody to take us."

"What about your friend José?"

"He don't have his own boat. He work on someone else's boat."

"Who's that?"

"Is the government. What they call a cooperative. Maybe ten men and a supervisor."

"So much for that idea. We shall have to find someone here in Havana."

"Elena, she say everybody needs money. She say is easy to find someone who will run past the patrol boats, for four, five thousand pesos."

"Then you've got to start hanging around the docks, Tomás. Try to befriend some of the fishermen. Stand them for beers. You're a fisherman yourself. You know how to talk to them. You think you can manage it?"

"Not without pesos."

"I'll give you whatever I can spare. Feel your way, Tomás. When you find someone willing to talk business, offer him whatever you have to, three thousand, five thousand, whatever it takes."

"You think Raúl, he will give us five thousand pesos?"

"We shall relieve him of it one way or another."

"What shall I say about when we gonna leave?"

146

"Whoever you hire will have to be ready to leave at a moment's notice."

"I ain't goin' without Elena."

"Nothing but trouble has resulted from your pursuit of that lady. The first time you tried to run away with her you landed in jail. Try it again and you may be shot. What's more, you're not risking your life alone. You're risking the lives of all of us."

"If she don't go, I don't go."

Dearborn decided to postpone discussion of Elena until a later date. He said placatingly, "All right, we'll see, Tomás. There's time before we have to make any decision about who will and who won't go."

"Just so you know how I feel."

"You have made yourself quite clear on the point."

Dearborn and Tomás parted company near the docks on Avenida Del Puerto, Tomás to embark on his quest for a boat and Dearborn to pick up Isabel's trail.

It was already ten o'clock, which meant that Isabel should have arrived at work. Dearborn didn't even try to intercept her at her apartment but went directly to the Sports Institute. He occupied himself for an hour strolling in the Botanical Gardens across the street and then, at noon, returned to the Institute to take up the watch.

His vigil was rewarded at one-thirty when Isabel and another young woman appeared at the door of the Institute and strolled to a restaurant on a nearby street. They took a table near the front window which made it easy for Dearborn to watch them, but so far as he could determine, no one joined them or spoke with them during the time they were there. After lunch they went directly back to the Institute and Dearborn once again positioned himself across the street.

At seven Isabel started for home. Dearborn managed to find an inconspicuous seat on the bus and when she entered her apartment building forty-five minutes later he was only a few yards behind. Three hours later he was still waiting for her to show herself again, having drained his memory of "Ode to a Nightingale," "The Ballad of Reading Gaol," and fragments from "My Last Duchess." He stuck it out until midnight, bogging down finally at "Tomorrow, and tomorrow, and tomorrow," and decided, with a melancholy last glance at her doorway, to call it a day and head back to Cabrahigo Street. Along the way he stopped at an open-air restaurant and ordered their specialty, *Pio Cuac,* which was advertised on a crudely lettered sign propped on the counter. It turned out to be crisp aromatic pieces of deep-fried duck which, with a glass of pineapple juice, went a long way to reviving his flagging spirits.

The apartment was only a few blocks south of San Ignacio Street and as he walked along the narrow streets, past the ancient buildings crowding in on one another, with their stained-glass arch windows, wooden doors, and galleried walkways, he tried to fashion an excuse for his extended absence. He decided to stick to the story of studying the city streets, perhaps adding that he had spent the last few hours in the Plaza de la Revolución getting the feel of the place, a taste for the battle, so to speak.

When he reached the apartment he wasn't called upon to present his excuse. Instead he found the full complement of El Cuerpo arrived and assembled. Señora Ortiz and Alberta Barrios were seated at the table, Alberta's dried apple face partially obscured by a floppy straw hat and Señora Ortiz's luminous eyes riveted to a handful of straws that Alberta was clutching. Carlos Naranjo, sans Panama hat but pince-nez in place, had situated himself in the armchair. Pablo Asturias's corpulent form took up most of the couch, and Felipe Mojica had squeezed his long spindly frame into what was left between Pablo and the wall. Enrique was leaning against the dresser, Tomás had settled on the floor with his back against the wall, and Raúl was observing the proceedings through the open bathroom door, having found himself a seat on the toilet.

"This is absurd," Dearborn burst out. "Is no one alarmed over the fact that we are nine people occupying a twelve-foot-square room, which barely translates to sixteen inches apiece?"

"We shall manage," Señora Ortiz said shortly.

"I've been in elevators that offered more breathing space."

"Señor Roycroft, we are discussing something very important right now."

"What's that?"

"We are about to decide who will take the microphone after Castro has been assassinated."

"Surely you aren't serious about that, are you?"

"I ain't gonna do it," Tomás piped up. "You betta not ask me since I ain't gonna do it."

"You are not under consideration," Felipe informed him. "It must be someone adept at public speaking."

"And," Alberta added, "someone who speaks excellent and grammatical Spanish which, of course, eliminates you, Señor Roycroft. I am sorry."

"That leaves seven of us," Señora Ortiz announced. "We shall choose straws."

"Who will win, we cannot predict," Carlos said in his mannerly voice. "However, it shall be a moment of historic importance. The assassin will be close by, standing among the spectators right in front of the stage. The shot will be fired. Castro will fall. A moment later a member of El Cuerpo will leap to the stage, take the microphone, and announce the coup d'etat!"

"Come," Señora Ortiz said impatiently, "let us get on with it. Señor Roycroft, will you hold the straws?"

Dearborn said fastidiously, "If you don't mind, I'd rather not."

"Your name will go down in the history books as the man who presented the martyr with his grand opportunity."

"Ridiculous."

"Revolutionists must not give way to squeamishness."

"I would never accuse you of that, Madame."

"I was speaking of you, Señor Roycroft."

Dearborn was disgusted. If they were bound and determined to go through with their mad scheme, who was he to stop them? He accepted the straws and turned his back on the group to arrange them. After all, the chances of any one of them getting past the guards at Saturday's celebration, much less succeeding in mounting the stage, were remote. However, he wasn't taking any chances with Raúl. Raúl was his responsibility and he did not intend to have Raúl's death on his conscience.

He separated the short straw from the others and bunched up the rest in his hand. Raúl stood a better chance if he went first. Dearborn placed the short straw in the curve between thumb and index finger, pushing it down until it was out of sight, then turned and headed for the bathroom.

"No, no," Pablo objected. "Ladies first. It is only common courtesy."

Gallantry prevented Dearborn from exposing the short straw, and first Señora Ortiz, then Alberta Barrios, chose one of the long straws and displayed it.

Again Dearborn headed for the bathroom, but Enrique stepped in front of him, deliberated over the remaining straws, and chose. "No estoy de suerte," he announced, holding up another of the long straws.

There were only four straws left, of which three were showing. Dearborn had no choice but to expose the fourth. He decided to reverse tactics. He turned away again and readjusted the straws so that the short straw stood taller than the other three, then approached Felipe Mojica. Felipe studied the straws carefully, then shot out his hand and plucked one of the three that remained. It was a long straw.

Raúl had by then come out of the bathroom and was hanging over Dearborn's shoulder. "Me toca a mí."

"Wait a minute, Raúl. Don't rush me." Dearborn reached past Felipe to hold the straws out to Pablo who crossed himself and made his selection. Another long straw.

Now that the odds had fallen to fifty-fifty, it no longer mattered who chose next. Telling himself that even if Raúl did choose the short straw, he would not permit Raúl to place himself in jeopardy, Dearborn held out the remaining two straws.

Raúl put both index fingers to his temples and concentrated on the straws like a magician about to bring off a feat of prestidigitation. Dearborn half expected the straw to rise of its own accord and float into his hand. It didn't happen that way. But it did happen. With a cry of delight Raúl held up the short straw.

# 27.

Sleeping nine people wedged wall to wall was only slightly worse than Dearborn had anticipated. He had arranged himself near the door, a precautionary tactic in case of emergency. Out of deference to her age and sex, Alberta Barrios was assigned the couch, an unfortunate arrangement, since she was accustomed to sleeping in a double bed and repeatedly rolled off onto Carlos Naranjo who was stretched out on the floor beside her. Pablo Asturias, who was sleeping upright in the armchair, wheezed, coughed, and choked his way through the night, while Felipe Mojica, lying under the table, woke himself up at intervals by smacking his long arms and legs against the table legs. Clara and Raúl slept next to one another on the floor in the middle of the room, their alternating snores like the scrape of bow against fiddle, while Enrique, head to head with Tomás under the window, whistled an unmelodious counterpoint.

Dearborn lay awake all night. At first light he got up, nudged Tomás and indicated that Tomás should follow him outside. It took Tomás a minute to blearily acknowledge him. Then he rose, hitched up his trousers and tiptoed after him out onto the porch.

"Well?" Dearborn whispered. "Any luck?"

"Yes and no."

"Speak."

"Yes, I found someone with a boat. He say he has takin' many pipples to Miami."

"And he will take us?"

"Yes."

"So then, what's the hitch?"

"He wants twenty thousand pesos."

"I should have guessed. Robbery, plain and simple."

"He say since the evacuation from Mariel, is much harder to get out. He say nobody won't do it except for a lotta pesos. He say we couldn't hire a rowboat for less than twenty thousand pesos."

"What did you tell him?"

"First I try and bargain, then I done like you said. I told him okay."

"You were right, of course. Has he agreed to keep himself available?"

"Anytime up until Sunday. On Sunday he has to report to the Reserve Guard for two weeks' trainin'."

"You mean I must find Benjamin by Saturday?"

151

Tomás shrugged. "If you don't, then we gotta go without him."

"We are not going without him, Tomás. Put that out of your mind. Where will we find this fellow when we're ready to leave?"

"He lives on his boat."

"Which is where?"

"At the docks by Desamparados and La Habana."

"What's the name of the boat?"

"*Estrella del Mar.*"

"All right, Tomás. You did your job well. There's nothing left now but to find Benjamin, gather up Raúl, and be on our way."

"Don't forget Elena," Tomás added matter-of-factly. I ain't goin' without Elena."

"Now see here, Tomás. Face the facts. When we leave, we shall have to leave quickly. There won't be time to pick up Elena."

"She can come here."

"She has no way of knowing when we intend to depart, and if she were to walk out on her husband now he'll come after her."

"He won't know where she is."

"You cannot bring another person into this apartment, Tomás. I forbid it. El Cuerpo would certainly forbid it. Besides, we live in constant jeopardy. Surely you don't wish to endanger her life."

"I don't wish to endanger my life neither."

"Yes, well that goes without saying. However, it is somewhat beside the point."

"It ain't beside the point to me."

"Enough, Tomás. Nothing is more destructive than self-pity. Now what did you say is the name of that boat?"

Thursday's surveillance proved no more successful than the previous two days' watch, and when Dearborn returned again to the apartment that night he found that his problems, far from being resolved, were being rapidly compounded.

To begin with, his new found associates had assembled a storehouse of terrorist paraphernalia. There were two army-issue duffle bags spilling out rifles, a wicker basket filled with pistols, a pile of cartridge belts, and a blow-up of an orange and green map of Havana that someone had taped to the Oriental screen in the far corner of the room.

Señora Ortiz was handing out jackets as he entered, peasant-type jackets of a rough fabric, more like burlap than cotton. With the exception of Tomás, who was sitting with arms folded and looking on with a brooding expression, everyone was putting them on and commenting vociferously on the fit and fabric.

"I must have a larger size."

"That is your size, Enrique."

"Why must it be burlap?"

"Because burlap is cheap and bulky."

"A suitable covering for potatoes, not people."

Señora Ortiz was elated when she saw Dearborn standing at the door. "Come in, come in," she called out. "I have a jacket for you too. But wait. You are about to see something wonderful!" She gave out a jacket to Alberta who put it on and buttoned it. "This is our uniform," Señora Ortiz explained. "All over La Habana there are members of El Cuerpo trying on the uniform at this very moment!"

Dearborn looked at Tomás who was staring morosely at the floor before he commented blandly, "A bit homespun, don't you think? Not particularly martial."

"That is it! That is it, precisely! We must not stand out in the crowd. We must infiltrate the Plaza, mix with the spectators, do nothing to attract the attention of Castro's guards. Then, when the moment has come, when the signal is given, when the first bomb goes off, we reveal ourselves!"

Señora Ortiz waved her hands at the group who reached into their jacket pockets, whipped out white visored caps bearing a graphic rendition of El Cuerpo's insignia in red, white, and blue, and clapped them onto their heads. Then they unbuttoned their jackets, peeled them off and flipped them inside out. The insides of the jackets were striped in red, white, and blue and bore a variety of patches which Dearborn presumed to be indications of rank and function.

"Well? What do you think? Excellent idea, eh?"

"All that's missing are the fife and drum," Dearborn noted dryly.

"Now, here is your jacket, Señor Roycroft. We have taken

the liberty of assigning you the rank of lieutenant. Normally the induction of a new officer would be accompanied by some ceremony, but in light of our situation we shall dispense with the formalities."

"For my part," Dearborn suggested candidly, "you can also dispense with the jacket."

Raúl, wearing a major's insignia on his jacket, beamed happily and said something which Dearborn couldn't understand and therefore paid no attention to until suddenly he heard Raúl utter the name "Pinch." "What's that? What's be saying?"

"He says," Felipe translated, "that he knows Benjamin Pinch. Benjamin Pinch is the name of the man the D.G.I. are searching for, the man who is presumed by them to be a C.I.A. agent and to have killed Fernando Solís. There was a report about Pinch on the radio tonight."

Raúl said something else.

"He says," Felipe added with a curious look at Dearborn, "that you know him too."

Dearborn's first instinct was to deny it, but he realized almost immediately that denying it would lead to an argument with Raúl. "Benjamin Pinch? Yes, I met him once in Florida. Young fellow. Athlete of some sort, I believe."

"Basketball player."

"Oh yes. Barely knew him. Passing acquaintance."

"We are relieved," Señora Ortiz joined in. "It would be unfortunate if he were a close friend."

"What did they say about him on the radio?"

"Dmitri Golovnin, one of Castro's advisers, was murdered this morning," Pablo said. "They theorize that it was the work of Benjamin Pinch."

"Preposterous!"

"Not preposterous," Alberta trilled. "Merely untrue."

"More of El Cuerpo's work?" Dearborn accused.

"Sí," Enrique replied. "It was necessary to force a temporary breakdown of communications between Cuba and Russia. Golovnin was the chief liaison officer in charge of emergency operations, and the only person permitted to transmit commands on direct order from the Kremlin. With him out of the way there will be no one to interfere with our operations on Saturday."

"But they have not thought of that," Carlos elucidated. "They say that the American C.I.A. is attempting to undermine the Cuban government with a systematic demoralization of its peace-keeping agencies."

Dearborn couldn't believe it. "They place the burden of responsibility on the C.I.A.?"

"And on the very clever and very elusive Pinch," Alberta qualified.

"Perhaps too clever," Señora Ortiz picked up in a troubled voice. "Pinch is looking for the agent of El Cuerpo who killed Solís."

"How do you know that?"

"I spoke with the head of Los Dedos this afternoon. He says that Pinch has broken into the homes of certain people who were present in his hotel room on the night that Solís was killed. He is looking for something. We do not know what. But if he finds it before Saturday he could conceivably ruin all of El Cuerpo's plans."

"It is already Thursday evening," Carlos reminded her. "If he hasn't found out anything by now . . ."

"Yes," she acknowledged, "and Los Dedos has people watching at a half-dozen places where he might show up next. If he does . . ."

"If he does?" Dearborn interrupted anxiously.

"Whoever sees him is under orders to kill him."

Dearborn was suddenly rubber-kneed. He reached for the back of the armchair and leaned against it. Tomás got up quickly and crossed to his side. "You okay, Señor?"

"What is it?" Señora Ortiz asked in an alarmed voice.

"A momentary weakness, Madame."

"You must not despair," Alberta broke in encouragingly. "Pinch will find out nothing and if he should, well then the chances are that he will not live to tell anyone about it."

"Alberta is right," Felipe confirmed in his well-modulated professorial voice. "We are too close to our goal to be thwarted. Tomorrow Enrique will bring us the bombs and tomorrow evening we shall take them to the Plaza. By then Clara will have received precise final instructions from headquarters on the role each of us is to play during the celebration on Saturday."

"There are nine of us," Pablo added ponderously, "and ten

155

bombs. We will draw straws to see who plants two of them instead of one."

"I ain't pickin' no straws," Tomás declared ferociously, "and I ain't hidin' no bombs. Not even one bomb!"

"Why Tomás," Alberta said in a shocked tone, "what's the matter with you? What are you saying?"

"I'm sayin' that I quit."

Dearborn said reprovingly, "Pull yourself together, Tomás. There's no backing out now."

"Speak for yourself!" Tomás shot back. "Maybe you are goin' to go and stick bombs in the bushes, but not me. But if you're smart, Señor, you're gonna say no to it too."

"I cannot believe you mean what you say," Señora Ortiz challenged. "What has come over you, Tomás?"

"Nothin'. I am just the same like always, and I am gonna stay just the same like always. I ain't got nothin' against Castro so why should I want to kill him?"

"Tomás," Dearborn warned, "say no more. You are merely overwrought. Think what you're saying!"

"This is incredible," Carlos exclaimed, adjusting his pince-nez and leaning forward to squint at Tomás. "You are defecting?"

"You cannot defect," Alberta proclaimed. "It is not permitted."

"I don't need no permission," Tomás answered defiantly. He got to his feet and trotted across the room toward the door. "If you pipples wanna get shot, you can get shot. Not me."

"You do not understand," Señora Ortiz chimed in. "A deserter at this point would be a danger to the success of our coup d'etat."

"Tomás," Dearborn pleaded, "I beg of you. Do not lose your head. Everything will work out."

"I been thinkin' about it. So far nothin' ain't workin' out. I'm better off takin' care of myself. I am gonna get Elena, find a boat somewheres, and get outta Cuba."

"Don't be a fool. You haven't a chance on your own."

"I ain't got no chance stayin' here, that's for sure. I'm gonna find some other way."

"You cannot leave," Pablo said severely, his chins vibrating with emotion. "We shall have to stop you!"

Much to Raúl's increasing frustration the entire confrontation had thus far been conducted in English. Now he jumped into the argument to insist that they speak in Spanish and when no one paid him the slightest attention he dove into the basket containing the pistols and came up brandishing one.

Without thinking, Tomás, who was standing next to him, grabbed it out of his hand, causing Alberta to cry out fearfully.

Suddenly Enrique, the spryest of the group, lunged toward Tomás, causing him to jump backward and fall against the door. Then the gun went off, the bullet splattering into the ceiling and raining down plaster.

In the brief, noisy encounter that followed, Carlos lost his pince-nez, Pablo was overcome by an attack of coughing, Alberta had the collar torn off her dress, and Raúl fell into the basket of pistols. When it was over no one knew quite what had happened, least of all Dearborn, who was by then sitting on the couch staring dazedly at the door through which Tomás had departed.

# 28

On Wednesday morning Carmen Bonilla arrived at the Novedoso, carrying what appeared to be her lunch in a paper bag, and emerged again in the evening to board the Siboney bus in front of the hotel. Benjamin took the next bus and followed her home. Playing Peeping Tom didn't reward him with more than the sight of her in bathrobe and slippers sitting at the kitchen table eating her supper. Four hours later, when she turned out the light in her bedroom, Benjamin gave up and left.

He called Isabel from a public phone to report on his uneventful day and promised to call again on Thursday evening. She wanted to meet him and wasn't happy when he insisted that it wasn't the best idea, but beyond eliciting another promise that he'd give it up on Friday, she didn't nag.

It wasn't any better on Thursday. The day was interminable and Benjamin was frustrated by the enforced inactivity associated with the waiting. He was sick of skulking around the hotel hoping that something would occur. And he was hungry, having had nothing to eat since breakfast.

He'd made up his mind that Carmen Bonilla was the one. It wasn't easy to think of her as a murderer but she was his last hope and he brushed away the disturbing questions that continued to plague him. Where had she gotten the gun? She had been wearing a thin rayon-type dress when she visited Benjamin's hotel room and he didn't remember her carrying a pocketbook. How could she have gotten downstairs fast enough to follow Solís out of the hotel? He had to have used the elevator, which meant that she would have had to run down three flights of stairs in less than a minute. But could she have done it? She wasn't athletic. Nor was she young. Most difficult of all to explain was Solís's wound. According to the newspapers he had been shot in the back of the head, the bullet traveling downward to emerge beneath his right eye. Yet Carmen Bonilla was a small woman. Where had she been standing when he was shot? On the steps of the hotel? But Solís had been fired at from close range and the newspaper account put him at the curb about to get into his car, at least twelve feet from the steps.

Benjamin was unwilling to accept the most logical probability, that the premise on which he'd based his suspicions was invalid. He reminded himself that the list hidden in his suitcase had been dated in pen, the date obviously tacked on at the last moment. And there was no question but that the person who had dashed off the date on the front was the same person who had written those letters on the back.

It was now or never. Benjamin was determined to stalk Señora Bonilla until she led him to El Cuerpo headquarters or until she gave herself away by some recognizable act. She didn't leave the hotel until nine, which was later than the night before and when she came out she was accompanied by Patricio Gómez, the hotel detective. Benjamin stayed well out of sight as he watched them saunter toward the bus stop.

He expected them to separate, but instead they continued

to walk to the corner. Señora Bonilla took Gómez's arm to cross the street and Benjamin noticed that she didn't relinquish it on the other side. Apparently they were going somewhere together . . . very together, judging by the possessive way she was holding onto him and his great attentiveness to her. Funny. They were such different people. It would never have occurred to Benjamin to link them romantically. They seemed to have nothing in common.

Or was that true? What if there were some common link? Something like El Cuerpo? Why hadn't he thought of it sooner? He had been thinking in terms of one person, a solo act. But suppose there were two of them acting in concert? Mutual conviction, compatible ideals, a common goal, those things could bridge the class gap like nothing else. And if Carmen Bonilla couldn't run down three flights of stairs in less than a minute, Patricio Gómez could. If she carried no weapon, Gómez always carried one. The angle of the bullet? Hard to square with her height, but not with his. He was a tall man, easily as tall as Solís.

Señora Bonilla and Gómez headed south on Pozos Dulces and west on the Avenida 19 de Mayo, then turned south again at the next corner, which brought them out onto the wide boulevard leading to the Plaza de la Revolución which Benjamin had begun to think of as home. He hung back when he saw Patricio Gómez approach a public phone kiosk at the entrance to the Plaza, put in his coin, make a brief phone call, then rejoin Señora Bonilla. What was that all about? Could it have been a signal of some kind? He hadn't spoken more than nine or ten words before hanging up. Benjamin was suddenly filled with hope.

They slowed their pace and began looking for a place to sit. It was a balmy evening and there was someone on every bench. Finally they settled themselves on a Parks Department equipment bin, padlocked and plainly marked *¡Las Manos Quietas! Hands off*. Benjamin realized that he couldn't get close enough to eavesdrop. Not that he could have understood most of what they were saying, but he would certainly have been tipped off by any key words they might have spoken, like El Cuerpo, or Solís, or even Benjamin Pinch. Since that was out, he sat down at the end of a bench some distance away to await developments.

He wished he weren't so damned hungry. He had stocked

his hideout with a couple of cans of beans and a loaf of bread, and the thought of them made his mouth water. He could see the television scaffolding from where he sat. It was only three or four hundred feet away across an exposed cement apron in front of the speakers' platform. Even if he'd wanted to take the chance of leaving Señora Bonilla and Gómez alone for a few minutes, he'd risk being seen. No, it was better to forget it. He'd been hungry before. It wouldn't kill him to go without eating for a few more hours.

Perhaps it was the word "kill" that made him uneasy or maybe it was a presentiment of trouble, but he felt an unexpected and uncomfortable prickling sensation at the base of his skull and found his eyes drawn to the far right side of the Plaza. It was dark, except for the fuzzy illumination that radiated from the park lamps, but Benjamin could swear that there were a couple of men watching him, the rough-and-ready type, reeking muscle and obstinacy. They looked, from a distance, remarkably like Tweedle-dum and Tweedle-dee, Solís's stalwart henchmen, and Benjamin was at a loss to explain how they, in particular, should have succeeded in tracking him down.

Then he saw two more men to his left, mirror-images of the first and he realized that what he was looking at was the archetypical goon, spit out of the D.G.I. like metal tokens from a vending machine. He glanced over at Carmen Bonilla and Patricio Gómez. They were looking at him too, and not as if they had just discovered his presence. Of course. Why should it surprise him? He'd made the mistake of treating them like amateurs, a couple of people whose survival depended on having eyes in the backs of their heads. How easily they'd outwitted him with a simple phone call to the D.G.I. "I've just seen the American, Benjamin Pinch. He's in the Plaza de la Revolución." That. No more. No need to identify himself. Just a quick phone call.

Benjamin rose slowly and took a few tentative steps. Both sets of men moved with him, not hurrying, but coming toward him from either side like the pressing ends of a vise. He judged the distance between himself and the safety of the television scaffold and decided that even if he could outrun them he couldn't chance leading them directly to his lair. On the other hand, he didn't stand a chance of escaping the park. They hadn't come with only four men. There were more, certainly enough to cut off his escape.

He decided to circle the masonry speakers' platform which offered some protection, lead them away from the television scaffold, and then double back. He didn't waste time weighing the pros and cons. They were already too close. He turned, dashed a dozen steps or so back toward the entrance to the Plaza, then whirled and tore for the left side of the speakers' platform.

The surprise strategy worked, at least momentarily. He couldn't see the men to his right, but the other two, the ones closest to him, bounded past him in the opposite direction. It took them thirty seconds or so to realize what had happened and by the time they slid to a stop and turned, Benjamin was already rounding the corner of the platform.

"Halt!" a voice cried out from behind him. "Halt!"

Benjamin kept going and was rewarded by the whistle and splat of a bullet grazing the cement wall a few inches to the right of him. A moment later he looked up and saw the second pair of thugs hurtling toward him.

He jerked to a stop, threw up his arms, and a moment later found himself being poked from several directions by four bayonet-tipped rifles. "I don't know what reminds me of it," he said, as amiably as he could feign, "but we had a housekeeper once who used to stick toothpicks into sweet potatoes and sprout them in mayonnaise jars."

"What?"

"No hablo español, that's what," he said agreeably.

They began pushing him around and one of them fished his wallet out of his pocket and began examining the contents. It hadn't occurred to Benjamin to get rid of the wallet or anything in it, his credit cards, his driver's license, his bank identification, his Blue Cross card. Not that it would have made the difference. His photograph had been in the newspapers almost every day for two weeks. He had used his head in regard to the list of addresses Quesada had given him, memorizing them and then disposing of them. But he still had the phone number for the Sports Institute which Isabel had written down, along with her and Nicasio Moya's extensions. The thug found it and stuck it in his pocket.

"Hey, that's private property!"

The response was a sharp jab at his stomach with the point of a bayonet, "Take it easy, will you!"

"Cállate!"

"Look Buddy, I could do with a little less of the rough stuff."

The fellow with the affinity for Benjamin's solar plexus gave him another jab with his rifle while one of the others slapped him on the back of the neck. "Damn it! I told you to cut it out!"

Benjamin wasn't feeling particularly heroic, but he didn't like the way things were going. They were definitely out to make bruises—and maybe a lot worse. "Listen, I'm supposed to have some rights. What the hell's coming off here?"

They began shoving him and when he continued to resist, one of them jerked down his right arm, and with a violent wrench, pulled it behind his back. The grinding pain was instantaneous and familiar. The son-of-a-bitch had dislocated his shoulder. Benjamin's rage was stronger than his anguish. He'd had his shoulder ripped out of its socket twice during his basketball career, once when he'd taken an ugly fall, once when he'd mixed it up with an astigmatic referee, but neither time had the violation been deliberate.

His reaction was extravagant and owed its success to the fact that he was a lefty and that no one ever seems to consider that a possibility. Certainly the muscle man responsible for the dislocation didn't because he relaxed his grip when Benjamin gave an agonized cry. A second later he was clutching at his groin as the heel of Benjamin's shoe snapped up and caught him in the crotch.

Benjamin grabbed the rifle jammed into his stomach and wrested it free, then swung it around wildly. The butt end slammed against one man's temple and he stumbled against the fellow next to him. Then one of the rifles went off and Benjamin felt the heat of the bullet sear his side. The bastards were out to kill him!

He swung furiously and took heart from a satisfying crack as the butt of the rifle struck his attacker's cheekbone. Then he hoisted the rifle up under his armpit and took off. Had there been only two of them he wouldn't have stood a chance, but four of them were enough to spawn chaos. It took them thirty seconds or so to sort themselves out and by that time Benjamin had run back to the end of the new stage. The television scaffold was only a few yards off, just around the next corner, and he broke for it, counting on the dark to act as a shield. He didn't look back. When he reached the base of the scaffold he squeezed between it and the stage, worked his way over to the loose board and, pushing it aside, slipped through feet first, working his way under on his haunches.

# 29

Tomás hadn't used his head, Dearborn thought. In the long run Tomás would suffer, not himself or Benjamin. The boat was arranged for. Raúl had the money to pay for it and it only remained for them to show up at the foot of Desamparados and La Habana and board her. What was the name? The something de Mar? Damn. Well, whatever it was, they'd board her with or without Tomás and be on their way.

What choices had Tomás? He couldn't leave Cuba without money. He couldn't return to Cojimar without taking a chance that someone would recognize him and turn him in. He couldn't run off with his inamorata because he had no safe place to run off to. Charming he might be—Dearborn admitted to himself that Tomás indeed possessed a certain raw-edged charisma, but basically he was shortsighted and lacking in character. What's more, he had let Dearborn down, not something Dearborn looked upon as defensible delinquency.

However, recriminations were pointless now. Dearborn still had to find Benjamin and he had to find him before those crazy Cubans set off World War III. He made a difficult decision. Considering the circumstances, he must trust his intuition, confront Isabel Quintana face-to-face, and tell her the truth. If she knew where Benjamin was, she would welcome Dearborn. If not, then he was going to have to extricate himself from a nasty situation. But either way, he felt that the risk was worth taking and the chances were in his favor.

He decided that the best place to intercept Isabel Quintana was out in the open where he had at least a reasonable chance of getting away should flight become advisable, but he was too late on Friday morning to buttonhole her at her apartment. Señora Ortiz had called an early meeting of El Cuerpo. "I was on my way out," he had objected. "It is my custom to take a morning constitutional."

"Yes. You may. In another half hour."

Dearborn had been forced to delay his departure. "Word has it," Señora Ortiz had announced, "that the police will close the Plaza this evening, so we shall pair off and leave here this evening at five. I expect everyone to be assembled here by four-thirty. When we return to the apartment we shall go to central headquarters where, for security reasons, we shall remain until tomorrow. Are there any questions? Is it quite clear?"

"Maravilloso!" Raúl had crooned rapturously. "Tremendo!"

"Raúl must practice his speech this morning and I wish to make him a sign to hold up. It will read *Listo Por La Cuba Nueva! Ready for the New Cuba!* Pablo, you are the artist. You will paint the sign."

"Must I do it now?" Pablo had objected. "I have written to my son. I want to mail the letter."

"Give it to Señor Roycroft. I need you here, Pablo."

Dearborn had finally been permitted to leave. He posted Pablo's letter, then went directly to the Sports Institute. He knew that Isabel Quintana would not come out of the building until lunch so he crossed the street to the Botanical Gardens, chose a bench in a shady spot, and sat down to wait.

After a few minutes he closed his eyes and permitted himself to doze, justifying the nap with a drowsy reminder that he'd suffered through two sleepless nights on Cabrahigo Street, lying on a hard floor squeezed in on all sides by wheezing, snoring strangers, and that if he were to remain at peak efficiency, he had to get some rest. He awoke to find that he had sagged from his upright posture into a sideways slump on the bench. He had a crick in his neck and one dead arm. He lifted the heavy arm and eased it into his lap, then began rubbing the circulation back into it.

He wasn't wearing a watch but he didn't need one to know he'd overslept. "Damn!" He got up stiffly and, still rubbing his tingling arm, walked over to a woman pushing a baby carriage. "Time?" he asked, pointing to his bare wrist. "El time-o?"

"Tres y media," she replied obligingly, lifting her wrist to show him her watch face.

Three-thirty? He'd slept the day away! Blast! he had to be back at the apartment by four-thirty. He couldn't afford to antagonize the members of El Cuerpo any more than he could abandon them so long as Raúl was still there. Not only did Dearborn have a responsibility toward Raúl, but Raúl had the money without which there would be no escape. There was no choice now but to confront the beast in his lair, or, to put it more simply, to visit Isabel Quintana in her office. Foolhardy, no doubt. Dangerous, yes. A reckless act, but necessary.

Once his mind was made up Dearborn wasted no time but cut across the grass, exited through the front gate, and crossed the street. As he approached the Institute he noticed there was a policeman guarding the side entrance. Odd thing that. Not ominous, but odd. Dearborn had no reason to think he'd be bothered but he paused at the curb anyway to study the situation. Then as he was making up his mind to go into the building he saw someone come to the Institute door and summon the policeman. Dearborn sidled up to the glass doors and peered in inquisitively.

The policeman was talking to a man in plain clothes, an official-looking person with a telltale bulge beneath his jacket. The word "stakeout" came to mind, as well as an image of Dearborn's frequent rival and sometimes nemesis, Chief Anthony Niccoli of the New York Police Department. Better not to call attention to himself, he decided. Discreetly, he eased open the door a crack and slipped inside. As he walked past he heard the men speaking . . . in Spanish of course . . . but one of them said something that caught his ear. It sounded like the name Quintana. "I must be hearing things," he told himself. "That's what comes of associating with a bunch of potty Cubanos."

He rounded a hall corner and headed down the corridor to the front reception area. There were no policemen in the lobby, but when Dearborn glanced out the doors of the main entrance he saw two more policemen standing outside with folded arms and stony profiles. The guard on duty at the front desk was the same one Dearborn had dealt with before. He approached warily and stated his business in a no-nonsense voice. "Miss Quintana please. Miss Isabel Quintana."

"Whasjornem?"

"Roycroft."

The guard, who was picking his teeth with the bent end of a paper clip, eyed him laconically, then picked up the phone. He pushed a button, spoke to someone, held up his forefinger to silence any remarks Dearborn might be contemplating, then after a minute or two, hung up. "Cheezcomindown," he reported.

"Down to the lobby? I see. All right."

Dearborn didn't know why she had decided it was better to talk to him in the lobby, but if it weren't for the police all over the place he'd have been grateful for it. As it was he hoped he could persuade her to accompany him outside where he'd have a head start in the event of trouble.

He sauntered back to the elevator and as he did so, the elevator doors opened and she emerged. But she wasn't alone. She was being held on either side by two rough-looking men who were propelling her forward in a determined and decidedly unfriendly fashion. Dearborn was astonished. He started forward but before he could intervene she spotted him and raised her voice to say scathingly, "I would not cooperate, so you arranged for my arrest. Now you have come to gloat over me. You are, Señor Whoever-You-Are, a most despicable man, even for a member of the D.G.I."

Dearborn pretended to be befuddled, raising his eyebrows and assuming a blandly curious expression as the men hustled her past him and out the front door. Inside, he was anything but calm. Why were they arresting her? He walked out behind them and watched as they shoved her into a car at the curb and drove away. Had her arrest something to do with Benjamin? Dearborn supposed it could be something else but he didn't entertain the notion with conviction. The connection between Benjamin and Isabel Quintana was too obvious.

He stared despairingly down the now empty street. With Isabel Quintana in jail he had no one to turn to. How would he find Benjamin? Another terrible thought presented itself. Had Benjamin been arrested . . . or worse perhaps? Fool! Lackadaisical numskull! Fuddlebrained idiot! He had warned Benjamin against coming to Cuba. Anyone with Benjamin's propensity for attracting trouble had no business being in a place where trouble was inevitable. Dearborn castigated himself for not having stopped him. He should have intervened more forcefully. He should have called the State Department and warned them about Benjamin. He could have nipped it in the bud. "Blockhead!" he agonized, and this time he wasn't referring to Benjamin. He turned and looked around him as if it were he who was lost. Where was Benjamin? Where was the boy? What had happened to him?

The answer was soon forthcoming. When he arrived back at the apartment on Cabrahigo Street he walked in the door to find Señora Ortiz standing behind the kitchen table on which lay ten packages, each one the size and shape of a cigar box, each wrapped in newspaper, and neatly tied with twine. The rest of the group were seated. Pablo, Enrique, and Carlos on the couch, Felipe on one of the kitchen chairs, and Alberta in the armchair near the door. All, with the exception of Raúl, who had developed a proprietory fondness for the toilet seat and was parked in the bathroom, were turned toward Señora Ortiz.

"Ah, here you are, Señor Roycroft," Señora Ortiz declared. "It is fifteen minutes before five. You are late."

"Sorry. I don't have a watch," he said shortly.

She clicked her disapproval, but turned her attention back to the group, smoothly making the transition from Spanish to English. "One of those arrested was Nicasio Moya."

"Who?" Dearborn broke in. "What's that you're saying?"

"A member of El Cuerpo has been arrested."

"Did you say a member of El Cuerpo?" Dearborn asked incredulously.

"That is correct. Nicasio Moya is one of our agents. He works for the National Institute for Sports, Physical Education,

167

and Recreation. They picked him up at his home early this morning. It is in connection with Benjamin Pinch having been shot last night."

Dearborn took a step forward, faltered, then sat down heavily on the arm of Alberta's chair.

"Are you ill?" Alberta asked.

"No."

"You staggered just then."

"I hope you are not getting sick," Felipe interjected severely. "We cannot afford to have anyone get sick."

Dearborn wet his lips with the tip of his tongue. "It's the . . . the water. I'm not accustomed to the Cuban water. Tell me. You say Pinch was shot?"

"It came over the radio this afternoon," Señora Ortiz told him. He was seen last night in the Plaza de la Revolución by two people from the Hotel Novedoso."

"Which two people?"

"The hotel security officer and the manager's secretary. They reported him to the D.G.I. The report is that he was shot in the back, and although one does not know whether or not he will die, for the moment he has evaded arrest."

"They think he is still in the neighborhood?"

"He could not have gone far," Pablo noted logically. "He was, after all, wounded."

"And losing blood," Carlos added succinctly, with a delicate adjustment to his pince-nez.

"He is the least of our worries," Alberta remarked. "I am more concerned over Nicasio Moya. A few minutes ago there was an additional news report that they have not only arrested him but the girl who works in his office. If Nicasio breaks, or if the girl happens to know more than is good for her . . ."

"Nicasio won't break," Felipe cut in, "and he is not so big a fool as to have confided in anyone at the Institute."

"Still," Pablo ruminated, "the girl was present in the hotel room when Nicasio Moya put the list into Benjamin Pinch's suitcase."

"This Nicasio Moya," Dearborn pressed, "it was he who killed Solís?"

"Oh no," Señora Ortiz replied. "He is not a member of Los Dedos. I told you before that we do not know the names of Los Dedos. They are a select group known to very few."

"But you just said that he is the one who put that list into Pinch's suitcase."

"That's right," Carlos verified. "But he did not shoot Solís. He is a colecionista. He collects information. He does not kill."

"It had to have been someone in that room," Dearborn insisted.

"No doubt," Señora Ortiz answered crisply, "but as I told you before, no one knows the identities of those members who are part of Los Dedos. It is information better kept secret, for our protection as well as theirs."

"Dońde están las bombas?" Raúl suddenly called out from the bathroom. "El tiempo apremia!"

"Yes, time presses," Señora Ortiz agreed. "We must leave. The police will close the park later tonight so we must get the job done quickly. Let us remind ourselves who will partner whom. Alberta and Felipe, you will go together and enter the park from the west. Enrique and Carlos, you will enter from the south. Raúl and I shall enter from the east. Señor Roycroft, you and Pablo will enter from the north. You see by the map which section of the park you are assigned. Stay within bounds.

"Now that Tomás has run off," she continued, "we have two extra cigar boxes to be distributed among us. Pablo, one of the extra bombs has fallen to you. I shall take the other. Be careful, all of you to watch for the police. Remember they are everywhere and that, thanks to Benjamin Pinch, among them will be members of the D.G.I."

"When is the first bomb due to go off?" Felipe asked.

"At one minute after twelve noon tomorrow, a minute after Castro begins to speak. Place them carefully. Do not leave them in the open under any circumstances. Metal refuse bins make good containers, especially since the refuse is collected every day in the early afternoon so we can be sure that they will not be disturbed after that. Proceed cautiously and take your time. However, as I mentioned earlier, the police intend to clear the Plaza early in the evening and so we must be finished by seven. Are there any questions?"

"It is all quite clear," Enrique assured her, answering for the group.

"Then let us proceed to distribute the bombs."

Enrique and the others rose. Raúl catapulted out of the bathroom shouting the Spanish equivalent of "Ready, set, go!"

"Preparados, listos, ya!" and Señora Ortiz began handing out the packages on the kitchen table.

Alberta had been eyeing Dearborn concernedly. Now she said again, "You are all right, Señor Roycroft? You look so pale. You will be able to carry on?"

"Shot in the back, you say? He was shot in the back?"

"Do not be concerned by it. Live or die, he will not interfere with our plans. Nor Nicasio either, who is a brave man and able to withstand torture. All will be well. Rest easy."

# 30

They bused to the Plaza de la Revolución, a practical mode of transportation, if not quite in keeping with the drama of their undertaking, and split up into pairs to enter the park.

Dearborn had no more intention of sticking to fat, slow-moving Pablo than he did of planting any bombs. He had only one objective, to find Benjamin. He quickly separated from Pablo with the suggestion that in order to save time they search for likely sites on their own. Pablo had already spotted a refuse container near the monument to José Martí and lumbered toward it while Dearborn followed his own circuitous route back to the park entrance.

The first thing Dearborn did once he regained the street was to drop his cigar box down the nearest sewage drain. If it exploded down there it wouldn't hurt anyone, and chances were that if it fell into water it wouldn't even go off. He tended, ordinarily, to take a cynical view of man's morality, but even he had been shocked by the callous insensitivity of El Cuerpo. Alberta and Señora Ortiz's talk of "harmless" bombs was absurd in light of what the bombs were intended to incite. The thought that innocent people would be caught in the panic was appalling. There was no way Dearborn could prevent it, but he wouldn't participate in it.

After ridding himself of the cigar box he began circling the park. It wasn't quite dark and he scanned the sidewalk, the street, and the grassy verge between sidewalk and street, searching for some sign of Benjamin. It took more than forty-five minutes to make the complete circle. Señora Ortiz had been right about the police. They were everywhere. Not actively searching for Benjamin as Dearborn was, but clustered at the entrances to the Plaza, looking bored or preoccupied or sleepy, but at the same time aware of everyone entering and leaving the park, their guns conspicuous at their hips and their handcuffs clipped ostentatiously to their gun belts. Trucks bearing wooden street barriers had drawn up to the park entrances and were waiting to be unloaded.

As Dearborn searched, the suspicion grew on him that Benjamin might never have left the park. There was no saying how far he had been capable of traveling, but he couldn't have gone far without leaving traces of blood, and although the idea of searching for signs of Benjamin's blood repelled him, Dearborn set about it with realistic fortitude. The police must have searched the park thoroughly before fanning out into the neighborhood and Benjamin couldn't have been in any condition to play hide-and-seek with them, yet as Dearborn studied the buildings surrounding the park and the wide streets spoking out from it, he became more and more convinced Benjamin had never made it this far.

It was past six-thirty when he arrived back where he'd started at the north entrance to the park. He looked beyond the statue of Martí to the stage from which Castro would speak the following day, envisioning the thousands of people who would mob the Plaza in their efforts to see and hear him, imagining the chaos that would erupt when the bombs went off and the first shots were fired.

It was dark now, the Plaza lit by street lamps, but still Dearborn could see Pablo waddling along at the base of the stage. He toyed for a moment with the idea of removing the bomb from the refuse container where Pablo had placed it and throwing it

171

down the sewage drain as he had done with his own bomb, but before he could act on the idea Pablo looked up, saw him, and signaled him over with a jerk of his head. He was still holding the second package and his expression was harried. "I am having difficulties," he whispered breathlessly as Dearborn approached. "Where did you place your package?"

"I found a street lamp with a rusted base," Dearborn improvised. "I pulled aside a jagged edge and shoved the box inside."

"Where?"

"Over there somewhere." Dearborn said, waving vaguely over his shoulder.

"I saw nothing like that." Pablo pouted. "We were assigned the most difficult area, all masonry and cement. I thought of prying a board free from the base of the television scaffolding and placing the bomb beneath but I am afraid that the bomb may be powerful enough to collapse the platform. That could be a . . . what is the word . . . calamity, since the assassin will be standing close to the stage."

"To say nothing of the bystanders," Dearborn reminded him dryly.

"What? Oh yes," Pablo commented in a preoccupied voice. He looked over Dearborn's shoulder. "Señor Roycroft, we must hurry. I am afraid the police will wonder what we are doing. There are so many of them. Look there! and there!"

He pointed to a group of three policemen leaning against the far end of the stage and to two other men dressed in plain clothes who were parading across the square. "D.G.I.," he informed Dearborn. "One can always tell the secret police by their . . . how do you say . . . their baglike jackets."

"Baggy."

"Yes, baggy. It is a sure sign that there are shoulder holsters beneath."

"In the United States it's raincoats. De rigueur for perverts and the F.B.I."

"Perhaps you noticed some spot I missed?" Pablo persisted worriedly.

"Well, let's see. Have you looked behind the stage?"

"I have already walked around back but there is nothing, only another open area filled with people and police."

"Let's give it another try," Dearborn suggested. "We'll separate, circle the stage and meet in back."

Pablo capitulated. With a careful eye on the D.G.I. men, he ambled toward the far end of the stage. Dearborn, imitating Pablo's casual pace, walked in the opposite direction. As he came abreast of the television scaffold he paused to take stock. The Plaza was large, but it wasn't a wooded setting like Central Park. There simply weren't that many places for a man to hide. Dearborn kicked the base of the scaffold. The slats were nailed tight as a coffin. It would have taken time for Benjamin to pull them apart. Not likely.

He continued orbiting the stage, looking for a place where a man might successfully conceal himself. He saw nothing except tropical flora, wooden benches, and an equipment bin that was large enough to hold a man but with a lock that wouldn't yield to Dearborn's fiddling. As he turned away from the bin he saw Pablo hurrying toward him.

"I have thought where to put it," Pablo puffed, one hand held to his heart. "Between the television scaffold and the stage. I looked there before and I could not fit in the space. But you can do it easily. Come. Let us go back."

Dearborn had no intention of planting the bomb. "Wait a minute, Pablo. That's too close to the television scaffold. You said so yourself."

"I said it was too dangerous to put the bomb *under* the television scaffold. Now I am talking about the area between it and the stage. It is not a heavy explosive. Merely a drop of dynamite."

"A drop? Equal to a soupçon or a dollop? No more than would blow the lid off a garbage pail or the head off a man?"

"It is a good place, I tell you. There will be no one standing there tomorrow. The worst it will do is scatter some fragments of wood."

Reluctantly Dearborn followed Pablo back to the television platform and peered into the narrow crevice that separated it from the speakers' stage. Barely enough space for a thin man like Dearborn to squeeze through. No doubt Castro's guards would keep everyone well back from the stage which meant that if the explosive were as innocuous as touted by Alberta, it would do less harm there than anywhere else. But was it innocuous? That was the question. Dearborn had far less faith in the proficiency of the bomb makers than did the members of El Cuerpo. Besides, he had promised himself that he wouldn't participate in this insanity.

"Here," Pablo said, pushing the package into Dearborn's hand. "I shall keep a watch for the police patrol."

Dearborn accepted the package. The only thing he could do at this point was put the bomb where Pablo wanted him to and pick it up again later. He eased himself sideways into the aperture and, facing the stage, slid his feet along for about six feet, which was the approximate midpoint of the alley. It was utterly dark and he felt his way along like a blind man. The stage was at least ten feet high and the television platform soared overhead to a height of fifteen or twenty feet. Although the sensation was claustrophobic, he felt ridiculously exposed like a fly caught between two panes of window glass. He could see by the slivers of paler black at either end of the passage that he was alone, but he didn't feel alone. There was a prickling sensation at the base of his neck, an ineffable awareness of some presence besides his own. Ridiculous, of course. The result of stress, something he mustn't give in to.

He decided to leave the bomb as instructed, then find some excuse to send Pablo back to the apartment without him. After Pablo left Dearborn would return, pick up that bomb and the one in the refuse container, and dispose of them. Then he would investigate the paths leading to the other park entrances and if there were still no sign of Benjamin, he would begin searching the streets outside the park. What he would do in the event that his search failed, how he would deal with El Cuerpo when he eventually returned to the apartment, were matters with which he refused to deal just now. Nothing would matter if he didn't find Benjamin. He *must* find him. That's all there was to it.

It was impossible to bend his knees in the confined space between stage and scaffold and Dearborn certainly didn't intend to toss the lethal little package. He bent sideways with stiff arms and legs like an unjointed marionette, and supporting himself with one hand against the base of the stage, carefully placed the bomb on the ground. He straightened up with a stifled groan, the groan echoing back eerily and adding to his almost hallucinatory feeling of being observed. He couldn't get out of there fast enough. He scuttled back through the tight channel, squeezed through the opening and walked rapidly away from the stage.

As he crossed the wide stretch of cement looking for Pablo, he thought about the excuse he'd give for wishing to remain behind. The only thing that came readily to mind was the excuse he'd given earlier in the evening to cover his indisposition. Water. He'd tell Pablo that he'd drunk some water out of the park's water fountain and was again feeling lightheaded. He'd send Pablo back to the apartment and tell him that he'd follow as soon as he was able.

With that in mind he began searching for a water fountain. He sighted one nearby and was making a beeline for it when Pablo, snuffling and huffing with exertion, intercepted him. "There you are. I did not see you come out. Hurry, Señor Roycroft, we must leave."

"What's the rush?"

"The police, they have already closed the park. While I was waiting for you, two of them told me to get out and when I objected . . . mildly, of course, trying not to antagonize them, humble to the core . . . they escorted me to the exit."

Dearborn was crushed. He made a futile stab at offering his excuse. "I'm feeling a little dizzy again. Perhaps I'd better find a bench and . . ."

"Certainly not! You will be arrested!"

Dearborn tried another tack. He slapped his pockets and stuck his fingers into the breast pocket of his jacket. "I think I dropped my wallet. Must have fallen out when I leaned over to put down the package. I'd better just . . ."

Pablo took a grip on his arm and pointed. "Are you crazy? Look. Do you not see them staring at us?"

Dearborn did see them, two cocky-looking policemen studying them with impertinent directness. As he watched, the pair began strolling toward them.

"They are the ones who ejected me," Pablo wheezed agitatedly. "Come quickly."

Dearborn hesitated while he cast around for some new invention to delay his departure, but the contemptuous swagger that characterized the approaching men was enough to convince him that Pablo was right. They had to get out while they had the chance.

"Hurry," Pablo urged. "They may not bother us if we leave immediately."

Dearborn glanced back at the stage before allowing Pablo to herd him toward the boulevard. No time to remove the thing after all. The best he could hope for was that the cigar box was as advertised. One bomb. Perfectly harmless. As for Benjamin, Dearborn didn't know what to do.

They were already crossing the street when Pablo asked with sudden solicitude, "Are you hurt, Señor Roycroft? Did you suffer an accident?"

"I?" Dearborn returned in bewilderment. "Why do you ask that? Do I look as if I'd suffered an accident?"

"You have blood on your jacket."

"I have what?"

"You have blood on your jacket."

# 31

Dearborn whipped off his jacket and held it up for inspection. The back was liberally discolored with reddish-brown stains. "I don't know what it is," he said steadily. "Must be paint. I probably brushed up against one of the equipment bins."

"Paint is something I am familiar with," Pablo said authoritatively. "I know all there is to know about paint. This is blood. The question is, where did it come from?"

"What's the difference," Dearborn returned brusquely.

"The difference is that a man was shot here in the Plaza last night."

"You are, of course, speaking of Pinch."

"Sí. Pinch. When they were chasing him he must have slipped between the television scaffold and the stage and from there made his escape."

Dearborn was relieved that Pablo's logic stopped short of what was apparent to Dearborn. "I see your point," Dearborn observed. "It's dark in there. Looks even narrower than it is. The police probably didn't realize he could negotiate it. He must have entered at one end and exited at the other."

"It is lucky for us," Pablo commented, "that the D.G.I. did not notice the blood on your jacket. They might have stopped us and begun asking questions."

"That's so," Dearborn conceded thoughtfully, "but I worry more about what will happen when they find my wallet."

Pablo waved away the thought. "You bought your wallet here in La Habana. There is nothing in it to identify you."

"Nothing to identify *me*, Pablo," Dearborn returned worriedly, "but something to identify you."

"How could that be?"

"The letter to your son. You gave it to me to mail this morning."

Pablo's chins began to quiver. "You did not post it?"

Dearborn felt only the merest twinge of guilt at lying to him. "I'm afraid not. I put it into my wallet intending to post it, but it slipped my mind."

"Ay, Dios. Where did you drop the wallet?"

"I seem to recall dropping it just as I squeezed out of the space behind the scaffold. At least I recollect the sound of something falling. Plop. Like that. A soft plop."

"The wallet may lead them to search the area further."

"No doubt," Dearborn agreed readily, "in which case they will find the bomb."

"And come after me!"

"One might logically draw that conclusion."

Pablo's face had taken on a ghastly pallor. "I am not sure how well I will stand up under torture. I am not physically strong. I am an artist, not a soldier."

"They will, of course, comb the city looking for you."

"They will not know where to find me."

"Until they question your son."

"My son? Ay, Dios! Mi pobrecito Heberto!"

"There is only one solution," Dearborn said gravely, "I shall have to go back for the wallet."

"You saw those men! They will stop you before you have walked three feet into the park!"

"I shall slip in from another direction and circle back."

"It will be dangerous."

"The alternative is no less dangerous."

"Perhaps we should look for Clara. She will know what to do."

"No doubt she and the others have started back to Cabrahigo Street. You must follow them, Pablo. Tell them what has happened. Say that I shall return as soon as I have succeeded in finding the wallet."

"Suppose . . . " Pablo's voice was unsteady, "suppose you do not succeed? It is not only my life you hold in your hands. It is all our lives. The life of El Cuerpo."

"Succeed or fail," Dearborn assured him, "I shall not betray El Cuerpo."

"The D.G.I. has its ways," Pablo warned.

"And I have mine."

"We must be brave, Señor Roycroft."

"Leave the bravery to me, Pablo. You just be sure you don't miss your bus."

Dearborn watched him cross the street and shuffle toward the bus stop. Poor fellow. A pity to frighten him needlessly. On the other hand, Pablo and his fellow conspirators would be the first to say all's fair in love and war. Dearborn patted his pocket where his wallet reposed. Then he started out on another half-turn around the park.

By the time he reached the west entrance the police had begun unloading and setting up the wooden barriers. There were a lot of curious bystanders and Dearborn joined them, slowly working his way into the park before breaking away from the group and nonchalantly strolling toward the center of the Plaza which had by then been almost completely evacuated.

Dearborn was somewhat conspicuous on the near-deserted paths, but there was a complementary advantage which was that everyone else was equally conspicuous. By avoiding street lamps, picking his way along the edges of the paths and keeping an eye out for anyone headed in his direction, he was able to avoid any disagreeable encounters. He chose not to cross the cement apron in front of the stage, but instead walked around the back, approaching the television scaffold from the far side and slithering between the stage and scaffold at the point farthest removed from the open plaza. As he inched along the narrow corridor he felt the boards in the base of the scaffold with his fingers, testing for one that might be loose or that could easily be loosened. "Benjamin?" he whispered. "Benjamin, are you there?"

There was no answer. Dearborn reasoned that Benjamin must be there, having taken Pablo's logic a step further with the knowledge that once the blood had soaked through Benjamin's clothing and begun to flow freely, he couldn't have left the park without leaving a telltale trail. When Dearborn reached the halfway point he felt around with his toe until he made contact with the package he'd placed there earlier. He picked it up and holding it in his hand, called again in a muted voice, "Benjamin, answer me." After a moment's thought he added, "It is your father speaking."

There was still no answer.

He continued to creep forward, pushing and pulling at the securely nailed boards, pausing to listen for a sign or groan, any sound that would indicate Benjamin's presence. The base of the scaffold was constructed of ten-inch tongue-and-groove vertical boards affixed to horizontal support beams. Benjamin would have had to loosen at least two of them in order to slip through. One would think they wouldn't be too difficult to locate, but although Dearborn went over them meticulously, he couldn't find any that were loose. "Nincompoops," he murmured balefully as if the fault lay with the carpenters. He repeated the process a second time, shuffling along in the constricted space, reaching, stooping, bending from side to side, aching from the awkwardness of the positions he was forced to assume in order to check every board. "Benjamin, do you hear me? Benjamin, answer me. I know you are there."

179

To Benjamin, who was speeding cross-country in his *SL 450* convertible, the whispers sounded like tires burning up the road. "Whooshmin, whooshmin." The desert stretched out as far as he could see. Isabel sat next to him. Eventually they would cut through the Sixty-fifth Street transverse, then flash down the West Side to Greenwich Village and home.

Benjamin had been dosing on and off for the last couple of hours and he didn't want to wake up. So long as he was only semiconscious he was able to bear the pain in his shoulder.

"Are you there?"

He wondered what his father was doing in the back seat. Dearborn hated the car and hated even more the way Benjamin drove it. Besides, this was supposed to be a dream about Isabel. Damn his father anyway. You'd think he'd have the decency to butt out of Benjamin's dreams. *"Of course I'm here. Who do you think's driving?"*

"Benjamin, answer me."

Benjamin decided to pretend he didn't hear. He put his arm around Isabel and stepped on the gas.

"It is your father speaking."

*"Speak away, Dad. I'm not letting anything bug me today. I've got my car and my girl and soon I'll be home free. Hey, what'd you say? Nincompoop? Listen, how come I can't take a simple little trip to Cuba without you calling me names."*

*"I think he's going to jump out of the car,"* Isabel cried.

*"Jesus, Dad, you can't jump out of the car when it's going seventy miles an hour. Dad? Answer me. I know you're there."*

Benjamin tried to turn his head to look into the back seat. It was a mistake. The pain was excruciating and jarred him awake.

Outside, Dearborn heard the groan and froze. The sound came from a spot directly opposite where he was standing. He flattened his hands against the boards and put his ear close to listen. There it was again, Faint but definite.

"Benjamin, Benjamin?"

The groan wasn't repeated.

"Will you answer me!" Dearborn tugged at the nearest board, then in frustration kicked at its base with the top of his shoe. "Tell me how to get in, Benjamin. I am here to help you." He slapped the boards with both hands. "I am reaching the limit of my patience, Benjamin!"

"Dad?" It was the barest hint of a whisper, little more than an exhalation.

Dearborn leaned his forehead against the scaffold.

"Dad? Is that you? Is it really you?"

"Don't be an idiot. Let me in."

"I can't believe it! I must be . . . "

"Benjamin, are you or are you not going to admit me?"

Thirty seconds passed, during which Dearborn could hear Benjamin shifting around and muttering. Then he heard the sound of an implement being applied to wood.

"What are you doing?"

"I hammered the boards shut from the inside and I can't pry them loose. Hold on. I'll get it. Give me another minute."

There was nothing Dearborn could do but hold on. He shifted his package from one hand to the other and checked the shafts of gray light at either end of the scaffold.

"Okay, I got one of them. See if you can feel which one."

Dearborn groped around for the loose board, located it and pushed it aside. "Give me your hammer, Benjamin. I'll try to pry the other one open from this side."

"It's not a hammer. It's a wrench. Anyway, it's okay. I've got it, Dad. Just push it aside."

Dearborn did as Benjamin instructed, parting the boards to form a V-shaped aperture wide enough to admit him. He slid down onto his haunches and wiggled awkwardly past Benjamin who was stretched out just inside the opening.

Benjamin grunted as Dearborn knocked into him. "Take it easy, Dad. I'm not in the best of shape."

Dearborn leaned over him and started to put one arm around his shoulder but reared back when Benjamin yelped with pain. "I appreciate the show of affection, Dad, but that hurt like hell."

"Affection? Consider yourself fortunate that I didn't simply leave you to your fate. It would have been no more than you deserve."

"How'd you get here? It's some kind of miracle."

"The miracle is that you're still alive. They said you'd been shot in the back."

"They nicked me in the side. Took out a nice wad of flesh, but nothing crucial."

"Painful, is it?"

"It's my shoulder that's killing me. One of those bastards got a hammerlock on me and dislocated my shoulder. I managed to break loose and dived in here."

How did you find this place?"

"How did *I* find this place? Is that what you're asking me? Jesus Christ, I'm lying under a television scaffold in the middle of a public park in Havana, Cuba, figuring there's no way to get out and no one in the whole God-damned world who knows where I am and you show up—if it *is* you and I'm not delirious or off my nut. The logical question is how did *you* find this place?"

"It was accomplished with some effort."

"It's got Stanley and Livingstone beat a mile."

"Can you walk, Benjamin?"

"I can walk but I can't get out from under this scaffold with my shoulder in the shape it's in. You'll have to straighten it out for me. You've got to grab my hand and arm, brace yourself against something, and pull. That's all there is to it. It'll slip back into the socket like nothing."

"I might make matters worse, Benjamin. I'm not a physician."

"Believe me, you can't make matters worse. There's no way you can make me hurt more than I'm already hurting."

"You are quite certain?"

"You've got to help me, Dad."

"Then show me what to do."

It didn't turn out to be as easy as Benjamin predicted. It took almost half an hour before Dearborn finally succeeded in manipulating the shoulder back into place, and even then the cure wasn't complete. "I've torn some cartilage," Benjamin said between clenched teeth. "Shit, I'm not going to be able to do much with my arm."

"Can you manage?"

"I can manage."

Dearborn was perspiring and his own shoulder muscles were sore from the strain he'd put on them, but he'd done his best and apparently his best had been good enough. "And please don't say *shit*, Benjamin," he reprimanded mildly. "You know how much it bothers me."

# 32

It was Benjamin who thought of calling Pablo Quesada. He began to explain in a low voice who Quesada was but Dearborn interrupted to say he already knew, that he had in fact already talked with Quesada.

"You talked to Pablo?" Benjamin whispered.

"And found him to be a gentleman. Not genteel, mind you, but a gentleman."

"Who else did you talk to?"

"Carmen Bonilla, Patricio Gómez, and Isabel Quintana."

"Isabel?" Benjamin repeated. "When did you speak to Isabel?"

"I met her at the Sports Institute a few days ago."

"She never told me about anyone visiting her at the . . . shit. The American passing himself off as a D.G.I. agent?"

"I see that I was correct in my assumption that she played a part in your escape."

"Wait'll I tell her who you really are."

"That may be difficult, Benjamin. Last night the D.G.I. took Nicasio Moya in for questioning. Today they arrested Isabel Quintana."

"Oh no," Benjamin agonized. "It was because of me. I had the Institute phone number in my wallet."

"Don't be overly concerned. I am sure they will lose interest in her once they dig into Moya's private life and find out who *he* is."

"What do you mean? Who is he?"

"He's a member of El Cuerpo," Dearborn informed Benjamin.

"Moya? That humorless little turd?"

"I haven't met him, but I have it on good authority."

"That's hard to believe, Dad. He doesn't fit the mold."

"Frankly I find most members of El Cuerpo atypical."

"How many have you met? Who the hell have you been hanging out with, Dad?"

"All in due time, Benjamin. Right now I think it advisable to act on your suggestion that we contact Quesada."

Benjamin agreed regretfully, muttering, "I hate like hell to put him on the spot."

"It will be for only one night. Tomorrow we will be leaving Cuba. I have hired an enterprising Cuban boatman to take us to Key West. All that remains is for us to pick up Raúl."

"Raúl who?"

"Raúl Baki."

"Crazy Raúl? Raúl from La Playa? He's in Cuba? I thought he was in the bughouse."

"Benjamin, this is not the Palm Court at the Plaza. We are not chatting over brunch."

"Okay then, how do we get out of here? You told me the place is crawling with cops."

"We shall emerge separately and cross the square to the north exit. You will follow me at a discreet distance. When we see the police I shall engage their attention while you slip by."

"Engage them? With what? With a couple of choruses of 'La Cucaracha'?"

"One would suppose that this unfortunate episode in your life had sobered you. Instead I find you as sappy as ever. No matter. Leave it to me, Benjamin. I know precisely what to do. Just make sure you make your move quickly and at the appropriate moment."

"I'm not looking to see you get shot, Dad."

"I have no intention of getting shot."

"I mean it."

"I'm touched by your concern."

They crawled out from under the scaffold and worked their way to the opening at one end, Dearborn in the lead and still toting the cigar box.

"What is that thing?" Benjamin whispered.

"What does it look like? It's a box of cigars."

Dearborn stepped out first and marched openly across the square, purposely making himself conspicuous in order to distract attention from Benjamin. There were a couple of men in plain clothes patrolling the square. He was quite certain they saw him, but instead of accosting him they turned and walked away, leading Dearborn to believe that they had taken him for one of the park officials. "Police are the same everywhere," he thought to himself. Inefficient and dense. He wasn't, however, inclined to malign them for their shortcomings, especially when, only a moment later, two other policemen crossed his path without giving him a second glance. "They've got the New York City Police Department beat a mile," he told himself, "but for once it works out to my advantage." As Dearborn approached the Paseo exit he saw threee more policemen lounging against the wooden barrier, but this time they spotted him, snapped out of their lethargy and drew their guns.

Dearborn accepted the challenge. He charged into their midst waving his arms. "How dare the police manhandle an American tourist," he shouted. "How was I to know the park is closed! Do you have any idea what the repercussions of this incident will be?"

They were flabbergasted by his unexpected attack. It was apparent from their utter confusion that none of them spoke or understood English and had no more idea of what he was saying than of what he wanted from them. Dearborn might have been reciting the Gettysburg Address for all they knew, but they seemed persuaded by his curmudgeon behavior to accept him as harmless. As least they put away their guns. He continued to command their attention, not to say their ill-concealed amusement, with his elaborate condemnation of Cuban officialdom. Meanwhile Benjamin stepped out from behind the monument of Martí, made his swift advance across the square, crossed behind them and slipped out past the barrier to the street.

It was at this juncture that one of the men pointed to the package Dearborn was carrying and with a sly smile began to question him about it. Dearborn decided it was time to withdraw and concluded eloquently, "International relations are not improved by an overzealous, indiscriminate constabulary. However, I'm not one to hold a grudge and so I shall not pursue the issue further."

He started to walk past the three men but the one with the curious bent and the fey sense of humor suddenly made a playful dart at the package. Dearborn grabbed the outthrust hand

185

and pumped it perfunctorily before releasing it. "Apology accepted," he said generously as he swung around the barrier. "Goodnight gentlemen."

They didn't follow. Once safely out onto the sidewalk Dearborn crossed to the curb and with a quick glance over his shoulder, surreptitiously dropped his package down the sewage drain, then crossed the street. Benjamin joined him on the other side. "Did I just see you throw your cigars down the sewer?"

"Butterfingers, Benjamin. The package slithered from my grasp."

"Listen, I could swear a couple of policemen saw me back there, Dad. The hell of it is they didn't make a move toward me."

"Slow on the uptake, like all of their ilk. We'd better get out of here before they come to."

Together they walked eastward toward the Novedoso Hotel. They telephoned Quesada from a phone booth. He was surprised to hear from them and naturally uneasy at being drawn into their dilemma but he didn't refuse to help. He instructed them to give him ten minutes, then to proceed to the hotel, enter through the back entrance which would be unlocked, and go up the back stairs to the third floor.

They were met by a tense Quesada and his equally tense doberman. Quesada was carrying a room key. He ushered them into one of the unoccupied guest rooms, slipped the dog's leash over the outside knob and closed the door. Benjamin was hugging his arm to his chest and Quesada regarded with concern the blood on his shirt and trousers. "You are hurt. They said over the radio that you had been shot in the back."

"The bullet sliced out a couple of ounces of excess fat. Unless gangrene sets in, I'll be okay."

"What is wrong with your shoulder?"

"I got a little roughed up while I was escaping. Nothing serious."

"And you, Señor Pinch?" Quesada inquired.

"Never mind about me. I'm fine. Let's take a look at Benjamin's wound."

Benjamin took off his shirt, peeling it off where the drying blood had glued it to his skin. A generous but not vital chunk of flesh was missing just south of his rib cage. It was a sloppy wound, still seeping blood, but not showing any sign of infection. "I feel as though I'd tangled with a barracuda," Benjamin noted sourly.

"A barracuda would have done a neater job," Quesada said, appraising the wound. "How does it feel?"

"It hurts like hell."

"I'll get you something for it. Wait here. I'll be right back."

Quesada returned five minutes later with disinfectant, gauze bandages, tape, and a couple of aspirins. He dressed the wound, then called room service and had them deliver a loaf of bread, a wedge of runny cheese, and a bottle of Portuguese wine. Benjamin waited in the bathroom until the waiter was dismissed. They ate and drank sitting on one of the beds. Benjamin propped up against the pillows at the head, Dearborn and Quesada settled at the foot.

"Quite frankly," Quesada told Benjamin, "I believed you must be dead by now. When you called me I was astounded, even more astounded when you said that your father was with you. Tell me how this came about."

Dearborn and Benjamin took turns describing their activities, breaking in on one another with questions. Quesada followed the cross conversation like a spectator at a tennis match. "You did not say anything about being involved with El Cuerpo when you were here, Señor Pinch."

"I'm not involved with them, Quesada. I was merely involved in an inadvertent encounter with them. Besides, when I was here last, we were talking about Benjamin and that scrap of paper with the incriminating *K*, not El Cuerpo."

"Is it not true that you have been planting bombs with El Cuerpo?"

"I have *not* been planting bombs with them. Quite the contrary."

"Dad, those weren't cigars in that cigar box."

"Quite true, Benjamin. Perhaps you will tell Quesada here, what I did with that cigar box."

"He threw it down the sewer."

"So much for my planting bombs," Dearborn informed Quesada sternly.

"But you did say," Quesada picked up, "that they intend to assassinate Castro tomorrow."

"They are certainly going to try."

"Did you know," Quesada continued, "that the police have arrested a member of El Cuerpo?"

Dearborn had been about to take a swallow of wine. He lowered his glass. "Nicasio Moya?"

"So you do know."

"The question is how do *you* know he's a member of El Cuerpo, Quesada?"

Quesada shrugged. "It was on the radio this evening. Under interrogation he confessed."

"What about Isabel Quintana?" Benjamin cut in. "Did they let her go?"

"Yes. There was apparently no reason to hold her since Moya confessed that it was he who gave you his phone number."

Benjamin was amazed. "What? He said that? Why would he say that? What else did he confess to?'

Quesada massaged the bridge of his nose between thumb and forefinger. "He said he was the one who gave you the list of names that were found in your suitcase."

"Gave?" Benjamin exclaimed. "The son-of-a-bitch. So he's the one I've been looking for." Benjamin dropped his bread and cheese onto the night table and swung his legs over the side of the bed. "He's trying to save his skin by pretending we were in it together. 'Sure,' he must have told them. 'Sure I gave him the list but he was the one who killed Solís!' How do you like that. It was Moya all along."

"Benjamin," Dearborn broke in, "Nicasio Moya did not kill Solís."

"Baloney." Benjamin got up and started pacing. "Why else would he make up that phony confession?"

"In order to protect the member of El Cuerpo who actually did the killing. You see, I know that Moya was not the only member of El Cuerpo who was in your room that night."

Benjamin stopped to regard Dearborn quizzically. "There were two of them?"

"That's right."

"I don't understand."

"There is a section of El Cuerpo called Los Dedos."

"It means, The Fingers," Quesada jumped in to explain.

"They are the ones," Dearborn continued, "who specialize

in assassinations. One of them was in your room that night and it was that person who killed Solís. Unfortunately the identities of Los Dedos are closely guarded, even from fellow members of El Cuerpo."

"You do not know who the person is?" Quesada asked.

"No," Dearborn admitted, "but I do know that whoever it is has been elected to carry out Castro's assassination as well."

"I had my money on Carmen Bonilla and Patricio Gómez," Benjamin remarked.

"Why?"

"Carmen Bonilla is the only one whose handwriting I never got to see. I fixed on her by process of elimination. Then I saw her acting very chummy with Patricio Gómez. Also, I'm ready to swear it was Patricio Gómez who sicced the cops on me."

"That much is true," Dearborn concurred. "He saw you in the park and reported you. However, one requires more than that to convict them." He got up and fumbled around for the scrap of paper he'd pocketed a few days before at Carmen Bonilla's house. "Ah, here it is. Take a gander at that, Benjamin."

Benjamin took the piece of paper and read aloud, "'Take the *F* bus on Kirov Street. Then take the *M* bus going north on the Avenida de la Independencia.' What is this, Dad?"

"It is a sample of Carmen Bonilla's handwriting. Notice the *K*s."

"Are you sure it's her handwriting?"

"I watched her write it."

Benjamin reached into his own pocket, took out the piece of paper he'd torn out of Solís's hand and held it next to the sample Dearborn had handed him. "So much for Carmen Bonilla. It begins to look like I've been running around like a lunatic looking for something that's got nothing to do with any of them."

"I think you're beginning to come to your senses, Benjamin, which leaves us nothing to fall back on but the old bromide about it being better late than never."

# 33

"I'm back where I started," Benjamin brooded.

"You are most certainly not back where you started. You will be back where you started when we drop anchor in Key West sometime tomorrow."

"What is this?" Quesada inquired. "You are leaving Cuba tomorrow?"

"That's right,"

"Not so quick, Dad," Benjamin said. "Not until I pick up Isabel."

Dearborn was taken aback. "Pick up Isabel? What do you mean, pick up Isabel."

"She's coming with us."

"Isabel Quintana?" Quesada said wonderingly. "She has agreed to go with you? I do not know her well, but I should have guessed she would not be the type to defect."

"Benjamin," Dearborn remonstrated, "have you no conscience? How can you inveigle a girl into giving up her family, her friends, even her country, for the sake of an infatuation?"

"It's not infatuation, Dad. Not this time."

"Oh, good Lord, Benjamin. You believe every female you meet is the love of your life until you meet another creature long on looks and short on inhibition. Well, I forbid it, Benjamin. Put it out of your mind."

"I'm in love with her, Dad, and I'm pretty sure she feels the same about me."

"You might be wrong about that," Quesada dared to suggest. "Señorita Quintana impresses me as being one of the new breed of Cuban women, passionate yes, but totally independent."

"I know you're trying to be helpful," Benjamin said curtly, "but this is between my father and me."

190

"First I had to put up with Tomás and his amorous nonsense," Dearborn proclaimed. "Now you too have joined the ranks of the lovelorn."

"Who the hell's Tomás?"

"He is the fisherman from Miami who brought me here. At the first opportunity he ran off with a C.D.R. official's wife."

"Really?" Quesada remarked. "Which C.D.R. official is that?"

"Which? Good Lord, I wouldn't know one from another."

"Did Señorita Quintana agree to go with you, Benjamin?" Quesada asked.

"Not exactly."

"Ah."

"But she will."

"Oh? Are you sure of that?"

"Damn it, I'm going to call her right now."

"The switchboard operator might wonder who is calling from an empty room," Quesada noted. "Let me place the call. What is her number?" He picked up the telephone receiver and, while Dearborn stood glowering at Benjamin, put through the call, handing the phone over to Benjamin when it began to ring.

"Isabel!" Benjamin exclaimed. "Jesus, are you okay? I heard about . . . When did they let you go? Of course, I'm all right. That's not so. I'm okay. I swear to you. I'm okay. I'm fine. Perfect. What about you?"

He glared at Dearborn and Quesada who were eavesdropping shamelessly. "Listen, Isabel, I have to talk to you. You and I are getting out of Cuba tomorrow. It's all arranged." Benjamin paused, then said vehemently, "There's nothing to think about. Just pack a few . . . " He paused again. "There's nothing to talk about either. Damn it, I'm not taking no for an answer. Didn't what happened to you today teach you anything?"

Benjamin looked up and saw Quesada nodding solemnly with an "I told you so" expression that infuriated him. "I'm coming over there, Isabel."

Dearborn raised his voice to say commandingly, "You most certainly cannot wander about Havana, Benjamin."

"Your father is quite right," Quesada seconded. "You cannot go back out onto the street."

"I'm coming, Isabel." Benjamin hung up and looked

defiantly at Quesada who had risen and was standing between him and the door. "Don't give me trouble, Pablo."

"Benjamin," Dearborn declared, "you heard the young woman refuse."

"She's been so brainwashed she doesn't know what she's saying. She's got some crazy idea that it's her patriotic duty to sacrifice her life to the system."

"You cannot browbeat her into going."

"You must listen to your father," Quesada joined in.

"Pablo, you're a hell of a nice guy, but I'd appreciate it if you'd butt out."

Dearborn said agitatedly, "We shall have enough difficulty persuading Raúl to come with us without trying to persuade Isabel Quintana as well."

"Raúl?" Quesada queried.

"There were three of us who landed in Cuba a week ago. I told you that. Or did I? Well anyway, there was Tomás and then there was Raúl who is a friend, rather an eccentric friend, as Benjamin can attest, but one to whom I owe a certain allegiance. He has joined the ranks of El Cuerpo and it is my duty to pry him loose before any harm comes to him."

"When do you expect to pick up this Raúl? Tonight?"

"Unfortunately, it is impossible. He and the others have, by now, left the apartment and gone to a central point of assembly. I shall have to intercept him at the Plaza de la Revolución tomorrow."

"If I may say so," Quesada commented, "you are even more foolhardy than your son. Either that or you have a suicidal impulse. You must not go to the Plaza tomorrow. I suggest you forget your friend and concentrate on getting your son and yourself out of Cuba with as much haste as possible."

"I can't go without Raúl," Dearborn said stubbornly. "Even if I didn't consider him to be my personal responsibility I'd be obliged to take him along."

"Why is that?"

"He's the one with the money belt. No Raúl, no boat."

"Still," Quesada persisted, "you would be mad to go to the Plaza. The crowds will be immense and the situation dangerous."

"Castro isn't due to speak until noon," Dearborn said. "By then we'll be long gone."

"You'll never find Raúl in that crowd, Dad," Benjamin said skeptically.

"I know precisely where he will be. Finding him will be the least of my worries."

"It certainly will be the least of your worries," Quesada predicted, "because if you go to the park tomorrow you will be arrested."

"Why should I be? I wasn't arrested tonight, was I?"

"The police were instructed to ignore you and your cohorts, merely to worry you a bit should a confrontation be unavoidable, and under no circumstances to detain you. Do you think you would have gotten out of the park otherwise?"

"What are you jabbering about, Quesada?"

Quesada's face had lost its look of benign concern and his voice sounded clipped and decisive. "What does it matter. Take me at my word and get out while you can. They know you and they know La Voz."

"That's nonsense," Dearborn declared.

"Is it?" Quesada snapped, "And if I name them? Alberta Barrios, Pablo Asturias, Felipe Mojica, Carlos Naranjo, Enrique Vargas, Clara Ortiz, Raúl Baki?"

"How do you know their names?"

"Can you not guess, Señor Pinch?"

"You belong to El Cuerpo?"

"No, Dad," Benjamin cut in grimly "You weren￲ listening. He said the police were instructed to ignore you. He's a member of the D.G.I."

"Impossible."

"Your son is right," Quesada said

"But when Benjamin asked you for help, you gave it to him. You made no attempt to arrest him '

Quesada shrugged. "We knew Solís had been killed by a member of El Cuerpo. Intelligence information had been trickling out of Havana to various unfriendly nations for some time. We recognized the work of El Cuerpo. We saw a correlation between ultimate destinations, times of arrival, and the arrivals and departures of various visiting athletes. It was my job to notify the D.G.I. Search Division whenever I thought it was warranted."

"You were the one responsible for that raid on my room?" Benjamin challenged.

Quesada showed by a slight inclination of his head that he accepted that responsibility.

"You son-of-a-bitch."

"We were fairly certain that you were an innocent victim of their intrigue since other athletes had been similarly duped, but by seeming to concentrate our attention on you, we hoped to put the main body of El Cuerpo off guard. Also it made for good anti-American propaganda. Lately the youth in Cuba are showing a marked fondness for United States culture. They are buying American blue jeans on the black market, tuning to the Miami rock stations, even speaking favorably of capitalism as if it were some new and intriguing economic theory."

"How long have you known about El Cuerpo?" Dearborn questioned.

"For a long time, although the particular cell with which you find yourself allied had eluded us until now. It wasn't until you paid a visit to me and I arranged routinely to have you followed that we learned their names. Frankly, it is the young, rather than the old, malcontents who pose the gravest threat and it is on them that we concentrate most of our attention. They are the leaders."

"Why?" Dearborn demanded suddenly, his dazed brain beginning to function again.

"Why what, Señor Pinch? Why are the young the leaders of El Cuerpo?"

"No. Why did you want to put the main body of El Cuerpo off guard?"

"Because we knew they were planning to assassinate Castro and we knew when. We did not wish to threaten them by seeming too close to their secret. We, like they, have been waiting for this moment for a very long time. They are like termites, El Cuerpo, breeding in out-of-the-way places. We could never hope to exterminate them all unless we could attract them out into the open. We had to sacrifice the commander of the Habana Guard to them, as well as Solís, but it will be worth it when tomorrow comes."

"You'll never to able to round them all up, Quesada."

Quesada laughed appreciatively. "Round them up? Does one round up termites? We arrested Nicasio Moya because it would have been thought peculiar had we not, but even he eats more of the people's food and takes up more of the people's space than he deserves."

"You mean you're going to massacre them?" Benjamin asked in a stunned voice.

"Their intention is to massacre us, is it not?"

"But *they're* the . . . what the hell are they . . . *they're* the renegades. You're supposed to represent the government. You're supposed to stand for law and order."

"And if they kill us and succeed with their coup, they will be the government and stand for law and order. No, when the first bomb goes off and they reverse their jackets so that we may identify them . . ."

"You know about that too?" Dearborn asked.

"We know everything."

"Do you realize," Dearborn declared angrily, "how many innocent lives will be lost? There will be thousands of innocent people in the park. You cannot gun them down in cold blood!"

"It will be regrettable," Quesada conceded, "but in the long run, justifiable."

"See here, Quesada," Dearborn exploded, "I am not taking sides, mind you, but I cannot stand by and see women and children murdered. Justifiable? You are a villain to suggest it!"

"I am not a villain, Señor Pinch. A villain would not have taken you and Benjamin in. A villain would have called head-quarters and arranged to have you arrested. I am a humane man. I offered you refuge and the freedom to leave Cuba. You should have agreed to it while there was the chance."

"This wickedness must be stopped," Dearborn maintained.

"Cool it, Dad," Benjamin cautioned.

"If your people won't stop it, I will."

"How?"

"Dad," Benjamin whispered. "Ixnay."

"I shall alert El Cuerpo."

"Surely you know that I cannot allow you to do that," Quesada told him.

"Allow me? How dare you presume to give me orders?"

"Dad, cut it out "

"I *do* presume, Señor Pinch," Quesada returned with composure.

"And I refuse to be bamboozled!"

"Shit," Benjamin muttered.

Quesada stood at the door with his hand on the knob. "In that case ' he announced, "I have the unhappy duty to inform you both that you are under arrest."

Benjamin made a move toward him but he had already opened the bedroom door a crack and grabbed the doberman's leash off the outside knob. Now he threw open the door to its widest and the dog, sensing the prevalent hostility, growled menacingly and strained at the leash.

"I am truly sorry it has ended so unpleasantly for the three of us," Quesada said.

He then stepped out into the hall and closed the door. They heard the key turn and Quesada's voice saying regretfully, as he and his dog moved off down the hall, "Father and son, so devoted. And such perfect fools."

# 34

Not only did the room face the street, but both windows were protected by decorative iron bars. Benjamin might have been able to force the door if he were in better shape, but there was no question of it now, and Dearborn, for all his agility, was not possessed of the requisite brute strength.

"Dad, how come you never learn to leave well enough alone?"

"I have asked myself that on occasion, Benjamin."

"What do we do now?"

"I'm thinking."

"You'd better think fast. Quesada will be back in a few minutes with the heavy artillery."

"Our only hope, as I see it, lies with the telephone. Unfortunately we cannot take advantage of our logical allies in El Cuerpo because there is no telephone in Enrique's apartment. That leaves only your sweetheart of the moment."

"Forget Isabel. Even if there were something she could do, it would take her forty minutes or more to get here."

They were seated on the edge of the bed staring forlornly at the door. "I don't suppose we could call the Swiss Embassy," Benjamin reflected.

"Not at night. By the time we got through to the right person, it would be too late."

"I could try calling Tony Olivares."

"Your basketball chum?"

"He might be willing to go out on a limb for us. Oh hell, it's Friday. He plays ball Friday nights."

"It wouldn't matter. Even a few blocks is too far. We need help closer to hand."

"In that case," Benjamin said desperately, "we're sunk." He picked up the wine bottle from the bedside table, shook it, then turned it upside down and watched the last few drops of wine dribble onto the bedspread. "I could use another drink."

"Excellent idea," Dearborn declared, suddenly enthusiastic.

"The bottle's empty."

"How do we call Room Service, Benjamin?"

"Dial six. Hey wait a minute. Room Service? Are you crazy, Dad?"

"Room Service is in the hotel and it requires only one waiter to deliver a bottle of wine."

"But if we're locked in, he's locked out."

"Not necessarily. Hand me the phone."

Benjamin picked up the phone, dialed six and handed the receiver to Dearborn.

"Room Service?" Dearborn shouted into the phone. "This is Room . . ." He opened panic-stricken eyes at Benjamin who made a face and shook his head. ". . . the room to which you sent Señor Quesada's order half an hour ago. Exactly! Room 304. I'd

197

like another bottle of wine immediately. Same label. Same vintage. Vino Portugal, 1980. Send it immediately please. Oh, and tell the waiter that I may be in the bathroom, in which case he should let himself in with his passkey. A tip . . . a generous tip . . .will be lying on the desk, provided that he gets here within five minutes. Do you understand me?"

"Did he understand you?" Benjamin asked when he'd hung up.

"Talk of money is understood in any language."

"I hope I'll be able to take him. I'm not in such good shape, Dad."

Dearborn rose from the bed, took the empty wine bottle out of Benjamin's hand and carried it into the bathroom. He returned carrying the bottle wrapped in a towel and handed it back.

"This isn't exactly my style."

"We're not concerned with form, Benjamin. Only with results."

The waiter was prompt. He tapped gently on the door and Dearborn signaled to Benjamin who was standing behind the door, waiting for it to open. The waiter tapped again and they heard the rattle of a key in the lock. Benjamin raised the bottle and Dearborn nodded in assent before slipping out of sight into the bathroom.

The door opened and a roly-poly waiter, carrying a bottle of wine on a tin tray, bounced into the room. He was exceedingly short and was humming happily. Benjamin was glad he couldn't see his face. It was bad enough looking down at his neatly combed hair and shiny pink ears. How could he hit a guy humming "Cielito Lindo." Well, it was now or never. Benjamin closed his eyes and swung. When he opened his eyes a second later the waiter was spiraling downward and the tray had hit the floor.

Dearborn rushed out of the bathroom. "Quick!" I saw two cars draw up in front of the hotel. Quesada is on the sidewalk waiting for them!"

"Wait a minute, Dad."

The waiter had dropped the room key. Benjamin picked it up and followed Dearborn into the hall. He closed the door and locked it from the outside. "Look, we haven't much chance of getting out of the hotel without running into them. I think we should wait behind the fire doors until they get to the third floor, then make for the stairs."

"Not the stairs, Benjamin. The elevator. We'll go up to the fourth-floor landing and take the elevator."

"If we do that we'll have to go through the lobby to get out of the hotel. They'll recognize me. Everyone knows me. The bellhop, the switchboard operator, the desk clerk, everybody."

"Perhaps, but the police will head directly for the stairs once they find us gone. It won't occur to them that we've gone down to the lobby."

"Let's hope you're right."

"I am usually right, Benjamin."

They hurried down the hall to the stairs, and Benjamin took up a post behind the fire door, holding it open just enough to afford him a view of Room 304, while Dearborn continued up to the fourth floor. When Dearborn saw the elevator indicator begin to move upward, he pressed the button. As he did so he noticed a door open farther down the hall and a pair of black gentlemen wearing embroidered skullcaps and silk caftans emerge. They fussed at the door for a bit and then one of them went back inside the room, while the other groped within his capacious sleeves for the room key.

Dearborn looked up at the indicator. The elevator was stopping at the third floor. He could hear voices through the shaft. One was Quesada and there were at least two others. He heard the elevator doors open and close and the pulleys groan as the elevator climbed to the fourth floor. Before the doors opened again Benjamin dove into sight, coming out the fire door at the end of the hall and loping toward the elevator. At the same time the black gentleman emerged from his room carrying a camera and hurried toward the elevator from the opposite direction while his companion, still fumbling with the room key, attempted to lock the door.

Benjamin got to the elevator first and he and Dearborn bounded into it. Dearborn pushed the lobby button, but before the doors could close, a sandaled foot and a very large hand shot out to block the doors. "One moment if you please," a resonant voice requested. The hand and foot were joined by a large dark face with an ingratiating smile. "My associate is coming now. Ah, he has dropped the key. Just another moment. Ah yes, now he has it."

Dearborn and Benjamin smiled back woodenly.

"Ah, upside down," the black gentleman said, still holding the elevator doors open with one powerful hand and motioning with his other hand to show his friend what was wrong. "Ah, good. Now he has locked it correctly."

The second gentleman joined the first and after an Alphonse and Gaston routine in which each insisted that the other enter the elevator first, they squeezed in together and the doors closed. The elevator began to descend. As they passed the floor below they heard excited shouts and cries issuing from Room 304, followed by the sound of footsteps galloping down the hall and then a fearsome banging on the elevator doors. They could hear a voice cry out in frustration. It was Quesada.

"Ah," one of the black gentleman said conversationally, "he has missed the elevator."

"So he has," Dearborn returned smoothly, his eyes remaining on the indicator overhead.

"Two," Benjamin counted aloud. "One. Lobby. Okay, Dad, here we go!"

They were standing in the back of the elevator, but as the doors opened they pushed past the two black gentlemen and sprinted for the front doors. One of the bellhops, recognizing Benjamin, pointed to him, but he was speechless with shock and unable to do more than croak unintelligibly. By the time he recovered his voice, Benjamin, with Dearborn only a step behind, had reached the sidewalk, dashed to the corner, and rounded it

Isabel didn't open the door immediately. When she did her eyes widened in fright and she tried to shut the door in their faces. Benjamin stopped her. "It's all right, Isabel. He's not who you think he is."

Isabel stared at Dearborn distrustfully. "I do not believe it. What is he doing with you?"

"You want me to explain it standing out here in the hall?"

She opened the door and motioned to them to come in, but

when Benjamin tried to embrace her she sidestepped him and walked away from him into the living room.

Benjamin followed. "What's wrong?"

"I expected you to come alone."

"Is that any reason for the deep freeze?"

She turned to face him. "Benjamin, it has been a terrible day."

"I'll say it has. You don't know the half of it."

"They kept Nicasio. I was so afraid they would keep me as well."

Benjamin was immediately contrite. "Oh hell, I'm sorry. I wasn't thinking. . . . They didn't hurt you, did they? Jesus, I'd like to get my hands on the bastards!"

"They didn't hurt me."

Dearborn had come into the living room behind them. "Benjamin told me what you did for him, Miss Quintana," he broke in. "You're a courageous young woman."

"I don't blame you for hating my guts," Benjamin said miserably. "If it weren't for me they'd never have arrested you."

Isabel's face became suddenly flushed. She reached out to touch him. "No, you are wrong. I do not blame you. It was not your fault." Her lips trembled and her eyes filled with tears. "When I heard they had shot you I wanted to find them and kill them for hurting you. When they arrested me I thought only that I should never see you again. I never blamed you."

Benjamin put his good arm around her and grinned at Dearborn over her head. "It's a hell of a way to introduce you, but Isabel, meet my father."

"Your father?" she whispered.

"The only one I've ever known."

Isabel stared at Dearborn. "Benjamin's father?" she repeated in a stupefied voice. "How did you get to Cuba? How did you know where to look for Benjamin?"

"It was not an easy task," Dearborn admitted, "but you know what they say . . . or perhaps you don't . where there's a will, there's a way."

"Tell me. Please tell me. Sit down and tell me about it. Benjamin, sit down. My God, this is all too impossible to believe!"

Benjamin did most of the talking, repeating the story Dearborn had told him about his adventurous landing at Cojimar and his subsequent affiliation with El Cuerpo, going on to tell her about his own ordeal during the previous twenty-four hours and ending with a recital of the events of the evening.

Isabel was shocked into slow-wittedness. "Tell me again," she insisted when he'd done. "You say they are going to massacre the members of El Cuerpo? But how will they know them?"

"When the bombs go off," Dearborn explained, "the members of El Cuerpo will remove their jackets and turn them inside out. Inside out the jackets become the El Cuerpo uniform, ideal targets in red, white, and blue."

"Something must be done to stop them!"

"We can't do anything about it," Benjamin told her. "We don't know where they are. All the members of El Cuerpo are meeting at some central location tonight but we don't know where it is."

"Oh my God! How terrible!"

"Somewhat of an understatement," Dearborn allowed.

"What will happen to you?"

"We shall get out as soon as I get my friend Raúl Baki out of the Plaza de la Revolución tomorrow."

"Who is Raúl Baki, a member of El Cuerpo?"

"Unfortunately yes."

"He's got the money for the boat," Benjamin told her. "Without it we'd have to swim to Florida."

"But you do not dare to go to the Plaza tomorrow, Benjamin. Neither does your father. If you are seen, you will be killed."

"We'll go around eleven," Benjamin told her. "That way we can use the crowd for cover and still get away before Castro arrives."

"We shall go through the east entrance," Dearborn said, "the entrance closest to the stage."

"Dad says that Raúl will be standing directly in front of the stage along with a couple of the others who intend to boost him up to the microphone once Castro's hit. All we have to do is get Raúl to come with us, work our way back out to the street, and head for the docks. You'll meet us there and we'll go to the boat. By tomorrow night we'll be safe."

Isabel was already shaking her head. "I cannot go with you. I have thought it over very carefully. My life is here."

"Your life's with me, Isabel."

"Benjamin, I have a job here, a good job, one I would not like to give up."

"You don't ever have to work anymore if you don't want to."

"I have family here."

"I know they're important to you, but I'm more important. Admit it."

"Benjamin," Dearborn interjected, "perhaps you should ask the girl if she's in love with you."

"Of course she's in love with me. You are in love with me, aren't you?"

Isabel was sitting on the couch facing him, with one leg curled under her and her hands clasped in her lap. She studied his face solemnly, almost absentmindedly, for so long that he became frightened. "Jesus, Isabel, you are, aren't you?"

"I am what?"

"In love with me, God damn it!"

She took a deep breath and let out a melancholy sigh. "Yes. Yes, of course."

"Then you'll cut the crap and come with me?"

"If I may say so, Benjamin," Dearborn interrupted, "your romantic approach leaves something to be desired."

"The hell with my romantic approach. What kind of life would it be without Isabel?"

"I will go, Benjamin," Isabel said quietly.

"How do you carry on a love affair with someone in Cuba? It's crazy. If you're in love with me, you'll come with me."

"I *will* go with you," Isabel repeated.

Benjamin finally registered what it was she was saying. "You will?"

"Yes I will."

Benjamin reached out toward her but pulled back as he felt a jagged pain shoot through his shoulder. "Damn! I can't even put both arms around you."

"Never mind. There will be time for that." She reached out, took his hand, and pressed it to her cheek. "Now you must rest. Tomorrow there will be much to do."

203

# 35

Isabel insisted that Benjamin and Dearborn take her room while she occupied the couch in the living room. They were too tired to offer even token resistance and fell into bed gratefully, letting their sore bodies melt into the mattress, and within minutes plunging into a deep stuporous sleep.

When they woke she was gone. At first Benjamin didn't realize it. He opened his eyes before Dearborn, saw the bands of dusty light filtering through the window slats, smelled the nutty aroma of brewing coffee and checked the time. Ten to ten. Late. Very late. She should have wakened them much earlier. "Dad? Dad, you'd better get up."

Dearborn opened his eyes and gazed at Benjamin. What was he doing there? Mrs. Woolley knew that no one, least of all Benjamin, was permitted in his bedroom before he'd breakfasted. "What do you want, Benjamin?"

"Isabel didn't wake us. It's almost ten. We've got to get going."

Dearborn landed in the present with a thud. "Ten o'clock? What's the matter with the girl?"

Benjamin was already out of bed and pulling on his pants. He grabbed his shirt off the back of the chair. "I'd better get the blood off." He went into the bathroom and washed the bloody section of shirt under the hot water tap, then put the shirt back on. The patch he'd washed showed only a faint discoloration. Once dry it wouldn't be noticeable. "I'll grab a quick cup of coffee while you get dressed," he said to Dearborn as he came out of the bathroom.

Isabel wasn't in the other room. Benjamin went to the front door. The hall was empty. He shrugged and closed the door. She must have gone out to get something from the store. Anyway, she'd made coffee before she left. He went over to the stove and picked up the coffeepot. It was cold. He lifted the lid and looked inside. An inch of stale coffee sloshed in the bottom. Funny. He must have smelled coffee wafting in from another apartment. He wasn't yet concerned, only annoyed that she had not wakened them before leaving. Time was tight.

"Benjamin." Dearborn came out of the bedroom wearing one shoe, carrying the other, and holding up an envelope for Benjamin's inspection. His face bore an expression of uncharacteristic sobriety. "I found this on the floor next to your bed. You must have knocked it off when you got up."

"What is it?"

"Take a look."

He handed Benjamin the envelope. It had Benjamin's name on it and the envelope was unsealed. Benjamin pulled out the sheet of paper and read what was written on it. "God damn," he whispered. He read it again, then with an anguished oath balled it up and tossed it onto the couch.

"She has left," Dearborn surmised. "Am I correct?"

"She says she doesn't want to be dependent on me. She's got some idea I might change my mind about her. She says she doesn't want me to have to take care of her because I was responsible for making her leave Cuba."

"She's a sensible young woman."

"What do you know about it?" Benjamin started for the door.

"Where are you going?"

"I'm going to look for her."

"You know as well as I that you won't find her. She said she was leaving Havana."

Benjamin stopped at the door and turned. "Okay, so I'll wait here. She's got to come back some . . . you read it, didn't you?"

"I scanned it to make sure it was for you."

"You didn't have to scan far to notice it began 'Dear Benjamin.' Who the hell do you think you are, reading my letter?"

"It is not I who am suffering an identity crisis, Benjamin. You are the one who has been transformed from a normal, if somewhat trying, individual, into a crazed adventurer. This is not a technicolor movie, Benjamin, and you are not the Scarlet

Pimpernel. We have more important things to concern us than your romantic antics."

"Antics? Jesus. It makes no sense. She's got no reason in the world to want to stay here."

"I have lived long enough to know that women are devious creatures. If she really wanted to go with you she would do so. She's simply letting you down easily. If I were you, I would not attach too much importance to her excuse for refusing you."

"All I'm trying to do is save her. After all, she is in love with me. She admitted it."

"She may be in love with you and then again, she may not. However, it is now ten-fifteen and if we stand here debating the question we shall sacrifice whatever chance we have to save ourselves."

"I can't believe it. I can't believe she'd walk out on me."

Dearborn sat down on the couch to put on his shoe. "Sooner or later we are all disappointed in love, Benjamin. I myself have had to face occasional rejection, not the least of which was your mother's elopement with a thoroughly dastardly fellow named Hogg when you were a mere infant. When I think back on it, it makes my blood . . ."

"Can it, Dad. I get your point, but it's not the same thing. Look, let's get out of here. If we're going, let's just go."

Dearborn scrutinized Benjamin through half-closed eyes, began to speak, changed his mind, then stamped his foot to settle himself into his shoe and rose from the couch.

Long before they reached the Plaza de la Revolución Dearborn and Benjamin found themselves pressed into a thick procession of people headed in the same direction. It was a mixed blessing because although they were able to conceal themselves easily from the police, they weren't able to move quickly or in the direction they wanted. They were jostled from every side and forced into moving toward the north entrance of the park when it was the east entrance that would have brought them closest to the front of the speakers' platform. They were afraid they wouldn't be able to work themselves through the crowd and it was a bruising snail's pace progress that left them, at eleven-forty-five, still a dozen yards from the stage.

"Do you see Raúl?" Dearborn asked.

"I can't see anything. Oh boy, look who's there. Keep your head down, Dad."

Dearborn peeked out from behind a man wearing a broad-brimmed straw hat and saw Pablo Quesada on the stage talking to a couple of khaki-clad members of the Habana Guard. There were soldiers everywhere, some carrying bayonets slung over their shoulders, some carrying rifles, some with a combination of both, but all looking like they knew full well how to use their weapons.

"Quesada is on the far side of the platform," Dearborn noted. "Let us hope he stays there."

"This is suicide, Dad."

"Keep moving," Dearborn ordered. "We must reach Raúl before those bombs go off."

"What if he won't come along? If he starts any kind of commotion, we've had it."

"You will be relieved to know that I have picked up a few words of Spanish, Benjamin. Enough to play the Pied Piper. I shall persuade him to come along with a few references to obliteración, violación, and combate."

"Are you sure?"

"Raúl is irresistibly attracted to any form of mayhem, Benjamin. Surely you remember that from our last encounter with him."

They continued to force their way toward the front of the crowd, each step accompanied by jabs and insults from the spectators dislodged by their advance.

"Do you see any of your pals?" Benjamin asked in a dry undertone. "I mean, where are they? Shouldn't we be able to spot some of them by now?"

"I am acquainted with only six of them and those six might be anywhere."

"Yeah? Well, it's five minutes to twelve, Dad."

Dearborn tapped a hefty matron on the shoulder. "Pardon me, Madame, but you are stepping on my foot." He peered over her head. "Raúl is quite tall. One would suppose . . ."

They were distracted suddenly by the crackle and whine of the loudspeakers. A technician was making adjustments to the microphone and a moment later a relaxed-looking official wearing army fatigues stepped up to the microphone, took it from the technician and made an announcement which was greeted by the crowd with deafening cheers.

"I think they must be getting ready to bring on the main attraction," Benjamin murmured. "You don't suppose he really intends to show, do you?"

"Undoubtedly."

"What are they going to do? Shove him out of the way when the shooting starts?"

"I don't imagine he shoves so easily, Benjamin, but they must have devised some means for protecting him. What time is it?"

"Three minutes to twelve."

With another surge forward Benjamin succeeded in moving them to the front row of spectators, although they were still considerably left of center. There were six-foot barriers placed ten feet or so from the stage and another ten feet of space between the barriers and the crowd that was roped off and patrolled by guardsmen. Dearborn leaned up against the rope and craned his neck to afford himself as good a view as he could get of the spectators close to the center of the stage. He didn't see Raúl. He was just beginning to shove his way in that direction when he looked up to see Quesada crouching at the near edge of the stage talking to one of the guardsmen below. As Quesada spoke he glanced up and, to Dearborn's horror, met his gaze. It took a split second for Quesada to realize who it was he was looking at. He jerked back startled, spoke excitedly to the guardsman and pointed first to Dearborn, then to Benjamin.

Dearborn turned back and grabbed Benjamin's arm. "Quesada has seen us."

"Where? Oh hell, you're right. Come on, we've got to get out of here."

"We cannot abandon Raúl," Dearborn insisted.

A half-dozen guardsmen were hurtling toward them as Benjamin roughly elbowed people aside to clear a path. "The hell with Raúl."

"I shall never forget that I have let him down," Dearborn declared as he started after Benjamin."

"You have your regrets and I have mine. Now come on, Dad."

As Benjamin and Dearborn began to snake their way toward the east end of the Plaza the crowd had taken up a mesmerized chant for Castro. The soldiers waded after them, impeded by the crush of bodies and unable to aim their guns, the spectators too thickly massed and too concentrated on the stage to comprehend the drama taking place under their noses. Behind them the microphone crackled and the call for Castro became a roar. Dearborn and Benjamin continued to thrash toward the exit without daring to look back, but they heard a deep voice, magnified a hundred times and issuing from loudspeakers all over the park. "Mis amigos, hoy congregamos a reverenciar Martí . . ."

Benjamin's shoulder was being battered, but he gritted his teeth and continued to plunge forward. "Dad, they've roped off a path leading from the east entrance to the stage."

"Head for it, Benjamin." Dearborn saw Benjamin wince as someone shoved up against him and Dearborn tried to ease his passage by making a half circle of his arms to ward off the blows. It seemed hopeless. They'd never make it.

Then they were there, slipping under the rope and running for the street. The soldiers who were patrolling the path shouted to them and when they didn't stop, rushed them. Benjamin managed to elude their grasp but Dearborn was less fortunate. He felt himself going down as two guardsmen tackled him around the waist and knees. "Keep going!" he shouted to Benjamin but Benjamin had already turned and begun running back. Benjamin slid to a stop, grabbed one of the men and pulled him off Dearborn, but by then two more guardsmen had arrived and were pointing bayonets at them. They hoisted Dearborn to his feet and both he and Benjamin put up their hands.

Then suddenly there was an ear-splitting explosion and a wooden bench a few feet away broke free of its cement base and blasted into the air. There was a second explosion and a third. Everyone within a twenty-yard radius, including Dearborn and Benjamin and the guardsmen, doubled over and covered their heads, and even before the bench landed people began ripping down the ropes and rushing toward the street. Benjamin and

Dearborn were borne on the crest, carried along like bits of jetsam until finally, as the throng slowed down outside the park, they were spewed out and left gasping.

Benjamin clutched at his shoulder but kept moving. "Come on, Dad, let's get out of here."

As panic began to subside many people slowed down and started to mill around. Benjamin and Dearborn crossed the street and along with a few dozen of the less intrepid spectators headed toward the Avenida Ayestarán, but before they'd gotten a quarter of a block they were alarmed to hear someone behind them shout, "Pinch! Stop!"

"Jesus," Benjamin groaned. "Out of the frying pan!"

"Don't turn around, Benjamin."

"Look, Dad, I'll handle it. You keep going. It's not you they want."

"Don't be an utter ass, Benjamin. I didn't go to all this trouble to lose you at the zero hour. Keep moving I tell you."

Benjamin's heart sank as he looked behind him and saw an ancient Nash Rambler pulling up alongside with the official seal of the C.D.R. painted on the door. There was a burly man at the wheel and another rough-looking character sitting next to him. "Dad, maybe you can still make it. When they get out of the car I'll try to hold them while you get away."

"Not necessary, Benjamin," Dearborn returned unexpectedly, veering toward the curb.

"Don't argue, Dad, and for God's sake, don't go over there!"

"It's about time!" the man called out. "Where have you been?"

"If I weren't so exceedingly glad to see you, Tomás," Dearborn responded dryly, "I would most certainly point out the irony in that inquiry."

# 36

The "rough-looking character" next to Tomás turned out to be his sweetheart Elena wearing no makeup and with her hair pinned up under a visored cap. If she was no beauty dressed as a woman, Dearborn thought, she was less so as a man, yet Tomás gazed at her as if she were the epitome of feminine charm. Dearborn wondered anew at the vagaries of the human heart which permit such eccentric obsessions, then banished the thought as the name Jessamine Moon flashed unbidden into his mind.

"Are you okay?" Tomás asked as he pulled away from the curb and turned north onto the Avenida Ayestarán.

"Reasonably so," Dearborn acknowledged coolly, not yet ready to forgive Tomás his treachery.

"I can't get over it," Benjamin declared. "It's a miracle you saw us! There must be close to a million people in and around the Plaza."

"We would have found you sooner but Señor Pinch, he didn't go in the east entrance like he say he was."

"How did you know where I intended to enter the Plaza?" Dearborn asked.

"Señora Ortiz, she told us."

"You mean meeting us wasn't coincidence?"

"Why should we come here except if we was lookin' for you?"

"I didn't see Señora Ortiz or Raúl in the Plaza. As a matter of fact I didn't see any of El Cuerpo. I was hoping to warn them off. Certainly to save Raúl. We could have prevented this terrible tragedy had we been able to find them in time."

"It ain't no tragedy."

"How dare you say such a thing, Tomás!"

"It ain't no tragedy because they ain't in there."

Dearborn leaned over the front seat. "Did you say they aren't in there?"

Tomás nodded and turned right onto the Avenida 19 de Mayo. "They changed their minds."

"When? Why?"

"I don't know when, but when Elena and me, we got to Enrique's place this mornin', Señora Ortiz, she say they called it off."

"That's where you saw them? At the apartment this morning."

"Sí. They had just come back from somewhere where they

211

have spend the night. I told them I was sorry I run away. I told them Elena and me, we have come back to join El Cuerpo."

"The truth being, I suppose, that you had second thoughts about your cowardly flight."

"I came to see if you have found your son," Tomás said unremorsefully. "I figure if you found your son maybe we can still get outta Cuba. Señora Ortiz, she told me you didn't know nothin' about El Cuerpo changin' it's mind, and she say you was goin' to be at the Plaza de la Revolución this mornin' lookin' for Señor Baki. They was goin' to send Enrique to find you but I told her Elena and me, we would come, so she say to look for you by the east entrance and we done that."

"Wait a minute," Benjamin interrupted. "There's something funny here. How did this Señora Ortiz know my dad was going after Raúl? Dad? What do you think?"

Dearborn slid back against the car cushions and gave Benjamin a long appraising look. "It would seem, would it not, that El Cuerpo has been tipped off as to what the D.G.I. had in store for them."

"Who by?"

"By whom, Benjamin," Dearborn corrected.

"Come on, Dad, who could have told them? Quesada's the only one who knew you were going after Raúl. Don't tell me you think he's a double agent. I won't swallow it."

"Quesada wasn't the only one, Benjamin."

"Who else? Oh shit, you mean Isabel? What good would the information have done Isabel? I know she was as anxious as we were to prevent a bloodbath but she didn't know how to locate El Cuerpo headquarters any better than we did."

"Unless . . ."

"Unless what?"

"Use your head, Benjamin. I am trying to prompt you into drawing your own conclusion."

"Unless *she's* a member of El Cuerpo?" Benjamin said impatiently. "Is that what you want me to say?"

"Precisely."

"That's all wrong. She would have told me if she were."

"Highly doubtful, Benjamin. You were hunting with a vengeance for a member of El Cuerpo. How could she admit to you that she herself was one of them?"

"Tomás," Benjamin demanded, "what exactly did Señora Ortiz tell you. Did she tell you where she got her information?"

Tomás was by now speeding northeast on the Calzada del Cerro, Elena affectionately clinging to his shoulder. He raised his eyes to the rearview mirror. "She say it was someone who seen Señor Pinch last night."

"Well, Benjamin?" Dearborn said.

Benjamin shook his head. "I don't buy it. Pretty soon you'll be claiming that everybody in my hotel room on the night of the murder were members of El Cuerpo."

"Only two."

"Three, Dad, three. You're claiming three. Moya's one. Solís's assassin is two and now you're telling me that Isabel's another. That makes three."

"Two, Benjamin."

Benjamin repeated in bewilderment, "Two? How two? Oh, I get it. You mean that Moya and the assassin are one and the same."

Dearborn didn't answer.

"Oh come on now. Surely you don't think Isabel . . ." His voice trailed off.

"When I first spoke to Quesada about Solís's murder," Dearborn said quietly, "he mentioned that Nicasio Moya had been talking to Solís's henchmen in the lobby when Solís was shot. Moya could not have been in two places at once."

Isabel's words came back to Benjamin. "I knew from the first Nicasio was innocent. I didn't bother to tell you. It was in the paper. Solís was alone when he went to his car. Nicasio had stopped Solís's men to speak to them. . ."

"The police didn't keep her," Benjamin argued. "They kept Moya but they let her go."

"I believe she was the one chosen to assassinate Castro and that Moya was helping her just as he had helped her the night of the murder by diverting Solís's men. He had no other reason for confessing to putting that list in your suitcase. He could have denied it. There was no way they could have proven it. He certainly had no reason for pretending that it was he, rather than Isabel, who gave you his phone number at the Institute."

In desperation Benjamin made his last-ditch stand. "She wrote something on a piece of paper for me. I compared her handwriting to the handwriting on the back of the list. It didn't match."

"Benjamin, I daresay she was the only one who knew *why* you had asked her to write what you did."

"You think she faked her handwriting? She wouldn't have done that."

"Hold on," Tomás cautioned as the car careened around the corner onto Máximo Gómez.

Dearborn grabbed hold of the tattered hand sling while he groped in his pocket and pulled out Isabel's wrinkled note. "I admit that until I saw this I thought you were chasing shadows. Here. Look at it." He handed the note to Benjamin who smoothed it and read it.

*Dear Benjamin,*
*I am leaving La Habana to stay with friends for a while. I will not be back until you are gone . . .*

"Do you see how she has written the *K*? Now look at the back of the paper, Benjamin."

Benjamin turned it over. It was a flyer advertising the Conjunto Folklórico.

"Last night you showed me the scrap of paper you tore out of Solís's hand. Show it to me again."

Benjamin took it out of his pocket and held it out.

"You see . . . *t–o* here and *l–k–l–o* scrawled below it. Conjunto Folklórico."

Benjamin raised stricken eyes.

"If you read the rest of her note to you," Dearborn went on relentlessly, "you shall see that the *K*s in three of her words, 'like,' 'look,' and 'take,' also display the same idiosyncrasy."

Benjamin opened his hand and let the note drop to the floor. Dearborn looked at his woebegone expression and decided to forgo his routine lecture on intestinal fortitude. "I daresay the girl wasn't lying about her affection for you. She must have been as distraught writing that note as you were reading it. Thus the careless slips."

"I think she wanted me to know. She just didn't have the guts to tell me herself. Lies. A pack of God-damned lies."

"It is what her way of life demands of her, Benjamin."

"It's a lousy way of life."

"Benjamin, I am not, as you well know, one to condone criminal acts or to justify immoral behavior, but there are those rare occasions on which one must exercise some understanding. This is one of them."

"You expect me to forgive her for deceiving me? For being who she is and what she is? My God, Dad, she's a killer."

"Forgiveness is not something she would expect, Benjamin. Credit her with appreciating the extent of her own iniquity."

"The hell with her," Benjamin said bitterly. "The hell with her."

"We're almost there," Tomás sang out suddenly.

"Almost where, Tomás?" Dearborn asked, peering out the window.

"At the docks by Desamparados and La Habana. I told Murillo to have the boat ready by one o'clock. We gotta hurry."

"Where is Raúl? We must stop for Raúl."

"Señor Baki, he ain't comin'."

Dearborn leaned forward again and pushed Elena aside so he could hang over Tomás's shoulder. "Are you serious? Even if I were ready to abandon Raúl, which I am not, we haven't the twenty thousand pesos to pay for the boat."

"Yes we do." Tomás spoke to Elena in Spanish and she fished around in her jacket pocket, pulled out a purse and handed it back to Dearborn. He opened it. A wad of bills was jammed inside. "Where did this come from? You didn't steal it, did you?"

"Señor Baki, he give it to us. I told him we must go back to Miami to buy more guns. He kept five thousand and he give us the rest."

"This is ridiculous. Raúl can't get along on his own."

"Señora Ortiz, she say her and Señor Baki gonna get marry."

"Married? Raúl and Señora Ortiz?"

"That's what she say. Is betta than livin' in the nuthouse, ain't it?"

"I should never forgive myself if anything were to happen to Raúl."

215

"Nothin' ain't gonna happen to Señor Baki." Tomás interrupted himself to announce, "There's the boat. That one over there."

Dearborn saw the name *Estrella del Mar* emblazoned on a small high-bowed open boat tied up to the dock. It had an outboard motor, no protective awning and for some inexplicable reason it listed radically to starboard.

"No," Tomás reiterated, "nothin' ain't gonna happen to Señor Baki. You know why?"

Dearborn eyed the boat with misgivings. Ninety miles through open seas in a nineteen-foot dory.

"I got it figured out now. Is because Señor Baki is crazy and God is always lookin' out for crazy pipples and fools."

Dearborn cast a dubious eye at Benjamin slumped morosely in his seat staring blindly out the window, and then said fatalistically, "In that case, let us hope he continues to run true to form, Tomás. If he does, we should make it home by nightfall."